AF253214

JILLIAN DAVID

EVERNIGHT PUBLISHING ®

www.evernightpublishing.com

JILLIAN DAVID

DEDICATION

To all of the pregnant patients who have trusted me with the most important events in their lives: Thank you for sharing your worries, hopes, excitement, fear, and joy. I am humbled to be a part of those moments.

JILLIAN DAVID

FALLEN COMRADE

Project Morpheus, 1

Jillian David

Copyright © 2022

Chapter One

Thanks to his tree-mounted security cameras that made the system guarding the crown jewels look amateur, it took less than ten seconds for Jake Zimmerman to identify the vehicle creeping to a stop in front of his remote Blue Ridge, Georgia, cabin. Silver Hyundai Accent, five years old, brand-new tires. Getting the registration info from the license plate, however, led to a dead end. His computer kept cranking through databases. So far, nothing had come up.

Odd. Normally, he could get the information right away.

Where was the convoy? When would they storm the compound?

He cocked his head to the side. No *whumps* of an incoming helo.

Sparks of adrenaline fired up his nerves, lasering all of his senses on the intruder.

His first thought was that the Army had finally

found him. He ran the pad of his index finger over the rough grip of the Sig nestled in his shoulder holster. How could anyone find him? He'd buried his personal intel deeper than a black ops mission file. The powers that be would have had to connect a hell of a lot of dots to figure out Jake's real identity and location.

Besides, if Uncle Sam wanted to storm Jake's castle, there better be a battalion coming. If Uncle Sam was smart.

He shifted, feeling the weight of a second pistol in the drop leg holster. With minimal concentration, Jake could detect the mild indentations of a Ka-Bar fixed blade in the sheath at the small of his back as well as the ever-present multitool tucked away in a pocket and ready to go for any occasion.

He peered at the … occasion … on the computer screen.

He kept the house lights off and waited despite a driving need to run out there and exterminate whoever had dared to invade his peace and quiet. *Control, dammit.* Drawing a hand over his face, he took several deep breaths and tightened and loosened a fist. The muscles in his neck clenched, refusing to loosen despite his automatic relaxation techniques.

The damned virus had started to take over his brain again until his entire world narrowed down to one mandate: destroy.

No, damn it. He was a man, not this … monster.

His ability to restrain those calamitous urges was slipping. Thanks to the top-secret Project Morpheus he had volunteered for almost two years ago in Special Forces, the part of Jake that had previously kept him from devolving into base violence now fucking loved it when he lost control. The darkness within Jake thrived on the anarchy that was his virally corrupted soul.

Add in an uninvited visitor, and it looked like tonight would bring even more fun for one of the U.S. Army's best-kept secrets.

Question of the evening: what idiot would show up at his place at 2:00 AM? Better yet, why? It was mid-March, still damp and at times freezing up here in the southernmost part of the Appalachian Mountains.

Did the person want to rob him? Jake had no material items of value. Not for lack of resources, thanks to his combat pay savings and mother's life insurance policy. But he didn't need much—just the ability to keep his demons at bay chopping wood out back and lifting weights until oblivion. That, and a deep-seated desire to not interact with any other humans suited him fine.

Something of value? Well, he had a locket with a clip of smooth auburn hair he should have thrown away long before now. Yeah, he was a bastard for preserving the keepsake, despite being technically faithful to his then-wife who did *not* have auburn hair. Could explain part of why he was no longer married.

He peered out the window again. Whoever was out there remained in the vehicle. *Come on, people, let's go.*

So. What to do about the person parked outside his house? Well, right now, his goddamned virus had a helpful suggestion. It wanted Jake to dismember whoever was in the car. Now.

Wiping his hands on his black cargo pants, he unholstered the Sig and crept to the front door. Time to eliminate the person stupid enough to visit him. Because one person could lead to two people, which could lead to being put back in the military "testing facility."

Unclenching a fist, he carefully released more of his tenuous control over the virus. It infused every cell in his body with unnatural strength and reflexes. But as the strength and acuity of his senses grew, his sanity ebbed.

The hellish yin and yang.

Ingrained training was all that kept him from falling over the cliff into psychosis.

The one person who knew he lived here was Mateo, and Jake hadn't seen his Special Forces buddy since Mateo and the rest of the Morpheus Squad had gone underground a year ago. Actually, strike that. He'd seen Mateo briefly at Brady McNeill's funeral.

Brady's funeral. And one particularly fucked-up night. Not in small part because of seeing Brady's sister, Kiera.

Seen? A bland word for the silky skin sliding over him and around him during their sweaty, heated reunion.

Since that night, nothing besides Jake's own misery mattered. Not his best friend's death, not the Morpheus Squad, his own emotional baggage. Nothing.

Which was exactly what he had now, wasn't it? Nothing.

Well, not completely. He had someone casing his house.

He licked his lips.

The figure closed the car door and stood, unmoving, facing the front porch.

Jake took stock in a matter of seconds: The person was around five-foot-eight, with a hooded jacket hiding the head and face in shadow. They favored one leg on those first few steps toward the house. Thin legs and what looked like a bit of a paunch. He squinted. Paunch or explosives vest? Damn it.

If the government had found him, they would attempt to take him back in for more experiments or wipe him off the face of the earth trying. *Best of luck.*

Maybe someone was lost out here in the mountains. The road petered out in another five miles, deep into the National Forest. Who the hell wandered around the Georgia mountains in the middle of the night?

He rubbed the back of his neck. The virus crackled through his nerve endings. Mental processes turned to sludge, making high-level analysis more challenging.

What a time to skip an antidote dose.

Too late now. Don't care.

As a swell bonus for volunteering to become a walking military biological experiment, each Morpheus Squad member had gotten extra goodies, like Jake, with his extraordinary upper body strength. He rolled his shoulders, upper back, and arms, priming for action.

Each muscle popped as poorly contained rage swept through him, turning him from Dr. Jekyll into Mr. Hyde.

Sweat broke out on his forehead as the shaking began.

Using his military training and what little humanity he still possessed, he fought to retain a shred of control. Adrenaline whipped like an icy breeze on naked skin.

He tightened up on the Sig's grip.

Neutralizing the guy was going to feel like nirvana.

On second thought, he could use a good brawl. Stuffing the weapon back in his holster, he flexed his hands. Mr. Hyde would much rather do this the natural way.

The hunched figure in the baggy jacket trudged up the gravel driveway, halting gait a little short on one leg. Jake spied a hint of a pale nose and cheek as the person looked up at the house, but he couldn't make out any other facial features with the hood casting a shadow.

Pressing his back to the wall next to the front

door, he waited. Listened. Biofeedback techniques and clenching and releasing his hands allowed him to slow his heart rate and focus all of his energy on the shuffle of footsteps up the porch stairs. The virus strained like a chained dog tempted by a wounded rabbit.

Jake became a metal spring, coiled and ready.

At a knock on the door, he didn't move.

The spring inside of him tightened. *Tick, tick, tick.* His body ratcheted down as tight as he could go.

A tap on the electronic keypad outside. *What the hell?* The bolt turned and the door cracked open.

The coil released.

His explosion of movement was a release of bliss and terror as power surged, unchecked, through every cell of his body. Grabbing the person's arm, he wrenched it behind their back and slammed the intruder sideways against the wall. He ripped the sweatshirt hood back. At a muffled, high-pitched gurgle, he froze.

In the two seconds before he flipped on the light, he registered several key things.

One, the guy came up to his nose, as expected based on Jake's assessment.

But what he hadn't expected to find was that the guy had curvy hips.

Oh, shit.

The … guy … smelled like a particular shampoo Jake loved. A shampoo that reminded him of his biggest regret.

He turned on the light, illuminating the intruder's shoulder-length auburn hair. The air squeezed out of his lungs, leaving burning fire behind. Spinning the trespasser around, Jake stared at the squinting, terrified expression of the one person he never expected to see again.

Kiera McNeill.

But his virus still wanted blood. All of his muscles clenched as the need to destroy surged. Desperate, he wrestled back control. The virus rushed through his veins, powering up muscles, pushing him toward the cliff's edge.

The view of her horrified hazel stare, with that pink mouth agape, knocked him back a step. For a nanosecond, his life split down the middle. One half of him remained in attack mode and needed to annihilate the intruder. The other half begged to bury his hands in her soft hair and kiss her lips until he lost his ever-loving mind, like he'd done last July.

Attack half won out.

He gripped the front of her jacket. "Kiera?" he yelled. "I almost killed you!"

She gave a strangled cry, and her full mouth twisted.

Oh, shit. Too fucking much. He had to relax or he'd hurt her … more than he had already. With a few deep breaths, Jake mentally shoved the urge to kill way down inside his mind and clamped the lid. Contained. For now. He glanced back to the kitchen cabinet. Damn it, he needed to get a shot of antidote, ASAP.

"What the fuck?" he roared. Then he cursed again when she cringed and flattened herself against the wall.

Okay. Wrong move.

God, what he'd give to run a finger over her skin, to see if it was as smooth as he recalled. He'd love to do so much more. What the hell was wrong with him? He had no right to touch her, not even on the night after Brady's funeral. He swallowed past a rock-hard lump in his throat. Besides, he couldn't trust any contact to be gentle, given his current state.

Her delicate features were fuller than he remembered. Come to think of it, even her curves had changed.

Then as he shifted position, he brushed against the sweatshirt-clad, rounded—

What. The. Fuck.

Doubling over like he'd been kicked in the nuts, he attempted to quickly put several pieces of critical information together. And failed.

"The fuck, Kiera? Are you okay? I pushed you into the wall without knowing—" He straightened up and reached his hand out to touch her belly, wanting to reassure himself that she and the *oh shit* were safe. But when she flinched and wrapped her arms over her middle, he stopped cold, curling his deadly fingers back away from her.

She stared at him, weary lines etching her drawn face. Pregnant?

Math. He forced his vapor-locked mind to do goddamned math. Brady's funeral. The night after. Her belly looked … he quickly counted on his fingers. Too small for…

Relief that it couldn't be his crashed against rage that someone else had put the child there. He fought to clear the red haze from his vision.

Then another wave of guilt mixed with fear blended into flashbacks from his ex-wife's miscarriage. The memories hit him harder than a right hook. He couldn't speak. Couldn't breathe. All the while, Mr. Hyde begged to be let out.

Forget it. Jake would kill himself before he harmed Kiera.

Too late. All of the color drained from her flawless face, and she swayed on her feet. What the hell?

"Jake?" Damn it. Her husky, broken-up voice bought him to heel.

"Yeah." He half-turned, hoping to hell she

couldn't see the area of his anatomy responding to the dangerous situation and adrenaline, needing release.

She swallowed, and he couldn't take his eyes off the elegant line of her neck. Damn her, she was even more beautiful than he remembered with those high cheekbones and wide eyes. Despite himself, he licked his lips. He wanted to find out if she tasted as sweet as when he last kissed her.

He also needed to know why she was here, where he could hide her car, and how quickly they could escape in case anyone else showed up. Special Forces multitasking 101.

When she tucked dark-red hair behind an ear, a ring glinted on her fourth finger.

He froze.

Math happened again in his brain. Ring. Pregnancy. Shit. No, he couldn't process the evidence that she had chosen someone else and that some other man's baby lived inside of her.

Her hand trembled as she rubbed her pale cheek. "Oh, God. I'm pretty sure…"

When her eyelids flickered closed and she wobbled, he grabbed her under an arm and shuffled her off-balance body in the direction of his favorite recliner. She always had a slight build, but for a pregnant woman, she hadn't gained much weight compared to what he recalled was normal. Was the pregnancy okay?

He wanted her to sit with her feet up. Because that was what you did when pregnant ladies were about to pass out, right?

No one could be less of an expert on the topic than Jake. But he had been Special Forces. Therefore, he would hydrate and feed her and then mandate that she rest.

Before he eased her into the chair, he glanced

down at her white sneakers. One shoe was tinged red. What the hell? Standing, he kept hold of her as he slipped the black jacket off her thin shoulders. She whimpered. Blood stained the back of her shirt. And the front. There were two holes in the fabric at each location. She moved her hands. Dark blood smeared over the palms.

His vision narrowed. Ears rang.

"Kiera? What happened?" With effort, he managed to keep his voice calm and low.

She swayed on her feet, and he tightened his grip around her upper arm. With his free hand, he clenched and released. *Do not hurt Kiera*. He rode the fine line between not supporting her enough and breaking bones into pieces.

"I may need a little help." Her strained whisper gutted him.

Grabbing the hem of her shirt, he lifted it a few inches to reveal red, angry, blood-covered skin around a bullet hole. On the same side, a jagged exit wound appeared on the edge of her belly. Bruising had begun in a line between the holes. His skin crawled. Fuck. Had the baby been hit? He clicked into medic assessment mode, scanning her from head to toe, cataloging injuries, and developing treatment options based on what he had in his kit.

"Why didn't you go to the hospital?"

There was a similar bloody hole in the fabric of her leggings. No second hole to indicate an exit wound.

Who the hell would hurt her—pregnant or not? His head buzzed as his brain heated up to a rolling boil.

Auburn lashes fluttered up. The fathomless hazel color of her gaze checked his inner beast more surely than if he'd mainlined a case of antidote into his jugular.

"I'm in big trouble, Jake."

Chapter Two

Mateo. Bless her mission partner's kind, deceased soul, but darn him. He'd sent Kiera to the one person who wanted nothing to do with her ever again: Jake. Even though he and Jake had been friends, judging by the fully armed reception up here in the chilly mountains, Mateo must have not warned Jake that she might drop by.

As if she had any other choice.

She scanned the holster straps outlining his chest. Glanced at the gun strapped to his thick leg and shivered. If he was anything like Mateo, there would be more hidden weapons on him.

The cold, hard glare from his gray eyes indicted her, even as her stupid heart fluttered with the proximity to him, reacting like…

She brushed her hand over the baby and winced. The bullet had gone through flesh only, thank God. A little nudge, a foot or a knee, reassured her that Little Bit was safe for the time being.

"I wanted to go to the hospital, but then they would find me. Mateo told me to come here. He said you would know what to do." She needed to tell him more. Clamping her mouth shut, she couldn't speak the words past the knot in her throat.

"Do you want some water?" he blurted.

Special Forces guys and their hydration. "I'm okay right now, thanks."

"How did you know the front door digital combination?" He kept a hand on her elbow, the touch light but steady.

"Mateo told me a few months ago."

"What?"

"Actually, no. That's not accurate. A few months ago, he told me how to reach the cache he set up which contained information on how to get here. I read all the information several hours ago, destroyed it, and came here."

"You remembered from then 'til now?"

She tried not to groan at a twinge in her back muscles. "Eidetic memory. By the way, you shouldn't use your high school locker combination."

A brief smile, then his mouth pressed into a hard line, and a muscle along his jaw jumped as he stared at her. Pregnant woman in trouble. Not what he wanted to see at God-knows-what time at night in his quiet mountain cabin. Her head swam as adrenaline seeped out of her body, rendering her boneless. If she didn't sit soon, she'd be on the floor.

"Mateo?" he repeated, almost to himself.

"Your teammate from the military? Brady's buddy from your Army team?"

"I know who he is!"

Was. "We'd been living together, and—"

"No personal details. I get the picture." His thick hand chopped air and cut off her explanation as he glanced toward her abdomen. "What the hell happened?" He barked out the words as he waved toward her bloody calf and side.

If he was angry now, wait until he found out about how she and Mateo freelanced a mission to avenge her brother Brady. Seemed safe enough at the time, or she would never have continued their work.

Seemed safe. In twenty-twenty hindsight, it was more of a nightmare. Speaking of a nightmare, she still had to address the result of that night after Brady's funeral.

"Long story. But I need to tell you—" A stab of

pain threatened to knock her down.

His vise grip under her arm pinched, but at least he kept her upright. He switched hands and stood behind her, lifting the hem of her shirt again. Chilly air on her wounded side grabbed her attention almost as much as his ripe curse.

"We're going to fix this. Sit down. And you have to hydrate."

Damn his strong hands, but he supported and steered her from the living room to the kitchen. Collapsing into a spindle-backed seat, she rested her arms on the table and leaned forward until her head lay on her forearms. She groaned in pain and relief as the cramped muscles in her back and legs relaxed.

"Stay put," he stated, depositing a glass of water in front of her and a damp washcloth.

As if she could go anywhere right now? Halfheartedly cleaning her hands, she stared at him, then wadded the cloth up in a ball. If she had any energy left, she would protest him ordering her around like another soldier.

Sweat beaded his brow as he fumbled in a metal box on the counter and pulled out a syringe filled with yellow liquid like the one she'd seen Mateo use from time to time. No alcohol swab for Jake, oh no, he just jammed the needle into his massive upper arm, bare below the tight short sleeve. His eyes shut and his entire frame went rigid then loosened, like a junkie getting a fix. Except his expression held no indication of euphoria, only tight-lipped resolve. Was he on drugs? He didn't act like what she'd expect to see if someone was going through withdrawal.

Was he even safe to be wearing weapons? While injecting stuff into his body? She glanced at the solid wood back door and counted the locks she'd have to throw to get out of here. No way could she move faster than Jake. Not right now.

What about when Mateo used a similar-looking syringe? He'd said it was for a medical condition and he had to take medicine every few weeks for his health.

What were the chances Jake had the same condition?

"Jake, what's that?" she mumbled. No way could she believe he was hooked on drugs. But she didn't care how exhausted she was. If he was using, then she and her unborn child would get the hell out of this place.

He flicked a tired gaze at her and quickly put away the supplies. "You know how a diabetic needs insulin? There's a condition, uh, a bunch of us got from … exposure in the Army."

"You're not doing drugs?"

"You're kidding, right?"

"I'm too worn out to kid."

Banging open cabinets, Jake yanked out a first-aid kit and tore open the top of the container. Harsh rips of packages and clanks of metal filled the silence. It took all of her will to remain awake. Her eyelids drifted closed.

She trusted Mateo's judgment in sending her here. Despite the weird behavior, Jake would take care of her because this was Jake, right? They had a history. He couldn't turn his back on their one-time … God, she couldn't give what they had a decade ago a name.

What about the night after Brady's funeral?

She rubbed her aching chest. What a mess. She was putting her faith and the life of her baby in the hands of a guy who had not once but twice turned his back on her, who had tried to attack her a few minutes ago, and who injected drugs. Okay, fine, treatment for a medical condition. The reality remained: he was still her best option for help.

Her only option.

His voice came from across the room. "Explain to me again why you didn't go to the hospital with bullet holes in you."

"Not bullets. A little shrapnel. It's complicated." Understatement of the year.

Returning to her, he lifted the back of her shirt and cursed under his breath. The icy fire of alcohol caught her so off-guard, she shrieked and jerked her head up.

"Sorry," he muttered, pressing her head back down to rest on her arms. He dabbed again, gently this time. "What happened to you?"

"Shrapnel," she mumbled.

"Could you expand on that statement?" His voice, deeper and harder than she remembered, made her shiver.

She stammered, "Metal exploded. The piece on my side went in and out. It missed the…" Groaning as he probed the wound, she gritted her teeth. "Not sure if the other piece went all the way through my leg."

"Answer me one question. How the fuck did this happen?"

"Long story." Her breath hissed between her teeth as he swiped the hellish alcohol swab over the wounds again. "Give me a minute to recover from your nursing skills and then I'll explain."

"Fine." He stalked back over to the counter and rustled through the kit. "I need to probe the wounds, make sure no more metal is in there. If there's material left behind, you're at high risk for infection. And you're right. I agree that it avoided the…"

Baby.

"Okay. Do whatever you have to." She buried her

head in her arms, willing herself to hold still. When he poked the wound on her flank with the metal instrument, imaginary razors sliced through her skin. Couldn't help it—she flinched. Then she opened her eyes and spied his scowling face a few inches away from her. Disgust twisted his hard features into warped stone as he glanced toward her abdomen.

She swallowed.

Fine, she'd hold still. Anything to limit the time he was forced to touch her.

"Do I need stitches?"

"No. It's best to let these areas drain. They're not bleeding much. But if you need stitches, it's no problem."

Glancing over, she caught his cocky smirk. "No problem for *you*. It's not your skin getting poked with needles."

A snort. That was all she got for a response, but it was enough to remind her of the old Jake. The one who *could* laugh.

He smeared ointment on the wound on her back, pressed a gauze pad to the area, and taped it in place. Then he repeated the efficient maneuver on the exit wound on her sensitive abdomen. Her heart sped up.

"How about your leg?" His frown summed up pretty much everything right now.

"Same song, different station." She pressed her hands to the table. "I can lift it up if it's easier with all the equipment you're wearing—"

His warm palm on her shoulder stopped her. "Don't worry about it. You're the one with the injury. I'll work around you." The sudden mellowing of his baritone voice caught her off-guard, making her eyes burn. "I'm used to working with full gear on. If you want, I'll put on a Kevlar jacket in case you kick me."

"Mmph."

Damn it if he didn't sit on the floor to examine the calf wound. She peeked at his dark-blond hair and broad back. Wow. She knew he'd bulked up since high school, but she hadn't exactly performed an in-depth analysis last July. In the dark. But right now, up far too close, he was big. Brady's Army pictures didn't do Jake justice. Muscles rippled under his t-shirt as Jake worked the hem of her legging up. Although there was restrained strength in his touch, he remained gentle.

Physical and emotional pain braided tightly together in her chest. She kept her arms crossed on the table and pressed fingers into her upper arms.

The quiet work was interrupted when he tapped her on the leg. "Shit. The metal piece is still in there. I'm going to have to get it out."

"Do what you have to."

He shifted to bend her leg and tuck her foot in between his knees as he knelt and cleaned the skin once more. His thigh muscles tensed, then with a sharp poke and a twisting and pulling sensation, a trail of fire burst from her calf. Stiffening, she bit her lip and dug her fingers deeper into the skin of her arms.

"Got it," he said. "Success."

Funny, he didn't sound pleased.

"I need to put stitches in. This one's bleeding quite a bit."

A wave of her hand and a mumble were all she could manage with the pulsing pain in her leg and side.

After one more trip back to the counter and rustling for supplies in what she assumed was the first-aid box, he returned.

"Let me numb up with some lidocaine." His exhaled breath was harsh in the quiet cabin. "This is going to hurt."

"More than getting metal projectiles embedded in my body?"

"Probably not."

Another few dabs with the awful alcohol swab, and then the fiery pricks of the needle. Then the pain subsided as she felt only some tugging, drawing sensations followed by more ointment and a dressing.

The wound on her side throbbed. As the last reserves of her strength faded away, all she wanted was to stay here and rest, if only for a few minutes. It would be comfortable enough, sleeping while sitting at the table.

"Kiera? Did you drink?"

"Water?" She made a halfhearted sip at the glass, because knowing Jake, he wouldn't stop until she floated away.

"Hey?" he said.

"Mm-hmm?"

"Can I get your shirt and pants cleaned up for you? They're stained with blood."

Yes, she should clean up. A normal thing to do after escaping death, watching her house blow up, having her friend die, and getting metal embedded in her pregnant body. Oh, and don't forget coming face-to-face with the man who wanted nothing to do with her. A manic bubble of laughter climbed her throat and stole the air from her lungs. She squeezed her burning eyes shut until she regained control.

When Jake helped her stand, the razor-sharp pain shot through her back and side again. She flattened her palm on the tabletop for a minute.

"Okay," she said, snagging the jacket from the table and draping it over an arm.

In silence, he preceded her to the bathroom and opened the door. For a big guy, he moved like a living shadow. He left for a moment, then returned with one of his own t-shirts and a pair of sweatpants.

Shrugging, he said, "They'll work for the short term. Hand me your clothes and I'll run them through a quick wash," he said, like they were a regular domestic couple. If regular couples typically fished out projectiles from each other's flesh and cleaned blood-stained clothing, that was.

After closing the bathroom door, she pulled off her maternity top, socks, and punctured leggings. His sweatpants were five inches too long, but she rolled them up. She unzipped her jacket pocket and removed an envelope and the thumb drive she had stashed before the house in Atlanta exploded. The former she had retrieved from the cache on her way here. Stuffing the items in the sweatpants' pocket, she patted the pants to make sure everything was securely stowed. As she tugged Jake's extra-large cotton shirt over her head, she took a deep breath. Oh, God, the soft, worn material smelled like simple detergent, a hint of spicy aftershave, and the faint aroma of hickory woodchips that was uniquely Jake. Flashes of memory, his warm, firm lips against hers, his hands roving over her breasts and lower over her hips and lower still… Her head swam, and not from the injuries.

Stop it. She had no right to feel anything for this man. He'd made his choice clear years ago. She was no longer that high school girl with a heart full of fluttery emotions.

The night together last July had been a mistake, if his fleeing the scene was any indication. Heck, he barely made eye contact with her tonight.

When she opened the door and held the soiled clothes out to him, he stared at her long enough for sweat to form under her armpits. Okay, maybe it was better when he wouldn't look at her. His posture went ramrod straight, and he leaned forward, rolling his hands into fists. Like he wanted to help but couldn't bring himself to touch her.

Or maybe he wanted to punch a hole through the drywall.

As much as she should turn away, God help her, she couldn't stop staring. He always was a solid guy, even in high school. Even though Jake carried much more muscle than she remembered, he moved with a grace unexpected with his big frame. The black t-shirt tucked into denim hugged hard ridges pushing against the fabric, his muscles emphasized by the shoulder harness straps lashed over his chest. Every inch of him vibrated with barely contained lethal power.

With anyone else, the sight of the man and the weapons would be terrifying. Anyone else but Jake.

Same dark-blond hair, although he'd let it grow out a few inches into waves that couldn't quite be tamed. Waves she'd love to run her fingers through. Nowadays, though, his hair was the only soft thing about him.

His face had matured. Wrapped in her own grief last summer, she hadn't noticed it then. He had never been typically handsome, but the way he focused on whatever was in front of him always made his appearance compelling. Now, the intense demeanor made him even more damned attractive. He'd been through his fair share of struggles as a kid growing up and since they had dated in high school. His personality had become even harder over time, what with Brady's death and Jake's wife leaving him a few years ago.

Wife.

Of course, Kiera had known about Jake's marriage. When her brother Brady had been recovering from his combat-related head injury, Kiera and her sisters had helped him access photos on his computer. She'd seen pictures of the small wedding where Brady had stood next to his high school friend. Jake had cut an impressive figure back then with his Army dress uniform, and his bride wore a simple and pretty white dress. Every time Kiera clicked on the picture, something twisted in her gut. Not jealousy. Not anger.

Regret.

Stop it. That train had long since left the station.

No, the train didn't exist anymore.

Today's harder Jake had fine lines at the corners of his intense steel-gray eyes, lines formed too soon for a twenty-eight-year-old.

What a world of difference the past ten years made.

Still standing in the doorway of the bathroom, he hadn't moved.

She met his gaze for a split second. Pain and anticipation both flashed through her. She had no right to any feelings for him. None. They'd passed a second chance up many months ago, and the idea of a third chance? Ludicrous.

She closed the bathroom door on the man she no longer knew and turned toward the sink. A haunted, empty expression filled the frame.

In the borrowed sweatpants pocket next to the thumb drive rested the crumpled envelope. Jake's name was on the front, written in Mateo's neat hand. A lump clogged her throat. Her friend Mateo was gone.

What about her baby's safety? This mission had gone from ho-hum to horrendous in a matter of hours. Her hands shook, thinking how close she had come this evening to … not making it here. The explosion, the chase. Now what? Beau Lequire would find her. His information net and desire to silence any threat to his business empire was unstoppable.

No. She would figure out how to keep this child alive and safe, no matter what.

Dealing with feelings about Jake was optional. Protecting her baby was not.

Now, if only she could figure out who could help her without putting their lives at risk. Although her father and sisters knew a bit about the work Kiera and Mateo were doing, no one knew the true extent of the project. It was better that way. Less chance of getting pulled into the morass. She prayed they were all safe for now.

Back to this baby. She needed to figure something out before delivery in, what? Less than six weeks. She braced her hands on the sink edge, too tired to think through a plan.

Incremental decisions. Each one had been driven by good intentions. Now she was homeless, injured, pregnant, on the run, and imposing on the one man who never wanted to see her again. Quite the accomplishment for the past six hours' worth of work.

After she'd been in the bathroom for fifteen minutes, Jake knocked on the door. "Everything okay in there?"

"Just taking some time to clean up."

A pause. "Let me know if you need anything." The tightness in his voice bored through the solid wood door like a hammer-driven nail. Her eyelids stung.

After another head shake, she scrubbed dirt off her face with the cold, damp washcloth and patted the skin dry. Carefully pulling the bottom of the sweatpants up, she tended to her scraped knees, avoiding the bandage on her lower leg. She eased the material back down and cleaned the raw skin on her palms. Then she stared into the mirror at the pale, exhausted woman reflected.

Chapter Three

As Kiera re-entered the living room, which was lit only by a single muted lamp, she took in the few pieces of warm, solid furniture with dark colors. The cabin had traditional Appalachian construction with pale chinking between the square wood beams on the outer walls. A small wooden desk in the corner of the room held several laptops with black and white images playing on four quarters of each screen. No dust on the shelves. No pictures.

No doilies, lace, or a vase of flowers. Not a single feminine touch in this home.

A cozy cabin like this shouldn't feel like a sterile collection of rooms. Even the sound of her footsteps echoed, the sound seeking substance to bounce off of and finding … nothing.

Jake sat motionless on the brown leather couch, staring into space. He leaned forward, corded forearms resting on his knees, fingers laced in a white-knuckled grip. The holstered guns were still strapped across his chest and on his thigh, like the equipment was part of him. In profile, his features could have been chiseled from granite. While he didn't look at her, she had no doubt he tracked her every movement, able to react in a split second. Her skin twitched.

Silence settled around her, making the thud of her heart sound far too loud in her ears. Time to talk.

She eased into the recliner with a creak of leather and a groan as the injury on her back protested, but she kept her feet on the floor. Reaching for the lever to put her legs up was too much work right about now. Besides, if she reclined, she would be asleep in a few seconds. She and Jake had to come up with a plan for her to deliver the information. Then she could get out of his life as quickly as she'd re-entered it.

As she sat, a hint of his aftershave and that faint hickory scent rose from the chair, tormenting her.

The spicy aroma from a mug of steaming tea next to the chair tempted her. Little Bit kicked. The baby must like tea. Would it be too much to ask for this kid to show their appreciation in a way that didn't involve pummeling her uterus?

Next to the tea was a PB&J sandwich, cut into precisely equal triangles. And another glass of water. Of course.

Also on the end table rested a pair of clean wool socks, neatly folded. Too large for her feet. Something in her chest twisted again.

"Thank you," she mumbled, trying to swallow past a hard lump in her throat.

Silence.

When she tried to bring her leg up, she only managed to do so on her good side.

In a ghost of movement, Jake knelt in front of her and tugged the wool sock over her other foot. His feather-light touch was at odds with the tight cords of muscles in his arms. The two of them created a weird image of raggedy Cinderella and muscle-bound Prince Charming. He returned to the couch, his movements whisper-quiet. She still felt the residual warmth of his fingers on her ankle. Wanted that touch elsewhere.

He pressed his mouth into a grim line.

Her vision blurred until she blinked a few times to clear it.

Finally, his gunmetal-gray eyes focused on her. "Do you need something else to eat? You should eat. Because of..." His Adam's apple bobbed and he stared somewhere beyond her right shoulder.

Holding up a corner of the sandwich, she smiled. "This is perfect. Thank you." She took a bite, despite the nervy sensation crawling over her skin.

"More water?"

"I'm good."

He stared at her.

Fine. She took a sip, only so he wouldn't witness her desiccating in front of him.

"So." Like a pebble tossed into a calm pond, his low voice disturbed the space between them.

"God, where to start?" She rubbed the bridge of her nose.

"How about explain why you're here?" He glanced at her and then toward the computers. "How did you even find this place?"

"You haven't been in touch with Mateo for how long? I thought you two were almost as close friends as you and Brady were."

"Things were complicated. I last saw Mateo at Brady's funeral." The tone, flat, lifeless. The time frame, precise. "Remember?"

"Of course." And how. Her thighs pressed together. "How did I find your house? After I ran from the people who shot at me, I followed Mateo's hidden directions."

"Wait. Someone *shot* at you? You said metal exploded and shrapnel hit you." His gaze scanned her, like he was searching for more injuries.

"It was kind of both things happening."

"What?" Every muscle went tight, like he could levitate off the couch.

"Not at the same time." She shifted in the seat. "So, you've heard of the Fallen Comrades charity?"

His spine ramrodded. When he pinned her with a glare, it felt like he was drilling laser beams straight through her body. "Fallen Comrades? The company run by that fake-disabled vet, Beau Lequire?" Like lashes of a whip, he bit out every word. "Why, yes. I'm extremely familiar with that organization. As well as that particular asshole. What does the organization have to do with any of this?" He slashed his hand in her general direction. "Why the fuck would someone shoot at you?"

"Jealous you didn't get dibs?"

Hands went up in a hurry. "Hey, whoa, uncalled for. You and I broke up fair and square years ago."

"Fine."

He reared back. "Shit. When you say 'fine,' it's never 'fine.' It's always the opposite. Usually my fault."

"Just like this situation is not 'fine.' But not your fault." She sighed. "Bear with me. It will all make sense."

"Fine."

She snorted.

"Hold on. Let me double-check the system." He uncoiled off the couch, strode to the computers, and tapped.

Kiera finished off the triangle of PB&J and washed it down with the water and tea. Her hunger pangs subsided, and she sighed. "Is my car okay out there?"

He glanced back at her with a smile so grim that the hairs on her arms rose. "Of course. I swept it while you were in the bathroom. No bugs. No identification at all. Not even a VIN or insurance information. Mateo put security and defensive tech in it that I can't let anyone else get hold of."

"Really? Anything else?"

"Couple of holes in the back window and bumper I'm not happy about."

"Makes two of us."

He paced the floor slowly, a lion on a stalk. "You

should get some shut-eye. It's been a long day."

She shook her head. "No. I need to tell you what happened." And yes, for the record, she would love to catch forty winks right now.

"Then you'll sleep?"

"I … guess so."

"Good." A curt nod. "Go on."

Despite his angry tone, she still loved his baritone voice. Every word slid in a soft southern accent when he spoke, and his voice riled her nerves in the best possible way, even now. Even after everything. Damn him.

"So. About Brady." She fought to keep her tone neutral.

Jake and her brother had been best friends in high school. When they had enlisted in the Army after a few years of college, she had made only one request of Jake: keep Brady safe.

It took all of her self-control not to blame Jake for Brady's injuries in Afghanistan. What happened to her headstrong brother had been out of anyone's control. By all accounts, he should have died in the explosion. Over time, she had come to realize no one could have prevented everything, while Brady served or since then.

But Kiera could damn well get revenge for some of it.

He turned. "Okay. About Brady." He scratched the light-brown stubble on his rigid jaw, the sound harsh and electric.

"You know how he wasn't … okay? Because of the traumatic brain injury and all?"

His eyes became two flecks of cold steel. "Yeah. I was there when the accident occurred."

She flinched. "Once he was discharged, Brady got tapped to be the 'poster boy' for Fallen Comrades. He did commercials and gave talks about how great

Fallen Comrades was and how the organization had helped him recover from his injuries."

"I'd heard about him working with the company, but I wasn't paying much attention to … the outside world … at that time." He pulled down a blind and peered out the front window. "Did they help him?"

"No." She sucked in a breath. "Well, let me back up. They paid him for the commercials and gave him a salary as spokesman, so it was something. He was proud to have a job again. Brady kept hoping Fallen Comrades would help more with rehab services for veterans who live far from their local VA facilities. Fallen Comrades were also supposed to retrofit houses for soldiers who had been injured. Set soldiers up with service animals. Provide additional mental health services."

"And?"

"A little over a year ago, Brady uncovered what was really going on." When she laughed, her voice came out hollow. "Well, some of it. He had only discovered the tip of the iceberg. He could have blown the lid off the entire company, even with the small amount he knew."

"Why didn't I hear about this?" His shoulders went rigid, and one hand curled into a fist that he pressed to the edge of the window sash.

"It wasn't public knowledge. Yet." She squinted with one eye at the pine ceiling beams. "I believe you had, um, been out of contact then." She waved a hand. "It wouldn't have mattered. Brady had an NDA placed on him by Fallen Comrades, complete with threatening boilerplate language. All the pressure didn't help his PTSD and brain injury one bit."

"So, he was a whistleblower? Happens all the time. Legal paperwork wouldn't stop Brady from doing what was right."

"It stopped him when the threats escalated into

unfortunate accidents."

"What." No inflection.

She rubbed her belly until she caught Jake staring. Deliberately shifting her hand to her knee, she continued. "When Mateo visited us in June, Brady told us about what was going on at Fallen Comrades. Shortly after, Brady died in suspicious circumstances. The police tried to chalk it up to 'random violence,' but I knew better." Her breath caught. "Mateo offered to help get to the bottom of Brady's death and go after Fallen Comrades. Mentioned something about how he had some resources from past work with a group of ex-military guys."

"He told you about the team?" One blunt fingertip ran the edge of the sash. Up and down. Like an absentminded motion, only Jake never fidgeted.

"What team?"

He froze and stepped forward. "Wait. You went undercover with him and he didn't inform you about the team?" He tapped his chin. "Actually, it makes sense. That would be need-to-know."

"What didn't I need to know?"

"Never mind." He huffed out a big breath. "You really should rest. We'll get a plan for the morning."

"No. Let me go over everything, then you can decide if you even want me to stay here."

"What?"

"I'm a liability, Jake. You might be in danger because of me."

He snorted. After snagging her empty glass, he stomped over to the kitchen. He popped a frozen dinner in the microwave. A few minutes later, he brought the noodles and more liquid back over. "Eat. Please. Then finish the story. Then you're staying here and resting. That's an order."

She snapped, "I'm not in the military. You can't order me around." Taking a bite of steaming pasta, she sighed as the tomato sauce and cheese met in harmony in her mouth.

"I never could make you do anything."

Nearly snorting a noodle, she managed to mumble, "Almost."

Was that a wickedly sexy smile on his face?

She set the food down after a few more bites. "Our mission was undercover. Kind of," she added in a hurry. "We concentrated on getting useful information out of Beau and from Fallen Comrades. I trusted Mateo because he's a good friend. We were both avenging Brady. I was focused on getting justice for Brady." Shaking her head, she creased the hem of the borrowed t-shirt. "Mateo always said the less I knew, the less of a liability I'd be if…"

Jake rolled his hands into fists, knuckles turning white. "If your cover got blown. If you ended up in a bad position. Shit." He blew out a breath. "What the hell was he thinking, putting you in danger? Especially with the—you know," He flapped a hand in her general direction.

"One, we never thought this project would be this dangerous, or I wouldn't have done it. Two, he knew I needed to avenge Brady's death. Even if Mateo had known there was danger involved, I still would have tried for Brady."

"I bet you would have." He circled back to the computer screens for a few seconds before straightening up and pacing again.

"Brady had two solid friends who would give the shirts off their backs for him: you and Mateo."

"No question." He stopped pacing, his voice only a decibel higher than a whisper.

"If you had come up with a plan to avenge Brady,

I would probably have gone along with it for the same reason: I trusted you. Like I trusted Mateo."

"Yeah, but there are better ways. Hell, send in the whole team."

Shaking her head, she said, "What we were doing had nothing to do with any team. We weren't official anything. Our project was never meant to attract attention. Besides, according to Mateo, the team was still rebuilding after…"

"After I went off the deep end and then refused to join them when they reformed here stateside?"

"He didn't share any details."

All she knew was that Jake and his wife had divorced. Kiera could imagine him picking fights at bars, throwing himself into workouts—anything to take his mind off of the pain.

A buzzer sounded, making her jump.

"Clothes are done."

"That's fast."

"I have really good tech." He walked midway down the hall, returned, and set the toasty garments in her lap. "Here." Like he couldn't stand for her to continue wearing his clothes.

"Okay." Wincing at her protesting muscles, she walked to the bathroom once more and quickly changed into her outfit, transferring the thumb drive and the folded envelope back into the zippered jacket pocket. The twin holes on the side of the tunic and jacket didn't look too bad. A little breezy, maybe. Returning to the living room, she folded the Jake-scented shirt and sweatpants and laid them on the end table, then leaned against the back of the recliner, stretching sore muscles. Her empty noodle dish and empty cup of tea were gone. The water glass? Full again.

He barely spared her a glance as he stood next to

the bookshelf with legs shoulder-width apart, arms folded over the holster straps that strained to contain his chest muscles. "About that bad time back then, a few years ago, when the team was forming up stateside. Look, I was in a rough place. Mentally. I kind of … broke down."

"Oh."

Raking his hand through his dark-blond hair, he grimaced. "*Oh* is right." He thumped his chest. "But no excuses. I didn't help Brady when he needed it the most. Didn't keep my promises. Couldn't help my—anyway. Ancient history." He paced back and forth, covering the length of the living room with leonine efficiency.

"Is that why you're so tense?"

"My training made me, um, extra vigilant." He rolled his shoulders. "Then you came into the cabin." His gaze slid away. "I'm sorry. If I'd known it was you, I would never have…"

"I get it. It's not abnormal behavior to be defensive if someone trespasses."

"Yeah. Anyway. I —I'm sorry. Go on with the story. It's going from bad to worse."

She blew out a deep breath. "So, after Brady was killed—" Her voice cracked. "We went to the authorities. Random violence, they said. No witnesses. No clues." Her eyes burned.

Damn Jake for the way he watched her, with a furrow forming between his thick eyebrows, as if he cared. As if he wanted to resurrect Brady—or move heaven and earth if she asked him to do so. The time for stark emotion was far in the rearview mirror. If he kept up the intense caring act, she'd start crying, which wouldn't accomplish anything.

Stalling, she took a sip of water.

A creak and a bang sounded outside the cabin.

She slammed the glass down on the table. Hard.

Chapter Four

In a flash, Jake went from semi-relaxed to lethally alert at her side. His tight posture vibrated waves of danger.

"Get down."

Awkwardly and with a wince of pain, she slid to the floor, putting the recliner between the front door and herself. "Jake?" Her heart skidded in her chest.

In an economy of movement, he snagged a tablet from the desk and returned, bracketing her with muscled legs that pressed against her back. As she glanced up, he held the device with one big hand and tapped on the screen. Then he pulled his gun in a *shush* of metal against the leather sheath.

He clicked off the lamp.

Her mouth went dry.

"Not today, Big Bob," he muttered, re-holstering his gun.

"What?"

Jake knelt next to her, his body heat warming her ice-cold skin. "Look."

Black and white images of the outside of the cabin flashed on the screen. With a tap of the pad, bright colors appeared.

"Thermal enhancement," he murmured. "Pretty cool."

"Sure. If the thing out there that is warm doesn't also want you dead."

On one feed, a figure moved across the screen.

She pointed with a trembling finger. "What's that?" A surge of longing for Jake to put those big arms around her made her muscles go weak.

"Hang on." He spread his fingers on the screen

and twisted them from side to side, making the image dance and grow. Another few taps and the images changed from color to black and white to a photographic negative. Two eyes blinked in the darkness. Jake's barked laugh made her jump.

"What?"

"This"—he enlarged the dark image of the round, menacing creature—"is my friendly neighborhood bear on his nightly rounds."

"Not a person who wants me dead?" A shiver laddered down her back at his proximity as she craned her neck to look up at him.

The brief squeeze of his hand on her upper arm shouldn't have brought tears to her eyes. "Not even close." The way his fingers trailed down to her wrist as he helped her stand left goose bumps on her arm. He flipped on the lamp. "But now you know. If anyone tries to get close, I'll see them. I'll know who they are." In a nanosecond, his demeanor flipped to cold and calculating. "I will neutralize any enemy."

In a few efficient strides, he dropped the tablet on the couch and sat, resting his elbows on his knees.

"Got it." She settled in the recliner.

He lifted his hard chin. "As for the cabin itself? So you know: I have this place locked down tighter than Fort Knox. With escape routes."

"Probably includes another stupid tunnel," she mumbled, leg aching as she re-lived her claustrophobic crawl to freedom from the exploding suburban Atlanta house which served as a front for Kiera and Mateo's mission, including their fake marriage. The after-scent of acrid smoke stung her nose.

"Huh?" He lifted a light-brown eyebrow.

"Nothing." The skin over her upper back twitched as she imagined hearing nonexistent vehicles approaching and ghost footsteps crunching through leaves and twigs as people surrounded the structure. Was that a patio door sliding open? *Stop it.* Jake didn't have a patio, much less a door to it. Her heart pounded.

"So?" Damn the smug lift to the corner of his mouth.

Fine. "So, I was pretty pissed off about Brady's death." Scowling at another of his smirks, she crossed her arms. "What? Like you Green Beret guys cornered the market on justice and revenge? Sorry, but no. Mateo also saw the connection between Brady's death and the organization. When it came time to solidify the plan, I asked him not to involve my family members. All they know is that we were checking on some things."

An image of what Beau Lequire would do with her family members if he made the connection from her fake identity to Brady and back to her sisters and father sent a blast of ice through her veins. "Mateo wanted proof of the company's business dealings before he took the information public. I had skills."

He tapped the screen and the bluish light made him appear otherworldly. "You never talked with anyone about this plan?" He looked up at her.

"Hello. I can make my own decisions."

The edge of his hard mouth rose. He settled back onto the couch with a creak of leather, lacing his fingers together over his flat abdomen. In no way did he appear relaxed. "Do you need something else to drink? Food? Sleep?"

"I'm not part of the squad, Jake."

"You should rest," he muttered. "Suit yourself. So Mateo's solid with tech, and he had a good reason to sink those bastards. But why did you go? What was your skill?"

Damn Jake's macho blinders. "Remember how I

have an eidetic memory? Not only have I memorized Lequire's spreadsheets, but with my background as an accountant, I could interpret financial data. Those figures didn't add up."

He tilted his head to one side, a flash of the high school Jake she had known. "How did I miss you getting your CPA?"

"Surprised? This"—she pointed to her head then made a picture-taking motion and a click sound—"is why I skipped a grade in elementary school. It's why I had no problem with the CPA exam. Helps when you can memorize big chunks of the textbook."

"Show off."

Another hint of a smile curving his hard lips? Her heart flopped over. Damn him.

And damn her for that response.

He kicked his muscled, cargo pants-clad legs out in front of him, booted feet resting under the coffee table. "Then what happened?"

"Brady threatened to expose Fallen Comrades for siphoning government-matched charity funds away from the vets and into the pockets of the c-suite guys. Someone in the company penthouse office took exception to Brady's vow to expose them."

"Someone?"

"The CFO, Beau Lequire."

He pivoted forward, big hands gripping his knees. "Holy shit."

"You got that right." She took another sip of water. "And you bet I wanted to get back at him. For the project, I pretended to be Mateo's wife. He got a job in the IT department of Fallen Comrades headquarters, and I worked my way from an overqualified entry-level assistant up to a position as an overqualified executive assistant for Mr. Beaumont Lequire." Even saying the name left a sour taste on her tongue.

"You actually worked for the sleazebag?"

"You know him?"

"In passing. He washed out of the Special Forces selection course I was in." He palmed his eyes. "Then I heard Lequire sprained his ankle playing flag football on base and got a medical discharge. The bastard parlayed his quote unquote disabled vet status into big bucks. Rode that gravy train all the way to the bank, sucking up preferential government contracts along the way. Since he was the one with ties to the funding, he ended up as CFO. Now he uses Fallen Comrades as a cash cow to help daddy dearest, Senator Lequire, with his re-election campaign."

"Knowing how he got to the top of the company makes Beau even more of a jerk."

"Oh, yeah, he's a real hero." Sarcasm dripped from his every word until his gaze narrowed. "Beau would be dangerous as hell and have everything to lose, what with his senator father in his back pocket and the government supporting Fallen Comrades as an example of 'the best of America.'"

Jake needed to know exactly what they were up against. She said, "It took several months, but once I advanced to the administration department, we discovered quickly that Beau was a real sucker for a redhead in a short skirt."

"I can imagine." He grinned. Then a frown creased his face. "Bastard."

"While he was busy trying to get under my skirt, I managed to get into his spreadsheets."

"Wait. *What*?" If he gripped the cushion any harder, Jake would shred it.

"Don't worry. He wasn't successful." She rubbed imaginary slime coating her cold arms. Kiera knew all too well Beau's inclinations and appetites. She had been lucky to get out of there untouched. "But his interest in me paid dividends when I gained access to certain files. You'd be amazed at how he cooked the books. The documentation is all right up here." She tapped her temple.

"No one will accept your memory as proof."

Well, there was additional information in the data stick in her jacket pocket, but Kiera had decided not to saddle Jake with protecting even more dangerous evidence. The reporter she had contacted a month ago had died suddenly, and their conversation included only a fraction of the information Kiera possessed. She knew the risks. She would carry the evidence herself. Her knowledge of the ledgers plus the data on the memory stick was enough to put Beau away. If that didn't work, she had extra dirt on him. Dirt that would attract the wrong kind of international attention. So she was holding that piece of info in reserve for a special occasion. "I know my memory isn't evidence. But I can connect enough dots for other people to investigate…"

"Makes sense." He cleared his throat. "So, what about Mateo? Where is he?" He indicated toward her belly. "What about the…"

"It's complicated." Her ribcage wouldn't expand. "About the baby, Jake, I need to—"

"I get it. You and Mateo." He chopped a thick hand like he could slice the truth out of the space between them.

"No. But—"

"Change the subject, Kiera."

He probably recalled their pregnancy scare in high school, so she could understand his point of view. But she needed to tell him everything.

"Jake."

"Please stop. I've got the picture." A muscle jumped in his jaw. "What about Mateo?"

"Mateo's who sent me here. He's—oh, God. I'm ... he's dead."

Chapter Five

Jake stopped breathing.

Mateo. Dead?

His ears rang. "No fucking way." Seemed like she could have led with that tidbit at the beginning of this little visit.

A growl died in his throat. When she pressed her lips into a sad line, holding her shit together like force of will was some kind of superpower, his arms ached with the need to pull her into an embrace. He wanted to take away her pain and then annihilate anyone who dared to hurt her. Thank God the Morpheus Virus antidote had hit his system well before she started this insane story, or Jake would have torn the cabin apart by now.

As it stood, his feelings rested firmly in the "inappropriate" category. Kiera had sought his services because of his connection to the Morpheus Squad. She wasn't here because of their history, but in spite of it.

As she straightened her shirt, the jewel green brought out the rich colors of her hazel irises glowing in the lamp light. What he'd give to drown in those eyes again. But he had his chance and then went and blew it. Actually, he had blown it twice, if he counted their inappropriate reunion last summer.

His gaze went to her face. He had long ago memorized the bow of her upper lip. It featured prominently in too many of his nighttime dreams, wrapped around his— He adjusted his seated position to relieve pressure. No harm in a little fantasy now and then.

The white lines around her tight mouth stopped his daydreaming cold. She was terrified. Of the situation. Sure. Of him? She should be. After all, thanks to the

Morpheus Virus, Jake had *become* the thing that went bump in the night.

Despite having the antidote on board, he still didn't trust himself to touch her for more than a second without the damned virus taking over.

She tucked a strand of auburn hair behind an ear. Uh-oh. Kiera's hair tuck equaled mad or upset. Ranked right up there with *fine*. God help him if she ever did both at once. "The best and worst day at work was the last one," she said. "Beau had left both sets of books—the real and fake ones—on his desk. Nothing computerized because that could be hacked. Which we knew, because Mateo had planted a crawler program to search for the data and had come up with nothing. Beau kept the important ledgers on paper, old school. It took less than a minute for me to memorize enough pages to know what he'd done. He caught me."

"Shit," he managed to choke out the word.

"I tried to play it off like I'd stepped into his office to drop off a few documents before going on maternity leave. He didn't buy it."

From the top of Lequire's perfect hair to his salacious sneer, to the soles of his shiny leather shoes, that snake hadn't believed a word she'd said. "You got out of there and left town right away."

"No. I made an error in judgment."

His stomach tightened. "What?"

"I was so darn tired. You have no idea. After months of working on this project, keeping secrets, and then with the pregnancy, I was exhausted. I—I convinced Mateo we would be fine leaving tomorrow morning instead of today." Auburn brows rose and her brow furrowed as her voice broke. She pinned him with a huge, hazel, thousand-yard stare. "Oh, God, that's what got him killed. Me. Being selfish."

"No way, Kiera."

"Yes. Beau showed up at our house tonight with some pals, his favorite weapons, and a heaping helping of pissed-off." Her cracking voice ice-picked him in the heart. "But you know how Mateo's always into survival prepping and setting up plans A, B, and C?"

"Yeah, he was an engineer, first and foremost. He could come up with a contingency for any situation."

Even now, the memory of his friend's earnest face, creased in concentration, haunted Jake.

"Mateo had my escape route dialed in to a T. His escape, too. But he never got a chance to execute his part." She rubbed her side but stopped with a wince. "He had everything planned out if we got separated, right down to coded instructions for how to reach the cache containing directions to get here. He had drilled me on how to run the escape route until it became second nature."

"Wow, you got out of there, even with being..." Even now, Jake couldn't say the word.

Pregnant. Going to have a baby. Mateo's baby. The mere concept punched a hole in his chest. Then flashbacks of his ex-wife, crying and screaming, echoed in his memory, creating a nasty overlay of images. The miscarriage devastated them. It broke their relationship beyond repair.

One corner of Kiera's sweet mouth lifted, drawing him back to the present. "Let's just say I'm not the fastest runner right now, and the shrapnel didn't help. But I got the job done." She leaned back in the recliner with a thumbs-up and a sigh.

He couldn't help himself. While her eyes were closed, he looked.

Her chest rose and fell beneath the rich green fabric of the stretchy long-sleeved top. Whoever designed this outfit obviously hated Jake. The top cinched under her breasts, showing off their fullness, and then the shirt flared over her softly rounded belly. He was no expert, but she seemed too thin, too small, for the pregnancy, however far along it was.

Extended on the recliner, her shapely legs, exactly like he remembered, were encased in dark tights. Raw skin peeked out through torn areas of fabric over the knees. Beau had caused her pain. Hell, the man had tried to murder her. Jake's head buzzed, so badly did he want to disembowel and then fillet the guy.

Even pregnant, Kiera's jaw had too sharp of an angle. Her collarbones were too prominent. Was everything okay with her and the…?

What he'd do to erase the circles from under her eyes. What he'd give to take away her wounds and absorb her fear. Stress couldn't be good for the baby.

See? He'd let the word enter his mind. *Baby*. How about that? His soul didn't rip in two. Gold fucking star for him.

Baby.

His gut took a nosedive.

Covering his reaction, he mumbled, "Well, I'll be." He couldn't sit still. Another check on the tablet reassured him that Big Bob had moved on, and none of Lequire's men or the U.S. Army had taken the nighttime creeper's place. Jake refilled her cup and added a protein bar. "Eat. Drink."

She opened her eyes. "You're funny."

"Special Forces. Can't help it." He sat again.

It did his heart a world of good when she took a nibble of the bar and washed it down. See? Hydrated and fed. Not so hard.

She swallowed, the delicate muscles in her throat working. "In our preparations, Mateo had said something about how you didn't want to be around the rest of the team. Wanted to keep to yourself, after…"

After Jake had failed as a husband then let his personal demons take over. Cracked. Unable to control his viral urges. Couldn't be trusted to participate in Morpheus Squad. All true.

She focused somewhere beyond his shoulder. "Sorry."

He waved his hand like he could swat away the past. If only. "No harm." He pushed to his feet, ostensibly to check out the window for the millionth time. Damn it, he needed to pace. It took more willpower than he possessed not to watch her sigh as she took another bite of the bar. Regular meals were important for a pregnancy. That, and not being shot at.

She folded up the empty wrapper, the sound too loud in the bare room. "Thanks. Didn't realize how hungry I was. Hadn't eaten since lunch."

No way should his chest swell with bizarre satisfaction that he had provided sustenance for her, humble as the offerings might have been.

Damned if he would lose focus because of the tiny ray of happiness her presence brought to his cursed, monastic existence. No way would he examine how he would gladly sacrifice his own safety and sanity for a chance to see her smile. He stopped by the desk to confirm the security settings on the computer feed. Perimeter still clear.

He leaned against the wall opposite Kiera, at a spot where he could glance into the kitchen or out the front window by only moving his head a fraction.

She smiled. "Mateo said this was a good place to go. Not only for the food." The corners of her mouth dropped. "No one else on the team knew where you lived, and I'm guessing Mateo didn't want to link your team to our project, in case we were caught. He said you'd know what to do next. I'm sorry to get you involved in this mess."

He crossed his arms but maintained a line of sight to the security system. "I'll think of something. Don't worry." Damn it, if he had to lay down his life, he'd do it to keep Kiera and Mateo's unborn child safe.

Oh, wow, he did it again. *Unborn child.* Almost like it was getting easier to think the words, like becoming conditioned to handle torture. Once he got past the first punch, the rest of the pain blended into a smear of manageable torment.

Shit. He equated his ability to process her pregnancy to getting tortured. Real fucking healthy association. If only the imaginary knife didn't twist deep down inside of him every time he thought about her life without him in it. As if he had any claim to her.

He had none. Never would, thanks to Project Morpheus. Blinking, he concentrated as she continued the story.

"When Beau and his men arrived, Mateo bought time for me to get away. My watch triggered a timer on explosives. I believe Mateo tried to remove other equipment before the house blew up." She gripped the cushioned arms of the chair until her arms shook. "He's gone. No one could have survived the explosion. So much fire."

"Man." He hung his head. "Mateo was one of my best friends. And yours. I'm really sorry." He paused. "So, he's the—?" No way could Jake say it out loud, but he gestured in the general vicinity of her swollen belly.

"Jake, I—"

"Makes sense. Because you two were...? The ring." He nodded at the glint of metal on her fourth finger.

As she shoved her hair back behind her ears again, he cringed. The hair tuck. Land mines ahead. Warning received. "It's complicated," she said. "Look, we created a fake marriage, thinking it would keep Beau's hands off me. Didn't exactly work."

Jake went momentarily deaf as an image of that snake touching Kiera blasted through his imagination. "What did Lequire do?"

"Don't worry. I handled Beau. But it was obvious he wasn't deterred by married women … or pregnant ones."

"Wait. So, you got pregnant to slow him down?" He snorted. "That's real commitment to the mission."

"Not exactly." Her cheeks turned pink, and she glared a hole into his forehead. Ouch. "Look, Mateo and I were in a stressful situation. We wanted justice for Brady, and we were trying to do the impossible and take down a huge, corrupt organization. We had no contact with any family or friends."

"And things happened?"

"Also complicated." She ducked her head. "I need to tell you—"

No. He couldn't hear her talk about Mateo like that. The words burst from his mouth before he could stop them. "Did you love him?" He had zero business asking, but shit, he had to know.

Kiera spoke slowly, like she picked her words one at a time. "Mateo was a good person whose heart was in the right place. We had friendship, and when things got rough, he was there for me."

"There for you?"

"The situation was beyond complicated."

"Even more so now, huh?" Damn it, as soon as she flinched, he wanted to take those words back.

Then, a new and awful idea sucker punched him

in the gut. Kiera shouldn't be pregnant. Not with a team member's baby. Shit.

What in the name of God would the Morpheus Virus do to an unborn child?

The entire team had been counseled to prevent pregnancy at all costs. Offered vasectomies. Those who didn't get the snip right away had all been careful, including Mateo. Or so Jake had thought.

What if the government knew she was pregnant? What if she or the baby contracted the virus? He visually scanned the room. Swept a glance over Kiera. Checked out the window again.

Shit. Jake's driving need to protect Kiera and her baby went thermonuclear, wiping out rational thought. He sucked in a deep draw of air and willed his body to relax.

One look at Kiera's guileless face told him that she had no clue about what she might be carrying.

For right now, the best he could do was keep Kiera and her baby safe. He'd love a shot at Lequire, but it would have to wait. Jake had to use his skills and protect her. He felt the virtual click as his brain went into a different gear. New mission: keep them safe at all costs. Roger that.

A thought dawned on him. "Question. How'd you keep Beau from knowing you were Brady's sister?"

"To my knowledge, Beau never made the connection while I worked for him. Mateo had created a solid fake identity for me. Also, before Brady had begun working at Fallen Comrades, my sisters and I locked down his social media and removed anything related to details of his time in the military and his family."

"That's not foolproof."

She shrugged. "We took a chance I could pass without Beau figuring it out. There was no reason for him to connect those dots."

"Wait. So, you went into the lion's den on a hope and a prayer?" He hadn't given her nearly enough credit.

Smoothing her shirt hem over her lap, she gave him a half grin. "Yes. But to be fair, I counted on him being distracted by my boobs."

Thanks to that visual, now Jake was also distracted. She wasn't wrong. They were amazing, and his fingers itched to trace the full curves. He shoved a hand through his hair and eased back into the cushions until he got his mind back on the task at hand. "Okay. I have ideas for our next step, but I'd like to hear from you first."

The resolute set to her jaw had him smiling as he got a flash of the old Kiera with the determined, take-no-prisoners attitude he appreciated. She pushed to her feet and walked over to him. Fishing around in the jacket pocket, she withdrew an envelope with his name on it and handed it to him.

"This is for you. And right after I go take that nap you suggested?" She shot him a tight and weary smile. "I say we finish the mission to take down Fallen Comrades and Beau Lequire."

Chapter Six

Jake lit the envelope and let it flare to ash in the empty grate. He couldn't burn the letter yet. He needed to re-read it.

Damn Mateo and guilt-tripping Jake to protect Kiera and the baby, now and after this child was born. Even from the grave, his friend made a problematic situation even more difficult.

Yep. The other Fallen Comrade information in the letter sealed the deal.

They were fucked.

Unless.

Unless Jake could get Kiera to a totally safe location.

Unless he could convince the team to take on a fool's errand and risk exposure and recapture.

Unless he could resist the urge to personally storm Fallen Comrades and destroy Beau Lequire.

They would be fine if he could keep his virally fueled Mr. Hyde locked away, and avoid freaking out about this woman. The same woman he'd tossed out like trash years ago. If he could do all of those things, then yes, there might be a chance.

So basically, they were fucked.

He glanced at her. His leather recliner dwarfed her slim frame. She had just woken up after a few hours' nap. Thank God. He'd work on scheduling his own rest period later.

He scowled at her half-full glass of water. Yeah, he had hang-ups. Fixating on hydration was minor compared to the other issues.

Now she sat still, watching him with those big, beautiful eyes like she could see into his soul. Truthfully,

Kiera would be shocked to know half of his thoughts where she was concerned. Even now, his memories flashed to that night last summer in Chattanooga, with their limbs tangled and mouths pressed together like air was optional but touching every inch of each other's skin was not. She had turned to him for comfort after the funeral, and damn Jake, but he could never refuse her anything. It was his chance for a do-over, and he'd messed up.

No way would Jake try to get back into her life now.

What woman would desire a hair-trigger killing machine with a future full of danger and a lifespan that was likely short? She needed protection and data analysis technology from Morpheus Squad, and Jake would make damn sure she safely reached headquarters.

If anyone asked the government, Morpheus Squad and its enhanced members were top-secret weapons that required further testing. Actually, no. For mainstream government and the general public, Project Morpheus and the team didn't exist. Only a few key lawmakers, military brass, and some twisted genetic engineers knew a fraction of the truth. Once returned to the U.S. and discharged from active military duty, Jake and his super soldier buddies had been destined to spend their retirement as glorified lab rats.

After the team's escape from the "reintegration facility," every day dawned with the chance of discovery and recapture. Guaranteed, if Uncle Sam ever caught them again, they would never escape a second time around. That was why all the Morpheus Squad guys did a great job of living bland, unremarkable lives well below the government's radar.

By helping Kiera, Mateo had risked his freedom. Jake understood why Mateo had done it. Besides, if anyone could hide in plain sight, Mateo was the guy to do it.

It made perfect sense why Mateo needed her to give the data to the Morpheus Squad. The team could collate, analyze, and determine how best to leverage incriminating information. Then they would release the data in such a way that undermined Fallen Comrades but allowed the team to remain in the shadows.

By helping Kiera, Morpheus Squad risked the one thing protecting them: secrecy.

"Fuck." He crammed a hand through his hair.

Her eyes flashed wide, and she dropped the footrest down with a wince. "What?"

"Shit just got complicated," he muttered, his brain churning.

Project Morpheus was the government's dirty secret—an ambitious experiment to solve the biggest military challenges gone horribly wrong. Shit, if other countries' governments ever got hold of the Morpheus Virus, there could be a world full of aggressive, super-strong, and unstable killers.

At least Jake and his Special Forces team had been selected for their focus and discipline. They were most qualified to handle the virus. He could only imagine the awful possibilities if the virus was given to rogue militia in the Horn of Africa or Russia. Or hell, anywhere.

"You want to tell me what the complication is?" she asked.

"Can't."

He had to reach the team. Kiera wasn't safe on her own. She knew too damn much, like the mere fact that the team existed. However, her presence at the compound would put the security and freedom of each and every member at risk.

Even scarier? God only knew what lengths that bastard Lequire would go to silence her. Any moment, Beau could connect the dots. Kiera to Brady. Brady to Mateo. Mateo to Morpheus Squad.

Everyone and no one wanted her, which meant a hell of a lot of conflicts of interest.

What about the baby? If the government had enjoyed experimenting on his buddies, then Uncle Sam would have a field day with a mutant child. Jake's hand rolled into a determined fist. Not on his watch.

"We've stayed here too long," he ground out. "Let's get out of this cabin. Keep moving. Stay far ahead of Lequire." Operation Get The Hell Out Of Here on deck and ready to implement.

"Okay." Her auburn brows knitted together, and she sucked in a deep breath as she pushed her way up and out of the chair. Waiting.

"After reading Mateo's letter, what do you think we should do?" Her low voice stroked him like a smooth palm on his cheek, bringing his attention back to the present. When she spoke, it felt like she whispered the words right next to his ear.

His gut clenched. *She doesn't know what Mateo wrote.* The air got stuck halfway up his throat. He couldn't do what his friend asked—not out of a sense of duty.

Holding the letter and lighting it on fire, he let the burning obligations join the ashes of regret. He turned back around. "First, we need to go to the compound."

"Compound?"

"It's time for me to rejoin the team."

"Rejoin? I don't understand. You were on the same squad in the Army, and then you all were discharged together, right?"

"In a way, yes. We all … exited the service at the

same time, and then reorganized into the covert working group stateside. I haven't been involved since we left the, uh, military reintegration facility. Then I took time off."

"What have they been doing while you were gone?"

"According to the letter, they have stayed in the southeast, training and maintaining readiness to regroup when needed. Hiding in plain sight." Yeah, he'd abandoned his buddies at the worst possible time a year and a half ago.

"So what will you do?"

"Do?"

She pinned him with a hazel stare.

He blinked first. "It's time to ask the team to take down Lequire."

"All right then, let's go. I've already been tracked down once this evening. Trust me, it sucks."

"I bet." He blinked, flipping into op mode. "All right. Be ready to go in five minutes. There's a backpack in the bathroom closet. Stash some bars and water bottles in it."

After snagging the pre-loaded ammo magazines from the living room table and stuffing them in his pockets, he went back to his bedroom. He pulled out his go bag. No need to check it. He inventoried daily. It was stuffed with all-weather gear, various sundries, enough cash to live on for six months, and what few identification documents he possessed. He stared at the locked gun case for a solid five seconds. No. The rest of the guns and accessories could stay here. He didn't need to withstand a siege or ping an insurgent at 500 yards with a scope. He just had to get Kiera to the compound.

What else? Back in the kitchen, he grabbed the small antidote box.

And two more bottles of water.

As he unplugged the computers, a beep on a blinking screen caught his attention.

Kiera's eyes widened as she approached.

He shoved the tech into an outside pocket of the go bag, took his jacket off the hook near the door, and flicked off the lights. "They're coming."

Chapter Seven

Kiera put her hand on Jake's back as they exited the cabin. Her breath misted in the pre-dawn light that turned everything around her into cloudy gray shades. Dark shapes snagged her peripheral vision, making her jump.

"How much time?" she asked.

He pulled the front door closed, patted the guns on his chest and leg, and pushed the digital code to lock the door. Whipping around, he stepped in front of her and peered again into the forest. "The first alarm triggers when people turn up this drive from the county road a few miles away, so maybe five minutes."

Her pulse beat double. "What then?"

"We try to get out of here before they arrive."

"If we don't?"

Half-shadowed in the darkness, his teeth gleamed white. "I get to have some fun."

The hairs rose on her arms. "What?"

"Kidding." Only, Jake wasn't the joking type. "Get in your car. Let's go."

"Where are you going?"

"Here's the plan. We're both going to drive with no headlights to a hidey-hole about a mile away, so whoever is coming up this road won't see your car. Should buy us some time. Then we'll hightail it to where I can dump your vehicle."

"Because of the tech?"

"I can't let that gear off the chain."

"Can't you just rip it out?"

"Not enough time."

"What if we get separated?"

"Stay right behind me and stop when I stop.

We're only going a little ways down the road and onto an undeveloped lot back in the woods. We can refine the plan from there."

He dashed down the road and disappeared.

Where did he go? Didn't matter. She had to leave. Now.

Acid coated her tongue. Hand shaking, she missed the first two tries putting the key into the ignition.

A black Jeep with headlights off backed up the dirt road next to the cabin, rocks flying out from the tires.

"Follow me," he called out from the driver's side window. "Hurry."

She quickly reversed out of the driveway and threw the sedan into gear, her palms sweating on the steering wheel as she struggled to keep up with the bouncing red brake lights in front of her. The cold air from her open window blasted her wide awake. She leaned forward, squinting.

Suddenly, the Jeep swerved and spun up another dirt road, barely an ATV track, which seemed to curve into the mountain and disappear into the forest. She slammed on her brakes and forced the sedan to lurch up the road after him. A hundred feet up the track, he swept the Jeep around on a building pad, facing downhill, shut it off, and ran back to her car.

"Turn it off," he bit out.

She turned off the ignition, and with deliberate effort, took her foot off where it was planted on the pedal. The red glow in the rearview disappeared.

Silence pulsed with every pounding beat of her heart. Only the rustle of some critters in the underbrush broke the false calm. Off in the distance, she heard the tinkle of a creek. The sharp scent of her fear and the loamy, damp earth created a thick taste in her mouth.

Jake remained next to her vehicle, unmoving, one

hand holding a gun, his other hand gripping the windowsill of her car. He focused toward the gravel road, as if daring anyone to approach their position. He'd always watched out for her, but this massive statue took protectiveness to a whole new level.

"Jake, what—"

He held up a finger.

In the distance, the whine of an engine slowly turned into a crunching rumble as a vehicle traveled up the mountain lane. Despite the frigid morning temperatures, a bead of sweat tormented her as it scudded down her temple.

"Can they see us?" she whispered.

"No. We're around the bend and uphill from their position, but I can see headlights through the trees. Sounds like an SUV. That's what I saw on my initial scan."

Craning her neck, she held her breath as blue-white xenon headlights stabbed through the trees, making shadows dance and lurch. After a few seconds, a red glow replaced the white, and then light and sound faded away to silence.

"Do we stay here?" She couldn't unclench her hands from their stranglehold on the steering wheel.

"No," he murmured. "If they knew to come right here, then they may guess that we're close. We have to put some distance between us and them. Then ditch this car."

"Why can't we leave it here?"

"I want every trace of you gone from here."

She couldn't stop the flinch.

Kiera stared up into the dark forest, backlit by the faintest glow of the sky. "Where does the road in front of your cabin go?"

"Way back into the hills. Dead ends on an

undeveloped parcel of land. But I set some lights to flicker up the road, which should distract them while they chase my fake foxfire. In the meantime, we need to go in the opposite direction. Get out of this area."

"The car?"

"While I hate splitting up during transition, the best thing is for you to follow me in your car to a spot where we'll dump the vehicle. We need to do it before daylight and before they can mobilize drones."

"Why couldn't they do it now?"

"They can. Heat-sensing for nighttime. But hopefully we're one step ahead, since they're only arriving at the cabin now."

"We're safe for now?"

She heard and felt the shift in his torso as he exhaled. "For now."

Chapter Eight

In the first pale hue of dawn breaking, Kiera wiggled her cold feet on the driver's side floorboard and tried to warm up. Fabric stuck to her back, where sweat had dampened her skin. Her tights and knit top did little to cut the frigid mountain air, even with wearing the jacket and the heat blasting. Thin, cotton-candy-pink and pale-blue clouds glowed on the horizon. Sunrise wasn't far behind.

Sunrise. Out of time to safely dump this car.

They had maneuvered the vehicles down the mountain road in first gear without using brake lights for the first mile. Finally traveling on a paved road in *drive* was a relief.

Following Jake's black Jeep through the sleepy Georgia town of Blue Ridge, she stayed close but not too close. When other vehicles approached on the highway, she couldn't keep from compulsively checking in her rearview mirror until Jake turned off the highway onto a deserted gravel road. As they traveled deeper into the National Forest, frost glinted off rotted stumps and shrubs on the steep hillsides. Thick mountain laurel leaves gleamed with dew. Water staggered down mossy, rock-littered stream beds and spilled across the gravel road every several hundred feet.

The mountains were beautiful in their stark chill, but every twist of the forest road could hide danger. She flinched at a large shadow looming out of the dawn. Squinting, she sighed—an uprooted hemlock next to a large rock. So many things could happen out here. Her car could get stuck in a ditch or slide off the side of the hill. There could be an attack by whomever tracked her to Jake's cabin. Every minute they spent out here put her baby in danger.

The sooner they ditched the sedan, the better. Then, she could reach the team, dump the information, and find a place to hide until this baby made an appearance.

She could let Jake return to his normal life. How did he put it? *I want every trace of you gone from here.*

The guy she'd loved in high school was gone.

Kiera had been so naïve back then. Of course, they'd both been careful, but when you were young, giddy in love, and fertile, things happened. When the first pregnancy test came back positive, she had sucked up her fear and told him. Even as a high school senior, he had promised to be responsible for the child and love them both. But the minute he'd discovered she wasn't pregnant, he had dumped her and left town.

That was it. No more dates, no more holding hands, no more all-night talks about the future. He had washed his hands of her. Message received.

The next time she had spoken with him was when he and Brady had enlisted in the Army a few years later. She'd asked Jake to look after her older brother.

Then? Radio silence.

By then, it didn't matter. She moved on. As people do.

She yanked on the wheel as the sedan drifted into the soft dirt on the edge of the road.

A piece of her heart had always remained behind. That night last July didn't help the move-past-Jake plan one bit. She bit her lip, remembering the sweaty and sexy hours where intense passion replaced pain for a short window of time. But like high school, when their bad decision-making was over, it was over.

Now here they were, in that future. Together. Not anything like she had ever envisioned.

Stupid hope. She should learn by now.

Like when Brady went missing after he had threatened to expose Fallen Comrades. Kiera had kept hoping he'd turn up. That he'd be okay.

Stupid hope.

Tears blurred her vision, and she had to stomp the brakes extra hard when Jake stopped his Jeep at a turnaround on a ridge top. Fifty feet ahead on the side of the road was a clearing and a drop off.

He stepped out of his vehicle, his breath puffing clouds of vapor as he stalked around the car, guns tucked into the ever-present holsters on his chest and thigh.

Damn his broad shoulders.

Damn her for still craving him, even though the timing could not be worse.

And damn Beau and his corrupt company for killing Brady and Mateo and putting her child in danger.

God. Somehow, she would make Beau pay. She patted the data stick still stashed in her zippered pocket. Closing her eyes, she called up images of written accounts. Images she had kept locked tight in her mind. Information, ready to be delivered to the right people. Between her memory and the data in her pocket, she had the necessary proof.

She could have dropped this information off at a press outlet. Could have gone public in a million different ways than this mess. Tried to, in fact. The reporter's death was on Kiera's conscience. But Mateo had made it clear: Beau Lequire had the means to reach into any media outlet and kill the story before it could air. Literally.

Jake knocked on her window, and she jumped, banging her hand on the door handle. She opened the door. The icy, damp air seeped right into her bones.

"We've got to hurry. Five minutes here, at most.

Give me the keys," he said. No preamble. He'd turned as cold as the outside temperature.

"Want help?"

"Keep your ears open for something unusual—on the ground or in the sky."

A zip of adrenaline was followed by a slosh of nausea. Threats could be anywhere.

With focused efficiency, he pulled off the license plate, emptied the vehicle of any remaining identifying information, yanked out small boxes with wires attached to them, and threw it all in the back of his Jeep. Then he wiped down the entire car with some cloths.

Pausing, he pulled out his computer and tapped away. The screen flickered with red dotted lines and radar-type images.

"What's this?"

He pointed at one dot entering the screen from the side and slowly tracking toward the center of the screen. "This is us running out of time."

"I don't understand."

"Drone." He shook his head. "Damn Lequire. Of course he'd have tech. He has access to the best equipment money can buy."

"So this means?"

His gray eyes turned to hard metal as he darted his gaze in all directions. "Dump this car, get in mine, and put distance between here and there."

"Jake?"

"We need to move," he muttered. "Let's get this over with."

A shudder rolled through her, and she laid her hands on her belly. She scanned the quiet woods with a growing sense of dread, expecting to hear a vehicle crawling up the mountain toward them or the buzz of a drone from above. She had led Beau and his men directly to Jake last night.

He folded his frame into the driver's seat of her car.

Keeping the door ajar, he drove her vehicle right to the edge of the road. The front wheels dug into squishy mud and gravel as the sedan stopped. Then he got out, planted his big hands on the trunk, and pushed the car.

Through the mud. Uphill.

Like it was no big deal.

Cords of muscles rippled, but his breathing remained steady and slow.

The front wheels teetered on the edge of the drop-off. He kept pushing.

After another shove, he jumped back right before the vehicle flew over the edge. Within seconds, it crashed into the draw, the sounds of crumpling metal and cracking tree limbs harsh in the otherwise quiet morning.

Jake flung the keys far into the woods and stalked past her, to the Jeep. "Let's go," he called over his shoulder.

Before following him, she pulled off the fake wedding ring, said a prayer to Mateo, and flicked it away and down the mountainside. A faint ping of metal on rock echoed the path all her relationships had taken.

As she approached the Jeep, he wrenched open the passenger door, barely sparing a glance at her as he scowled at the woods. "Get in. We need to get away from this place. And there's still a hell of a lot of work to do."

The compound. Answers. Depositing the data.

Revenge for her brother. And Mateo.

With a backward glance in the direction of the jettisoned ring, she bit her lip.

Fine. She shoved her feelings about Mateo into a box, shut the lid, and labeled it *deal with later*.

When Jake handed her up into the Jeep, the texture of his sure, work-worn fingers against her skin sent frissons of heat up her arms. The hint of his hickory scent tormented her senses. Shaking her head to clear the sensations, she buckled up.

"What's next?" she asked as he slammed his door shut.

His head whipped around, expression stone-cold and businesslike as he started the vehicle and made a quick K-turn. Squinting up toward the sky, he said, "We may have to ditch this vehicle, too. If Beau could track your car, then he'll know it sat at my house for several hours. If I can get us out of their initial search grid, then we'll have more time to play with."

"Also, the sooner you can get back to your life." She rested her hand on the grab bar as he quickly maneuvered the Jeep down the dirt road.

"My life? It's done. He's got the resources and tech to figure out the connection between that location and me. It'll take him a while to dig through the legal layers, but at the end of the day, my name is still buried in the LLC that owns the property. When he figures out the part about my connection to Mateo and Brady, you and I will be fucked. Possibly along with the entire team."

She pressed a hand over her chest, anything to calm the frantic thudding. "I'm so sorry."

"Not your fault." He shrugged massive shoulders. "You were trying to stay alive."

"Given the lengths Beau went to silence Mateo and me, I should have guessed he would track us." Another horrible thought hit her. "What about my sisters and father? If Beau realizes the connection between me and Brady…" Acid coated the knot in her stomach. Ruining her own life in the name of revenge was one thing. But putting her family in harm's way?

What had she done?

"Shit." He rested his fist on the steering wheel and blew out a long gust of a breath. "Okay. I think they'll be fine."

"You *think*?" The air through her tight throat came out thin and hot.

When he studied her, his expression softened. "Look, I know we don't have a hell of a lot of options here. But if Beau didn't immediately connect you with Brady, then it will take him some time to track down your real identity and then dig deeper to find your family members. We're not even certain he'll put all the pieces together. Or that he'll go after anyone else."

"You just said there was a great chance he would figure everything out. We know he's vindictive."

"Well." He shoved his hand through his hair. "Yeah. I was trying to make you feel better."

"Beau won't stop until he gets what he wants," she muttered, folding her arms close to her chest in the cold air.

"He wants you. By any means." Jake's profile froze as he maneuvered the vehicle. A muscle in his jaw jumped several times. He glanced at her and wordlessly flipped on the heater. "Do you need some water?" He reached behind her seat, pulled out a metal bottle, and handed it to her.

"Sure." She chuckled, taking a sip not because she felt thirsty but because it was obvious he needed to see her drink. "You're not kidding about the hydration, huh?"

"Old habits."

She kept quiet as she rested her hand on her belly, noting the occasional nudge against her palm. At least the warm air from the vents took the chill out of her bones. After they turned onto an asphalt road and drove for another thirty minutes, she broke the silence. "Where are we going?" Her voice came out tight and too loud in the small space they shared.

"To get you some breakfast. Dinner was many hours ago."

"Don't you need to get rid of the Jeep?"

"Eventually, yes. We'll get farther away from here." He spared her a quick flick of his eyes. "You and the baby need food and rest. No way are you getting sick on my watch."

"We can't—"

Her stomach growled in response, and he chuckled, the first honest-to-God laugh she'd heard from him in ten years. A shocking sound. "You still like Waffle Palace?"

"Oh, my gosh." Her favorite breakfast chain. Her mouth watered.

He stared up toward the sky for a moment, then nodded. "I know where to go. It's way off the beaten track." When she opened her mouth to protest, he added, "Besides, your bun in the oven is hungry." He clamped his mouth shut.

Her cheeks burned. "We can talk about the baby, you know."

"I don't want to discuss it, thanks." His knuckles whitened as he gripped the wheel.

"We need to."

"Nope. You and Mateo. Got it. End of story."

"No, that's not the—"

"Don't."

"But—"

"Kiera, please. Stop." Like the words had been ripped out of him.

The baby kicked, taunting her. "All right." Her eyelids burned. Later. After they got to safety and she gave the information about Fallen Comrades. Then they would talk.

Another twenty minutes down an empty country road and they reached Highway 74. A sign read *Murphy, North Carolina, 10 miles*.

"Murphy?"

"They have a real nice Waffle Palace there. We should be good to grab a quick meal." He spared a tap and a glance at the tablet mounted to the right of the console. "No eyes in the sky over us. We're far enough away from where we dumped your car. It's a good stop."

Her stomach rumbled again. "God, I love Waffle Palace."

Chapter Nine

They entered the small diner and seated themselves in a padded vinyl booth. Clinks of silverware on sturdy plates and murmurs of patrons filled the restaurant. The warm scent of fresh eggs, waffles, and sizzling breakfast meats made Kiera's mouth water.

She stared out the diner window into the morning sky that had turned as gray as Jake's eyes. The silence between them hung like the low clouds, heavy, uncertain, waiting for change.

The waitress bringing their coffee—and water, of course—provided a welcome respite. She took their order and dropped it with the short-order cook.

Jake's gaze never stopped moving, outside, around the restaurant, and back to slide past her, over and over. It wasn't lost on Kiera the way he had kept his big frame partially covering her back as they entered the restaurant, and how he stood at the end of the table until she sat. It also wasn't lost on Kiera how he had picked a booth where he could sit with his back to the wall. He had moved the thigh-strapped gun to his lower leg where it was concealed by his pants. Before getting out of the Jeep, he had pulled his leather jacket on and kept it on, hiding the chest harness and gun there.

He seemed twitchy. Did it have to do with the stuff he injected into his arm last night? Maybe he did have a medical problem like Mateo. She had more questions than answers. Given his tight-lipped response to even the mildest query, she wouldn't get a response.

She studied him from under her eyelashes. His broad shoulders took up all of the space in the booth across from her. Every inch of his body vibrated with coiled strength.

He drummed his thick fingertips on the table until he snapped his steel gaze up to her. He stopped tapping and pressed his palms into the fake wood finish.

"So how's your family?" he finally spoke.

Her jaw must have dropped.

One side of his mouth lifted as he raised a hand. "Truce. We were friends once."

If by *friends* he meant *lovers*, then sure, friends.

"Thought you would want to plan our next move," she said.

A big breath made the leather jacket creak. "Already mapped out. Factored in time to have breakfast. Then we'll move on to the next steps."

"I was kidding."

"I wasn't." His face relaxed into a big smile. "I did enjoy talking with your folks when you and I dated back in the day. Your old man was a little intimidating, though I guess it wasn't personal. I didn't get a chance to talk much with him at Brady's funeral."

Because she and Jake were too busy … consoling one another. Her face heated up.

The muscles in her neck and shoulders loosened as she sat back in the booth. "He didn't like any of us kids dating."

"No kidding." He rubbed a hand over his face. "Brady was protective, too. During our time in the service, he always talked about you and your sisters. I felt like I knew your family better than my own."

A nicer, more conversational Jake? Talk about a curveball. Okay, then. She would accept the proverbial olive branch. "Dad's still a postmaster. Might retire in another five years."

"He's not that old."

"He'll have enough years with the postal service then. Mom and Dad were pretty young when they got married."

His mouth twisted into a scowl. "Because she was pregnant with Brady?"

"Yes." A kick from Little Bit encouraged her to change the topic. "You remember Mom passed away from breast cancer a while back."

"Yeah. I was sorry to hear about it. I knew she'd fought it years earlier, too."

"She was diagnosed around when I graduated high school. Then the cancer came back two years ago in a more aggressive form. She died a few months before Brady. I think she worried so much about him after his injury. Maybe affected her own recovery." She shoved her hair back behind her ears. "It was a rough period."

"Man. Your mom and then Brady. Hell of a one-two punch for the McNeill family."

Damn how the hard lines of his face softened, almost like he cared. Those gunmetal-gray eyes made something inside of her melt. Made her want more of this closeness. Damn it. Her defenses were far too low where Jake was concerned.

Lifting a shoulder, she continued. "We got through it. At least Mom had us all around her at the end."

His gaze tracked out the window, toward the parking lot, then back to her. "How about your sisters?"

"Britt is finishing college in Atlanta this spring."

"Still premed?"

Kiera chuckled. "Not even close. Joke in the family is that undergrad was the best seven years of Britt's life."

The rare sight of his grin made her heart flop. "What major did she finally pick?"

"Last I heard, she was finishing up at Savannah College of Art and Design, but on the Atlanta campus.

Something about needing to be in a location where she can 'feel the pulse of the fashion world.'" She lifted her hands, palms up.

"A fashion designer?"

"This week, yes."

He lifted his coffee cup. "Long may it last."

"You got that right." She took a sip from her own steaming mug of decaf.

"What about Reagan?"

"Big sister is still nature girl, working in the Smokies. All flannel-clad, rugged, and tough as usual. Works at the camp as a year-round outdoor education instructor. Self-reliant to a fault."

The sounds of cookware and murmurs of staff and diners filled the silence for a moment. "So, what about your mom?" She cut the question off as soon as she asked it. "I'm sor—"

Raising a palm toward her, he interrupted. "It's history. She was my mom. With all her erratic behavior and manipulation." He cut her off again when she opened her mouth. "Look, can we talk about something different? I don't want to dwell on my crappy past."

Trying to ignore the fact that *she* was part of his crappy past, Kiera looked anywhere else but at Jake. "So, what are our next steps?" she asked after a minute.

He stared at the table. His mouth went tight, and he fingered the car keys, which rested on the smooth surface. "I texted my CO, Hunt, before you and I left this morning, and he's prepping the team."

"You had a cell phone? Isn't it traceable?" Mateo had drilled into her not to carry any personal tech devices.

"Burner phone that was turned on for the sole purpose of sending one message. Don't worry, I ripped the SIM card out and destroyed the phone." He palmed the keys and shoved them in his pocket. "For now, you and I need to kill time until everyone gets to the compound. They'll ensure it's secure before you arrive."

"It's not?"

Gaze roving the half-empty diner, he lowered his voice. "You're the source of information we need to take down Fallen Comrades. Morpheus Squad needs to remain secret. Lequire's on the hunt. We have to increase our base level of security."

"That's what it's called? Morpheus Squad?"

"Shush. You can't know that information, by the way."

"Why is it so top-secret?"

"Can't tell you."

She pretended his statement didn't hurt. He had his secrets and she had hers. Fair was fair.

He continued. "Yes, we have a secure compound, but the guys need to be certain the tightest security measures are in place."

"Where are we going?"

"Our compound."

"Nearby?"

"Somewhat. Look, as much as I'm hardwired to go over every minute detail of this plan with you, I have to keep the location secret."

Her head shot up as she peered at him. Being excluded by Jake hurt. "You don't trust me?"

The intensity of his stare made her blink back tears.

"Of course, I trust you." He dropped his gaze. "But I also have to regain the trust of the team. Us. Me." He huffed out a lungful of air. "It's a thorny issue."

"Clearly."

When he ran his thumb over his cup handle, the tiny movement made her swallow. Then he tapped the table with a knuckle. "Meantime, we have some work to do on you."

"What do you mean?"

"Well, for starters, you strike me as more of a dark brunette." The lines around his eyes crinkled as he shot her an equilibrium-tilting grin.

She gripped the table edge. "What?"

"We've got to change your hair. You stand out like a sore thumb."

Tugging self-consciously at the strands, she ducked her head. "I kind of like my hair."

"Me too," he mumbled.

She whipped her head up.

A muscle popped in his jaw. His pupils dilated. Then he blinked, breaking the spell. "It needs to be changed so no one recognizes you."

"Is that part of your plan?"

"Yes."

Taking in his dark-blond hair, she pointed. "How about something like your color?"

"No." He tipped his head to the side. "A deep chestnut color would go better with your natural tones and highlights."

She nearly snorted her coffee. "I can't believe those words came out of your mouth."

"I've read my fair share of fashion magazines, trying to understand women…" He clamped his mouth shut.

There it was, the past which never quite went away.

Fortunately, the waitress brought their food, rescuing them from more awkward conversation. Kiera spent the next few minutes devouring bacon, eggs, and hash browns. Her baby wiggled in happiness. Great. A big breakfast kind of kid.

They finished the meal in relative peace. The sounds of customers' low voices and the hum of traffic on the nearby highway mixed into relaxing background noise.

After a trip to the restroom, she met Jake at the cash register.

His frame had gone stiff, shoulders tense beneath the leather jacket. By some trick of the light, he had grown bigger. Broader. In a slow, too-casual movement, he pivoted his head toward the door.

"What?" she whispered.

He stared out the bank of glass windows and the glass front door and placed his hand on the small of her back, rotating so she stood partially behind him. His murmur was for Kiera's ears only.

"We've been followed."

Chapter Ten

Kiera's hazel eyes went wide. When she bit her lower lip, Jake wanted to kiss her fear away. Erase the furrows between her brows. Use his own body to shield hers.

He studied the black SUV in the parking lot. It was conspicuous in its blandness.

Damn it. He had known full well the risk he was taking by coming here. But one look at her too-thin frame and the excitement in her eyes when he mentioned a nice meal? Years of training gone out the window in a flash. And he called himself a professional.

Flipping into high gear, he formulated options.

Kiera's mouth pressed into a firm line, and she raised her chin. His icy heart melted a tiny bit. This was the stubborn and determined Kiera he remembered.

Remain calm. Work the problem. Don't draw attention.

He draped an arm around her, pulling her close but tempering the impulse to yank her into his chest and never let her go. He inhaled the hint of floral shampoo. As the scent hit his brain, his thoughts coalesced into the only goal that mattered: save her life and the life of her baby.

After the waitress left the register to serve a customer, he dipped his head and whispered in Kiera's ear. "Walk slowly into the storeroom." No kitchen in the back, damn it. The Waffle Palace staff cooked on flat tops right in front of the bar.

Not many escape routes from the—he double-checked over the top of her head—two nondescript men who exited the SUV. He mentally plotted out the distance from where he hoped the back door of the diner would be to his Jeep. Too much distance, not enough time. And Kiera couldn't move quickly.

What about his virally enhanced upper body strength? He rolled his shoulders. Nope. Damned virus wasn't anywhere close to full strength yet thanks to last night's antidote dose.

Sure, he was strong even despite the antidote coursing through his system. But not strong enough to fight both men and keep Kiera safe.

His mouth went dry.

He glanced back as he and Kiera strolled toward the storeroom. One man headed toward the restaurant. The second guy leaned a hip against the vehicle.

The vehicle which was parked two spaces away from the Jeep. *Shit, shit, shit.*

"Let's go." He spoke in measured, slow syllables while his mind whirled like the state fair Graviton ride pushing him against the spinning cylinder wall.

He took stock of his resources: Sigs on his chest and leg, Ka-Bar tucked into his lower back, a set of car keys, and one unstable ex-Green Beret infested by a military-grade virus. Oh, and an injured, pregnant woman. Fuck it all, but they were in big trouble.

Guiding her through the metal door to the storeroom of the diner, he confirmed an exit on the back wall. Even if it was locked, he could break it down. He stopped the swing of the door to the main diner with his hip and quickly scanned the space, looking for materials they could use for step one of his plan.

"What do you need?" she whispered.

"Something flammable." He kept an eye on the restaurant entrance. To protect Kiera, he would kill whoever came through the swinging door. Simple as that.

"How about those?" She pointed to a cardboard box full of cooking spray aerosol bottles.

"Oh, yeah."

Now, how to light the contents. *Think.* The waitress had smelled like cigarettes. He zeroed in on the shelf next to the back door. Bingo. Bic lighter.

Next, he flung open drawers. Under a sink, he found another ingredient he could use: steel wool pads.

The faint tinkle of bells on the front entrance triggered a fiery rush of adrenaline. His heart banged in his ribcage. *Faster. Work faster.*

Even in Afghanistan, he never had to deal with fear like this. Why not? Because Kiera wasn't involved in ground ops there. When he handed her the box of steel wool pads, he cursed the unfamiliar tremor in his hands.

This cinder-block room would not be the place she died.

First, he needed to create a diversion and buy enough time to escape. But the diversion couldn't hurt Kiera or any of the innocent bystanders in the restaurant. Also, the spectacle had to not only draw the enemy into a trap, but also motivate the patrons to exit safely.

There was zero margin for error and no guarantee of success. He stopped cold and stared at Kiera's bent head as she searched under the sink for more supplies.

He forced his whirling brain to focus. "Take the steel wool pads and fluff them up as much as you can. Quickly. Make a stack. Put them in the sink. Then get fuel for the fire like paper or cardboard, place it all around the pads."

Voices at the register—he had to hurry.

Not enough time.

They had maybe thirty seconds to pull this shit off or that bad guy out there would quickly become a bad guy in here.

While Kiera crumpled up paper towels, he searched for more potential deterrents. Ah, a jug of cooking oil. Nice. He splashed it all over the room and drizzled it in the sink. Maybe the asshole would slip and break a hip.

Not with Jake's luck.

However, someone might rush in here to check out an explosion.

Now, how to incapacitate the lookie-loo long enough to buy Kiera and Jake time. Nothing deadly, in case a bystander entered. Just the right amount of pain to slow someone down. He scanned the room. Two bottles on a high shelf caught his attention.

Bleach and window cleaner. *Party time*. He grabbed a yellow mop bucket, dumped the bleach in, and uncapped the window cleaner so it was ready to be added to the mix.

More sounds drifted back to him from the front. A man's voice asking a question, then a woman's answer. The waitress.

"Get ready to run out the door, okay?" He stared into Kiera's wide eyes until she nodded and sidled toward the back door, testing the handle and cracking the door open.

Dumping the ammonia window cleaner into the bucket of bleach, he stirred with the mop until his eyes watered as chlorine gas released. Good. He propped the container so anyone coming through the door would step into a cloud of pain. Not deadly, but noxious enough to provide a few seconds' more delay.

Kiera leaned over with her jacket lapel pressed over her mouth and tears rolling down her cheeks. Fuck. The fumes. Her baby.

Stifling his coughs, he pivoted to the sink, flipped the lighter, and lit the steel wool. Then he dumped the cooking spray bottles on top. For good measure, he tossed the lighter into the pile. If he was lucky, the whole mess would blow right as the guy entered the room.

Nothing even close to the precise demolition timers he was trained to use.

Fumes and thick, greasy smoke choked him.

"Go!"

Chapter Eleven

Jake's heart stopped as Kiera fumbled with the door handle. He stepped in, yanked the door open, and exited first, scanning for danger as he reached into his chest holster.

She staggered out into the brisk air right behind him, her muffled coughs ratcheting up his guilt. He'd exposed the baby to toxic gas, smoke, and God knew what else.

Dragging her behind him down the side of the building, he peered around the brick corner toward the parking lot, all the while keeping his body in front of Kiera and his Sig ready. The second man, a burly SOB, hadn't moved from his position. The fucker still leaned against the bumper, trying to look nonchalant as he cased the front of the restaurant.

The Jeep, two spaces away from the asshole, at least was closer to the back of the restaurant. But it wasn't close enough. They'd never get to Jake's vehicle before the SUV man intercepted them.

Intercepted Kiera.

Damn it, he needed the second dude to go inside. Now.

Sure enough, after about thirty seconds, a scream and a blunted crash came from within the restaurant.

A series of small explosions shook the brick wall next to him. He checked over his shoulder. Deep-fried bleachy smoke poured from under the back door.

People rushed out of the Waffle Palace and into the parking lot. They had phones out. Shouts echoed off the glass windows.

Confusion took over. Fire alarms wailed. The guy two cars away from the Jeep ran straight toward the restaurant. Perfect.

Jake yanked Kiera forward in a sprint, half supporting her off-balance frame and gritting his teeth at her awkward, too-slow pace.

Five feet from the back of the Jeep, she stumbled.

His heart stopped.

He gripped under her arm and somehow kept her on her feet.

God bless her, but she kept up as best she could as she dashed to the passenger side. By the time her door closed, he'd turned the key in the ignition and re-stowed his Sig.

People milled about in the parking lot, pointing and blocking the exit to the highway.

The two SUV guys staggered out of the restaurant, coughing, spitting, and doubled over as they threw up.

So, how did you fuckers like my little chlorine gas surprise?

Then one man stood, swiped a hand over his eyes, and fished at his waist.

Shit.

"Belt in and hold tight!" Jake yelled. He didn't wait for her response but threw the vehicle into drive.

He forced the Jeep to jump one curb, then two, almost tipping the vehicle over as they crawled down and up a drainage ditch to an adjacent parking lot.

High-pitched pings, impacts on metal, had him pushing Kiera forward.

"Oh, my God!" she yelled.

"Shit. Stay down!"

"Hard to do." Her voice came out muffled.

Moving his hand from her head back to grip the wheel, he lurched over another curb, peeled out through an adjacent parking lot, and squealed wheels getting onto

U.S. Highway 74 South, heading away from Murphy, NC.

Sitting up, she brushed her auburn hair back from her sweaty forehead. "How did they find us?"

"I got sloppy." He smacked the wheel. "Fuck!" Taking a cleansing breath that in no way did its job, he glanced at Kiera's pale face. The face he couldn't say no to. The face that made him jettison good judgment and go to a public diner. Shit. He was in way deeper trouble than from the guys chasing them.

For now, though, he had to take care of Kiera. He'd deal with the whys of his bad decisions later after he re-tooled this operation ASAP. "Are you okay? Can you breathe? Do you need medical help?" When Beau's minions recovered, they would be coming for Kiera and Jake. What he would have given to stick around and permanently incapacitate those two cowards. Hunting down a pregnant woman—real brave.

She ran her hands over her head, abdomen, and hips. After a strong inhale and exhale, she shook her head. "No injuries. Lungs seem okay." She grimaced. "Baby is moving even now. Probably thinks there's a party going on."

Turning onto a less-traveled state highway, he said, too loudly, "Are you sure you're okay? Because if you and the baby need medical attention, I will get you to a facility right now and figure out the security issues later."

"I'm good."

"You're not hearing what I'm asking." He shoved a hand through his hair. "Like, do you really want to continue down this path? The mission." Hell, did Jake want to continue down this path? Protecting a pregnant woman who had become the most interesting target for Beau Lequire. Right now, Jake's precious privacy had been destroyed. His life was destroyed. Maybe the team's safety, too. *Crap.*

"Yes." She sat up straighter, and he caught a determined tilt of her chin from the edge of his field of vision.

"Yes, what?"

"Can you keep me safe until we get to Morpheus Squad?" She snagged the grab bar on the front dash as he took a corner too hard.

He eased off the accelerator. Thank God he knew these southern Appalachian mountain roads like the back of his hand. He'd driven them enough, logging hundreds of miles as he tried to outrun the memories of his fuck-ups. At least he'd gained a hell of a lot of knowledge of the terrain, the roads, and about a million places where a person could disappear. "I will keep you safe," he said. Eyes on the road, but ears attuned to the woman next to him.

"Once I'm at the compound, the baby and I will be okay?"

"Hell yes." His statement held more confidence than fact, but he could create a plan to ensure it happened.

"Then let's keep going. We'll be more careful. We only have to lay low until tonight, right?"

"Right."

She sat back with a sigh. "Once the information is turned over, things will be less dangerous."

"We don't know that."

"Why would Beau want to keep me silent then?" Her guileless wide eyes pinned him.

Shit. She thought all this would end in a neat package where she returned to a normal life. "He's got all the motivation in the world to shut you up for good." Imagining what Lequire's revenge might look like sent a wave of searing rage through Jake. "Our solution to the problem with Lequire won't be simple, that's all I know for sure."

A whiff of bleach and burnt oil drifted by him, and he rubbed his hands on his cargo pants. Glancing at Kiera, he flipped the levers to roll down both windows. He prayed he hadn't caused lasting harm to her and the baby with the toxic fumes and cooking spray bomb.

"Either way, I'm taking a risk," she said. "If I keep going or stop." A statement, not a question.

"Yes." God help him, but he wanted her to stay.

His reasons weren't completely altruistic.

"Then let's take the risk that includes avenging my brother's death. And Mateo's."

His thawed heart re-froze. Mateo. There was one way Jake could honor his fallen brother, which meant protecting Kiera and her baby. So it said in the letter Mateo's letter to Jake. Honoring Mateo's memory probably did not include making a pass at his buddy's pregnant fake wife.

Honor. Giving death meaning. If they could complete the mission Kiera and Mateo had been working on, then all the better.

They flew down the state highway, far into the mountains between Tennessee and North Carolina. Careening around blind corners and hairpin curves, Jake remained calm. He knew where they were ultimately headed and at least six different ways to get there from here. He turned off the state route onto a secondary road.

Those men knew what car he drove. Might have a tracker on this vehicle by now. Probably had used drones to find him in Murphy. No time to check on the computer.

Thank God for the thick tree canopy surrounding these narrow mountain roads. But the cover wouldn't last. He needed to ditch this ride. Fast.

Although he kept checking in the rearview mirror, he hadn't spied the vehicle from the Waffle Palace parking lot. Yet. Didn't take a rocket scientist to realize it was only a matter of time before the bastards caught up with them. With reinforcements.

As he crested a hill, he spied a *For Sale* sign on a rusted, late-model Ford Taurus parked on the side of the road. Jamming on the brakes, he turned toward Kiera.

"Can you memorize that number?" he asked.

She shot him a tight smile and tapped her temple. "Does a bear poop in the woods?"

Despite the knee-deep shit they were in, he loved her sense of humor. Had seen precious few flashes of it since she arrived. The impish quirk to her lips warmed the cockles of his cold, dead heart.

"Want me to call about a car?" she asked.

"Please."

He drove around while searching for cell phone signal. Then she sweet-talked the owner into meeting her at the vehicle in fifteen minutes.

While she waited on the wooded dirt driveway next to the Taurus, Jake ditched the Jeep on a nearby road cut. With efficiency, he removed the plates and any identifying information and wiped down the car. A thorough check did not find any trackers. Good. He might have bought them enough time to get out of this area and later make it to the team. As he checked his go bag and stuffed the extra tech from Kiera's car in a second duffel in the back of the vehicle, he ensured the antidote vials were also safely stowed in a bag. A chill stopped him in his tracks. What would happen if he lost his supply and didn't get the next dose in time? What if the antidote stopped working?

No one knew.

But the military doctors had made it clear: one day, the antidote wouldn't contain the relentless chemical reaction occurring in their bodies and minds. Each of the guys would turn into a soulless monster.

Then?

No one ever talked about what that next step involved. Not yet, anyway.

By the time he jogged back to Kiera, he had his shit pulled back together. The car's owner was happy to sell them the car for exactly the asking price, no haggling needed. Jake's shoulder blades prickled as he expected a black vehicle to appear on the road behind them.

He ground his molars as the owner proceeded to describe every trip he and his family had ever taken in this car. In painful and minute detail. Complete with a listing of each Cracker Barrel they had stopped at between here and Myrtle Beach. Shit, man. This fellow needed to stop talking already. Every car passing by took another year off Jake's life.

Finally, papers were signed with a fake name, Jake handed over a wad of cash, and he had himself a real nice family vehicle.

The car smelled like cigarettes and pulled to the right, but it would do for now. First stop was the Jeep, and he offloaded the supplies into the Taurus's trunk. Heading west, they wound away from Murphy, traveling on forest roads and doubling back on little-used highways for several hours until they passed through the small town of Tellico Plains on the Tennessee side of the mountains. A little farther down the highway, he turned onto I-75 and drove south for thirty minutes, then pulled off at an exit chock full of cookie-cutter, four-story, two-star hotels.

It killed him to leave her in the car. He checked in to the hotel as quickly as possible, cringing as the front desk staff wrinkled their nose at the residual odor of bleach and burnt oil still clinging to Jake. His goal to remain unnoticed had already failed.

He checked his watch. Early afternoon. They had about six hours before it was safe enough to arrive at the Morpheus Squad compound. Ushering her through the lobby and into a quiet elevator, Jake held the duffel bags with his left hand, keeping his dominant hand free to protect Kiera.

He examined every inch of the clean and nondescript hotel room. Safe. No bugs. No recording devices. No dangers he could detect. He pulled the heavy upright chair next to the door.

"Bolt the door behind me and cram the chair under the doorknob." He paused. "Is it safe for you to push the chair into place?"

With a flash of a smile that quickly fell, she said, "If I can crawl through a three-foot diameter tunnel as a house explodes behind me, run through the woods with shrapnel in my leg, and help to blow up a Waffle Palace, then I'm pretty sure pushing a measly chair a few feet across a vinyl floor is totally in my wheelhouse."

He snorted. "How is your leg? Your … other injury?"

She glanced at him then to the floor. "Achy but not bad. I peeked while we waited to buy the car. No pus on the bandages or redness, like you said to watch out for."

"Good."

Then he went very still. How badly did he want to kill someone for putting her in danger.

"Jake?"

He blinked back to the reality of Kiera standing in front of him and the foreign sensation of shakiness in his gut when he looked at her. "I'll be back in less than a half hour," he said. "If it's more than an hour, go to the Travel Suites two buildings down and stay in their lobby where the front desk worker can see you." Although, shit, public places didn't deter Lequire's men, did they?

Remaining on high alert, he exited the room and waited for the clunk and scrape as she bolted the door and pushed the chair into place. In record time, he went through a drive-through for some food and rushed in and out of a nearby drug store to get necessary supplies before returning to the hotel.

The pause between his knock on the hotel door and the moment she threw the metal door guard? Torture. He willed his damned shoulder muscles to relax.

It took her too long to drag the chair away. All he wanted to do was break down the door and rush in there.

After closing and locking the door, he blew out a lungful of air. Kiera stood in the room, a small, pregnant figure all alone. If someone came in here, intent on harm, she wouldn't stand a chance. That concept sucker punched him.

"Are you strangling lunch?" Her voice cut through his black thoughts.

"What?"

"You have a death grip on my hamburger."

"Damn it. Sorry."

Unclenching his fingers, he handed her the bag of food. "It's not fancy. Or particularly nutritious," he mumbled.

"You kidding? Right about now, I'll eat anything not nailed down."

"Then by all means, dig in. And don't forget—"

"Water?" A flash of a smile, and she waved the plastic hotel cup, half full. "I'm on it." Then she tore into the bag and took a bite, sighing as she sagged in the vinyl armchair.

Something tight in his chest gave way at the image of her enjoying her meal. It had absolutely nothing to do with the fact that he had provided sustenance for her. Nothing at all.

Then the corners of his mouth rose, a foreign sensation for unused muscles.

Stick with the mission. He tried to review the next few steps of the plan. He checked outside the window once more, pulled the drapes shut, and joined her at a laminated desk for the meal. Only he didn't sit. He stood.

Or more accurately, he hovered next to her.

Pausing after chewing a salty, crispy fry, he said, "After lunch, it's time for your bad dye job. Then a rest period." He hated the idea of changing the color of her beautiful, deep-red hair. Couldn't be helped. Another thought hit him. "Uh, any idea if the hair dye is okay … with the pregnancy? I did get a box of ten-minute hair color, thinking it would be less exposure. But I didn't want to ask the pharmacist."

She squinted at the ceiling with that eidetic-memory look he'd seen plenty of times before. "It's fine as long as it's not black aniline dye." She focused on him and winked. "Page forty-three from one of the pregnancy books. The super dark, goth hair dye contains a chemical that uncouples DNA. I believe uncoupling DNA is bad for growing babies." She giggled.

He did not. Because the DNA inside of her was more than uncoupled.

He had to get Doc to check her out, make sure the baby would be okay. Then what?

Then they would wait and see.

When Jake had agreed to test the virus, the scientist in charge of the program had made it clear: do *not* get anyone pregnant. Ever.

Vasectomies were recommended. Some guys did

it right away. Others swore to use protection. After his wife's miscarriage, Jake couldn't get the snip. He couldn't wrap his mind around the finality of never having children. No legacy … nothing. So he had been careful, except for that one night. He had dodged the proverbial bullet then.

After the night with Kiera, he'd been so rattled that he had gone to the doctor the next day and done the deed. Now? No possibility of Jake, Jr. or grandchildren, or any future family. Probably better that way, all things considered.

His gaze swept Kiera's small frame that carried a small baby. Damn it. Mateo knew the rules. He had protection. Why the hell did he take the chance with Kiera?

A question Jake would never be able to ask his friend.

Kiera was saying something. He asked her to repeat the question.

Her brow furrowed as fear shot across her features. "After the dye, then what's the next step?"

"Then we wait."

"Here?"

"I swear you'll be safe." He said it like maybe this time around the statement would be true.

He said it like a threat.

Chapter Twelve

After the meal, Kiera took the bottle of hair color into the bathroom, followed by the squeak of a faucet and water running in the sink.

Jake reassessed his weapons, the knives, the contents of the go bag. He mentally rehearsed the best route from this location to the compound until he had the highway numbers burned into his retinas. He went over to the door and unlocked and locked the bolt and privacy bar. Were the windows securely shut? Yes. Through a small slit in the curtains, he scanned the parking lot visible from their room. Nothing suspicious.

Then he did it all again.

Anything to focus on the op.

Anything to keep him from imagining Kiera …

Splashes and bangs came through the door, followed by a hearty *oof*. When a few ripe curses drifted out into the hotel room, Jake gave up on his professional duties.

Knocking on the door, he asked, "Everything okay in there?"

"Fine." Another grunt.

"Doesn't sound fine. Can I come in?"

"No. Damn it." A groan. "Okay, come in."

He had to stifle a laugh at the sight when he opened the door. Her half-treated, half-auburn hair formed damp clumps and wild arcs. Puffing, she tried to apply the color while leaning sideways against the sink. Her position was made awkward thanks to her belly. The towel to protect her shirt kept slipping off her shoulders. Dark-brown dye dotted the white countertop.

He kept the door open for ventilation. Funny, he'd tried to asphyxiate her with low-grade mustard gas, but apparently had no qualms about exposing her to toxic hair-color fumes. Turning his laugh into a cough, he finally managed to speak. "I'm no stylist, but I might be able to help."

She opened her mouth, then snapped it shut and sat on the closed toilet seat. "Fine. I give up. Have at it." Pointing to a box, she said, "But hurry. The color is done in ten minutes." She tugged the towel more snugly around her neck.

Pulling on the vinyl gloves she offered him, he took a glob of hair color and started at her roots, then ran it down the length of the warm copper strands. Strand after strand, he worked the color through until all of her hair had been saturated, creating an adorable, damp mess on top of her head.

The warmth from her scalp seeped into his fingers, making the tips tingle with the desire to touch more of her body. Even suppressed by the recent antidote dose, his virus flared, flooding his arms with power—and the urge to hold her. Wait. That last part wasn't from the virus.

How many times had he fantasized about being this close to Kiera one more time?

He wet a washcloth and gently rubbed away the dots of dye on her neck and cheek.

With her hair piled on top of her head, he couldn't resist studying her elegant neck. How many times had he kissed her right under the hairline? Nipped at the tender, soft skin? How many times had she shivered at his touch?

Not nearly enough times.

He licked his lips. One taste was all he wanted, then he would forget her again.

Liar.

Dragging his attention from the back of her

smooth neck to her delicate ears and the light pink flush on her cheeks, he tilted her chin up and met her clear, steady hazel gaze. She blinked and pressed those full lips together, tempting him even more.

Then she grimaced and touched her belly.

Damn it. The need to stay professional went without saying. But where Kiera was involved, the *staying professional* part proved to be an impossible task.

"Are you okay?" he asked. The bathroom had become far too small. Her floral scent swirled around him, despite the sharp hair dye odor.

"Yes. Little Bit is demanding attention right this minute."

"Boy or girl?"

"No idea. At the twenty-week ultrasound, this kiddo wasn't cooperative. Couldn't see gender."

"Were all the tests, uh, normal?"

"Why wouldn't they be?" She frowned. "That's exactly what Mateo kept asking, over and over. He had a lot of hang-ups about the pregnancy. Didn't like there being ultrasound pictures of the baby in my medical records. Knowing his computer skills, I wouldn't be surprised if he didn't hack in and delete them."

"I can see him doing that." His pulse quickened. "So, *has* everything been … okay with the pregnancy?"

"Textbook." A downward turn of her lips came and went. "Why wouldn't it be?"

Right. Textbook. Except not at all.

He worked hard to form words with his suddenly dry mouth. "What are your plans for delivery?"

Looking down, she mumbled, "Not sure. What to do … or where to deliver. I've still got some time to figure it out."

At her tiny sniff, he froze. The glimmer of her tears derailed any rational thought.

He had a decision to make, right here. He couldn't change the past, but he could ensure her future. He could give her child a fighting chance against someone like Lequire.

And the U.S. government.

With one finger, he tipped Kiera's chin up to him. The whisper of her sigh swept over him like a feather. Her skin felt silky, like he remembered. He wanted more than a fingertip touching her. He wanted to drag his mouth all over her forehead, cheeks, and lips. Her breasts, her body, everywhere. Until she writhed and gave the breathy moan he loved to earn.

He leaned forward.

But.

It wasn't about what he wanted.

He cleared his throat and thought about anything other than the impossible tightness below the belt. *Focus on Kiera.* "Hey. I'll make sure you have a safe place to deliver. If you want company, I promise you won't be alone." Could he really make promises like that?

Well, he'd better damn well man up and find a way to follow through.

"Really?" she asked.

"You got it. I'll even stand there while you're in labor and you can yell at me. Then I'll pass out cold. Basically, I'll be the perfect new father."

He mentally face-palmed at the insensitive remark.

With a furrow to her brow, she pressed her mouth closed, then gave a tight smile. "About that."

"Never mind, Kiera. I'm sorry I said anything."

"No—"

"Seriously. Drop it." His brain couldn't get the words out fast enough. "Let's finish your hair so you can rest before we leave for the compound."

Like blinds yanked down in a room, the lightness in her eyes faded. He knew her fake, it-will-be-fine expression. "Sounds great," she muttered.

Shit. He was losing her. He needed to do something to prove he'd be a stand-up guy instead of his current fuck-up status.

Think.

"Eyebrows!" he said, too loudly.

She reared back. "What?"

Dropping his voice, he continued. "Um, need to get your eyebrows colored, too. They're red."

"Oh. Kay?"

"Close your eyes. There's a little goop left."

She obeyed and tilted her head up, eyes closed. The image stole his breath. And broke his heart. Her sweet face, beautiful and trusting, shone up at him. It humbled him to the core to see how she gave herself into his keeping. How many times had he imagined the gentle slope of her nose and high cheekbones? How many times had he recalled the ruby tint of her soft lips? Shit, he wasn't worthy.

But today, he'd sure as hell try to provide something he'd failed to give her ten years ago: security and support. This time, he wouldn't run.

"Don't move," he said.

He applied the brown dye to her auburn brows, hating all over how he had to dull the vibrant color. He'd always liked her hair. Loved to run his fingers through it and watch how it glinted in the light, like a glowing bed of embers. He craved the feel of how it fanned out on his chest when they had hung out together, during one of those many nights when they had talked about fixing all of the problems in the world and making life plans.

None of which worked out, thanks to him.

What about now?

Maybe he could make one solid choice today.

He leaned down. With his desire rising, the virus flared in response to heightened emotion, wanting Jake to possess her, to sling his arms around her and use his unnatural strength to keep bad things away. Destroy anyone who dared get close to her. Use his body to claim her as his own. Like last summer, those stolen hours of sweaty, slick passion. Limbs and lips tangling. Her hot, tight warmth surrounding him. How she shook every time he thrust into her and drove her higher and higher until they both found the release they needed.

Again. He wanted her now. Here. The virus pushed him.

Damn, it hadn't been a full twenty-four hours since his last antidote shot. It should be providing more control to overcome these wild impulses.

Was it the virus itself or Jake's own will driving him?

His knuckles cracked as his fisted hands tightened and released over and over. *Control. Tamp it down. For her.* It took several seconds, but he suppressed the urge until he was safe to be in the same space as Kiera.

But, shit, how he wanted to remain like this, hovering over her, protecting her. Daring the world to try to come through him to get to her.

Kiera's eyes fluttered open, and her soft lips parted.

Perfect.

He paused a millimeter away from her mouth. Only a taste, right?

"Kiera," he breathed.

She smiled and leaned forward. Into him.

When their lips met, he took one taste of her honey lips and his willpower fled. His careful plans to kiss her and then step back? Scrapped. His mind spun.

Restraint was all a lie. No way could he stop with one kiss. A jolt of desire tightened his dick. He widened his stance to help relieve the pressure. Didn't help. He didn't care. He covered her mouth with his, moving over her lips. Savoring. Loving the brush of her skin against his. He started slowly then increased until their tongues tangled, and she groaned.

"Jake," she whispered into his mouth. "It's been too long."

He breathed her words in as he trailed kisses over her jaw and back up to her mouth. One tiny taste was never going to be enough. Sliding his hands over her smooth neck and collarbone, he stroked the skin with the pads of his fingers, fighting to keep his touch gentle, even when there was nothing gentle about what he wanted to do with her. Warm sparks flew through his palms and into his chest.

Her breathy gasp encouraged him to take the kiss deeper, his tongue tangling with hers. Like last summer. How had he lived the last ten years without the taste of her on his lips? How had he walked away—twice?

More. He took the kiss deeper, laving her lips, filling his senses with her scent, her taste. His thumbs trailed lower, over the top curve of her full breasts. Was that her groan of pleasure or his?

A beeping sound wormed its way into his consciousness.

She tapped his forearm and made a tiny sound as she pulled away. He kept a hand on the back of her neck and another on her sternum. It physically hurt him to break contact.

The image of her swollen pink lips and upturned face nearly drove him to his knees. He would beg for more.

The beeping continued.

He frowned. The timer on her watch.

Her hair was done.

She took a deep breath and looked away with a bright red tint to her cheeks. "Um…"

Swallowing a hard lump, he gritted out, "Shit, Kiera. I—"

"Rinse?" she said, standing with a wince.

The churning desire finally slowed. The woman wanted to rinse. He would help her. "Let's rinse!" Good ol' Jake, all business and to hell with feelings.

Helping her maneuver so she could lean over the sink, he poured cups of water over her head several times until the water ran clear. Once her hair was toweled off, he wetted a washcloth and rubbed the dye from her eyebrows. Then he removed the dye that had transferred to his face during their kiss. Worth it.

When she looked in the mirror, the corners of her full mouth dropped open. "Wow."

"The red is gone. You're a dark-brunette bombshell now." He picked up a strand of her damp hair.

"A brunette bombshell who stuck her finger in a light socket!" Her little self-deprecating grin made his heart flop. Her smile fell and she leaned on the counter, shoulders dropped.

He dried his hands. "Come on. Time to rest up until we leave for the compound." Leading her to the bed, he helped get her settled. He then moved the cup of water to the nightstand, thankful for a concrete task.

She smirked at him before closing her eyes and turning her head to the side with another sigh.

He opened the curtains a few inches to squint in the cloudy mid-afternoon light and then parked himself in the armchair in front of the window.

When he glanced back at her, the air stuck in his throat. It had taken all of ten seconds for her to fall sound asleep. Dark smudges beneath her eyes marred her otherwise perfect, relaxed face. Tiny dots of sweat beaded her upper lip and forehead.

Her bare hands rested on the top of the blankets. She no longer wore the ring.

Chapter Thirteen

"Is this the place?" Kiera asked, teeth rattling as the poorly aligned Taurus lurched and dipped over gravel, dirt, washed-out portions of the road, and oil-pan-destroying rocks. Jake had explained the team kept the access rough to deter casual citizens from exploring what lay at the end of this awful road.

Mission accomplished: Kiera was deterred.

They had passed through the small mountain town of Bryson City, North Carolina, and then headed due west into the Smokies. According to Jake, the Morpheus Squad compound backed up to a remote portion of the National Park. Literally the end of barely a road.

This trip was nearly over. Thank God, because the 300-plus hairpin turns on Highway 129 as they traveled east from Tennessee back over the mountains, almost ruined her. That stretch of road was called the "Tail of the Dragon." More like hair of the dog. Between the smell of cigarette smoke permeating the seat fabric, the lingering scent of hair dye, and the bumpy ride, her unsettled stomach pitched and rolled. One minute she was sweating, the next minute she had goosebumps. It was past time for this day to end.

At least he hadn't blindfolded her before driving over here. His rationale was that once she was safe in the compound, no one could get to her and pry out the information about the team's location. He also didn't want to clean up the car if a blindfolded Kiera had a mishap in here.

A few flakes of snow drifted down, illuminated by the car's headlights. Late snow showers in March, but in the mountains, the weather changed quickly.

She pushed her hands deep into the jacket pockets. The thumb drive was still there. She literally held the key to obtaining justice for her brother. A shiver ran through her.

For his part, Jake appeared oblivious to the weather, still wearing the t-shirt and pants from this morning. The chest holster remained in place, spanning the expanse of his chest. His leather jacket lay on the back seat.

He flashed a little grin. "Almost there." His low voice warmed her insides and triggered the memory of their steamy kiss in the hotel bathroom. Talk about curling the ends of her hair. She pressed her thighs together. Their kiss had to be a fluke. Or a stress-reliever. At minimum, it was a bad decision.

One of many.

Once she delivered her information to the team, Kiera would settle down somewhere for a quiet, boring life where nothing interesting occurred. A sigh lodged in her chest. And yes, she would leave Jake to return to the privacy he prized. Even on the ride here, he dodged questions about the Morpheus Squad until she had given up and stared out the window. She understood—Brady couldn't talk about his Special Forces missions when he had served. But it still rankled. This was Jake, her first boyfriend, the guy who had blown up a Waffle Palace for her. Seemed like that sort of in-the-trenches history earned her an insider peek.

Trying to ignore the awful ride, she prayed for the rough terrain and snow to end soon.

The Taurus hated big divots in the rough road, and she winced every time they bottomed out and rock screeched against the undercarriage. She kept imagining important parts of the vehicle falling off or sparking an explosion as they traveled uphill, deeper into the mountains.

Jake had long since stopped apologizing for the bumps over the rutted gravel road. He kept his steady hands planted at ten and two.

Little Bit seemed to enjoy the journey and jumped around like he or she rode a rodeo bull. When the baby tossed in a kick for good measure, Kiera groaned.

The dashboard etched stark shadows into Jake's face as he turned his head. "You okay?"

She braced her hand on the dash as the vehicle heaved over exposed rock. "Baby's going nuts in there."

"Sorry. It'll be done soon." He paused. "Unless, maybe we need to stop for a while? Will this cause problems with…?"

"My bladder? Of course, it's a problem. This kid is acting like I'm its personal trampoline."

At least his features relaxed into a rueful smile.

"I meant like it wouldn't jostle or do something … bad … inside?" he stammered.

"If nothing has happened with all I've been through in the past twenty-four hours, then I'm sure we're fine." Rubbing her belly, she grimaced. "I'm more concerned about what kind of kid enjoys this sort of terrain."

The laugh came from deep in his chest. "You always liked waterskiing and ATVs."

"How many days did we spend on Nickajack Lake back in the day?"

"Enough for you to burn to a crisp too many times to count."

"I wanted to get a base tan."

"With your red hair?"

"Everyone else tanned." Did he still have a light-brown color on his chest and back? It wouldn't be the worst thing to find out. "I finally gave up and went full-on sunblock and big floppy hat after that summer and ever since."

"Your wild youth."

"Parts of it were wild." Like the part where she and Jake made love for the first time under the stars. True, the back of his truck wasn't the most comfortable place to be, but the company made up for the backache.

"Yeah. Those were the days." He gripped the steering wheel and wrestled the vehicle through a deep, uneven rut. "They're gone now."

He clamped his mouth shut and stared straight ahead.

Wild youth. She'd tagged along with Brady and Jake for too many childhood adventures to count until middle school. Then they became "too cool" for Kiera and didn't want her around.

A few years later, something changed again. During high school, she and Jake stuck together like taffy to a pull as their teenage love bloomed.

An image of those hands roving all over her body hit her out of nowhere. A wave of memory from last summer made her nipples tighten. The kiss earlier today kept him front and center in her thoughts, damn it. She brushed a hand over her lips.

When he spoke again, his low voice dragged vibrations up her spine. "Here we are." Tension laced each word.

The featureless thick forest and rutted dirt road gave way to more thick forest and dirt road. They stopped at a small metal box where Jake rolled down the squeaky car window and punched in a code. She blinked out of habit. Code memorized. A red light glowed as he stared directly at the box until a low beep sounded.

He put the car back in gear.

She instinctively braced her feet against the

floorboard and winced as pain lanced through her wounded leg. She slid a hand down. The area felt warm, even through the legging fabric.

"That's it?" She studied the dark forest. "No gate?"

His teeth gleamed against the dash lights and he pointed under the moving vehicle. "If I hadn't passed the biometric testing, gate spikes would have risen."

"Under the car?"

"Through the car."

She swallowed.

He chuckled. "With the computer systems in place, they've known we were on the property for at least fifteen minutes. The security box is mere formality." Pointing out his window, he added, "One of the guys is out there with a scope on us as well."

The skin on the back of her neck itched, and she had the urge to duck.

Another five minutes of driving, and a group of several one-story buildings appeared. In one of the buildings, lights were on, but the illumination seemed muted. Or something filtered the light. Overhead, moonlit clouds were blurred from full view. Weird. Even when she squinted, she couldn't bring anything into sharper focus. Maybe the flurries had something to do with the effect.

When they exited the car, the ground muffled her halting steps. Very few snowflakes trickled down to the ground.

She must have given a strange look because Jake pointed upward. "Sound and light absorbent materials. Special fabric blocks infrared and satellite detection as well as camera-wielding drones from seeing what's down here. To any eyes in the sky, this place would look like more forest and nothing else interesting."

"Wow. Pretty fancy. You all must have a hell of a product supplier."

"You have no idea."

Stomping with her uninjured leg and making no noise, she asked, "Is that what we're walking on? Soundproof material?"

He nodded, a barely detectable movement in the shadows. "Basically, yes."

"Wow. I thought you said this place wasn't fully functional?"

He shrugged. "The guys have been busier than I thought."

"Are they all inside?"

"No. There's at least two out here with us." He planted his feet and scanned the property. "One when we arrived. One over there." He pointed fifty feet away in the trees. "The other one will be patrolling the back forty."

Squinting in the direction indicated, Kiera shivered. "I don't see anyone."

"That's the idea."

Taking her elbow, he led her up two steps to a central building's front door. She stumbled on the front mat, and another zap of pain shot through her leg, accompanied by a hot flash, despite the freezing temperature.

He tightened his grip. "Tired?" he asked.

"Something like that."

After a pause, he pulled open the heavy door, then placed his hand on her back for her to precede him. Once they stepped inside, he moved to stand partially in front of her.

The large room contained several oversize couches, recliners, and TVs, but also large tables and computer desks. There was no clutter anywhere.

Whoever laid out the room had done so in a grid where all furniture was either parallel or perpendicular to the other pieces. In the corner of the room sat an empty foosball table. Five men, each sporting weapons in holsters stood or sat in random locations in the room.

When the door closed, the men turned almost as one—in silence. Without looking at each other for reference and without any obvious signal, they somehow ended up in a perfect semicircle of huge muscled frames around Kiera and Jake.

Morpheus Squad.

Chapter Fourteen

Kiera didn't miss how Jake's stance widened. His shoulders had widened, or maybe it was a trick of the light, but he seemed more intense. He had barely moved, but she felt surrounded by his presence. Goosebumps rose on her arms.

Six men stood in the room. Seven, counting Jake.

Jake had told his team leader about Mateo earlier this morning. So by now, each man knew how Kiera was linked to Mateo's death. If their glares were laser beams, she'd be incinerated.

She swallowed, her mouth dry. A dull headache had built over the past few hours, creating a low-level throb in her temples. Sweat cooled on her neck.

The men stared at her. She fought the urge to cower even further behind Jake's big frame.

One man, around forty and sporting precisely cropped black hair graying at the temples, strode forward. His stern air of authority made it clear: he was in charge. When she moved out from behind Jake to shake the man's hand, her hand disappeared in his big paw. Cords upon cords of muscles rippled along his tattooed forearm. His grip was confident and powerful, but he didn't hurt her. He also didn't release her hand.

The way he frowned unnerved her, like he had memorized her face and read her character, all in the space of a split second. "You're Brady's sister." His voice reminded her of a rock tumbler.

It was difficult, but she maintained eye contact. "Yes."

"I knew that you and Mateo were working on a project together, but he didn't give details. He needed resources and extra funding." With a raised brow, he glanced at her pregnant stomach. "But there were big parts of the story he left out."

"That's not exactly true," she said.

"If you say so." His mouth pressed into a line.

Her quick survey of the men revealed expressions ranging from closed-off to downright furious. Strange reactions. A shiver rippled down her spine. Suddenly, she wanted out of this building. She'd take her chances on her own if this barely contained aggression was the type of help she could expect here. The walls of the room drew closer.

Letting go of her hand, the leader crossed his big arms, bare below t-shirt sleeves. Come to think of it, all of the guys wore short-sleeved shirts. Someone hadn't given them the memo about the freezing temperatures outside. She pulled the jacket around her, pitiful protection it afforded.

Jake hovered behind her, heat radiating off his frame and warming her back. He made quick introductions. "Guys, this is Kiera McNeill." He pointed at the team leader. "This is our CO, Captain Hunt."

"Your brother was a good guy." His lantern jaw clamped shut. "Good to see you again, Jake."

Too tense to say anything, she endured the scrutiny of seven sets of eyes, all riveted on her.

"You're safe here," Jake said. "This bunch of the guys are grouches, that's all."

"Hey, not all of us," a tall, Black man sporting a tan Stetson tipped his hat. "Ma'am."

Jake snorted. "Don't let the yuck-it-up cowboy shtick distract you. Rodeo here is the most badass weapons guy around."

With the angles of his face, the guy could model for a fashion magazine. Even the guy's smirk looked like a camera-ready expression. "Surprisingly accurate. Here

I didn't think you noticed all of my … assets."

Jake waved his hand toward another teammate. "This here's Gonzo."

The stocky, heavily muscled Latino man had a deadly gleam in his eye. Then he flashed her a boyish grin, complete with dimples.

Unable to help herself, she smiled back.

His neck flushed red. Not so tough after all. Kind of like Jake. Hard on the outside, but inside … well, not exactly soft. Soft and gentle inside described Jake from years ago. Who knew what lay beneath the hard exterior now?

"And this ugly mug is Stumpy." Jake grinned.

The White man with a black goatee knocked his cane against his leg. A *thunk* of metal filled the room, and Kiera froze until the other guys snickered. Stumpy winked.

For a group of big, scary ex-military guys, these men had a lot of inside jokes.

The way her week was going, maybe the joke was on Kiera.

Next guy was Curly. Pale, tall, quiet, and bald. He didn't shake her hand. Barely looked at her.

Message received.

Her gut twisted. There was something … extra … about each one of them. She couldn't put her finger on it. But Mateo had been the same way: more perceptive, too quiet, but ready to uncoil and strike at a moment's notice. It was like each man vibrated at a higher frequency than normal humans. Unnerving. Lethal. She fought the urge to run.

"There are other guys, right?"

Hunt gave a curt nod. "Rivera, Pele, and Red. They're patrolling."

Jake pointed. "This is Doc."

The tall, tanned man in his mid-thirties had the best poker face she'd ever seen. Never changed his expression. If he had any opinion about her standing there in front of him, she couldn't discern it.

"I'm a physician." His calm voice came from lips that barely moved. "Would you like me to check on your … pregnancy later, Ms. McNeill?" The team's doctor ran a hand unselfconsciously over his straight, black hair, pushing the ear-length strands back off his face.

"If you wouldn't mind, then yes, I'd appreciate it," she said.

Jake nodded vigorously as he hovered near her shoulder.

Doc stepped close to her and sniffed while he gave the slightest frown. Weird. Did she smell strange? She resisted the urge to do a chicken wing deodorant check.

"Are you feeling well?" he asked.

The throb in her lower leg tormented her. The ache on her temples and burning behind her eyes made her long for a cool cloth, a horizontal surface, and about twelve hours of uninterrupted sleep. "I'm fine."

"All right." He clamped his mouth shut, stepped back, and didn't move.

In such close quarters, the men's attention both reassured her and unsettled her. In this room was the protective demeanor of Jake multiplied several times— except she sensed they were waiting for her to make a mistake and then they would pounce.

Jake broke the thick silence. "So, guys, can I have Kiera debrief y'all on her project with Mateo and Fallen Comrades? Then she should take a rest period." Just like that, he took over the meeting. She gave a tiny *hmmph*. One part of her took offense. However, his suggestion sounded pretty good right about now. Her shoulders sagged.

His gaze landed on her with more weight than she'd experienced before now. What gave? "Do you need anything?" he asked.

"Maybe some water."

Like a group of dangerous Keystone Cops, three men sprang to action and scrambled to fill a glass like they were putting out a five-alarm fire. Rodeo must have won, as he handed it to her with a big, gleaming smile and a flourish.

Jake snorted.

One of the squad members behind Rodeo frowned and shook his head. Her mouth went dry beneath the unnerving scrutiny as the bald man glared at her pregnant belly. Curly. The guy who had taken over Brady's duties when her brother had been injured. She looked away.

Handing the glass to Jake, she said, "Let me grab a quick bathroom break." She needed a few seconds to breathe. With these guys looming, the air in this place was too thick. Too warm.

Once finished, she walked toward a couch, and the men scattered like she parted the Red Sea. Easing back into the cushion, she sighed with relief. The throb in her lower leg lessened. "Hey. I don't have the plague, guys. It's a pregnancy. It's not contagious."

A nasty silence descended on the room as all seven men froze.

Sweat prickled her chest.

Peeking at Doc, she added, "Not that I'm aware of, at least."

His unemotional demeanor creased into a thin sympathetic smile for a beat of two. Then it unfolded into solemn professionalism.

A few mumbles later, and everyone arranged

themselves either in a seat or stood nearby. Jake perched next to her on the arm of the couch, a hand planted behind her on the cushion. He didn't touch her, but heat and tension flowed out from his frame. The proximity was not exactly comfortable.

He'd sacrificed his uncomplicated life to get her to safety. A knife-like twist deep down inside her gut indicted her. Or was it a queasy stomach from a bug she was getting? Hard to tell.

No time to dwell. Time to provide information to the people who could do something about her knowledge and what Mateo had died to protect.

"Tell us how you ended up here." Hunt's rough voice cut through the heavy silence.

She took a sip of water and carefully replaced it on the low table in front of her before beginning. "So, Brady had been injured."

"We were there." Hunt stared past her, like he watched a scene straight out of a nightmare.

How could her mouth be dry again? "Once he was discharged from the Army, he took a job with Fallen Comrades as their spokesman." More nods. "He started noticing odd patterns in the company. Funding drives that raised millions of dollars but never materialized into promised services. He talked with some of the so-called beneficiaries of services from Fallen Comrades." She tucked her hair behind her ear. "Nothing. The veterans had received no funds or services. He started asking hard questions. At first, no one took him seriously because..."

Stumpy muttered and shifted his leg, "Because he had been injured."

"Exactly. Due to his traumatic brain injury, his conclusions were dismissed. Until he made a too-accurate connection. He shared his findings with Mateo and me." A jagged breath escaped. "He also had told his employer. Shortly after, he died under … odd circumstances."

"Explain," Hunt said.

"The official report said it was gang-related, random violence. That was BS. He never went to the part of Atlanta where his body was found. He had never gotten into drugs or ran with any bad crowd. Heck, the *only* crowd he hung out with was you all." She rubbed her eyes, like doing so could remove the image of his still, quiet body in the casket. "So, yes, Brady figured out who was siphoning money from the donors and straight into his own pockets: Beau Lequire."

"God damn it," Hunt snapped. "I hated the entitled prick the minute I laid eyes on his privileged ass years ago at Special Forces Assessment and Selection." His wave was more of a karate chop of air. "Go on."

"Mateo and I decided to find out for ourselves what was going on at Fallen Comrades. It was a way to give Brady's death meaning. Frankly, we wanted revenge."

The men all murmured agreement and nodded along with her story. They might not like what she and Mateo did, but they understood the motivation.

"So we gathered information, especially about how Beau moved funds in and out of the company. His methods were undetectable, unless…"

Rodeo's grin gleamed white against his dark skin as he jiggled a thick purple disc in one hand. "Unless you were good with computers like Mateo." With a negligent flick of his wrist, the yo-yo climbed up and down a string in a whir, softening the hard silence.

"Or if you can interpret financial databases and have an eidetic memory." She pointed a thumb toward herself.

"Oh?" Hunt asked, peering at her.

"Yes." Unzipping her jacket pocket, she drew out the gig stick. "Also helps when some of their transactions are backed up on a drive."

Jake leaned forward, his eyebrows up. "Where'd you get that?"

"Mateo."

"You've carried it this whole time?" he bit out.

"Yes." She did her best not to cringe as his frame went rigid and his expression closed. She didn't need his approval. Truly, she didn't.

"You should have given it to me."

"Last person I entrusted with the information died. The reporter. Remember?"

"Damn," Rodeo gritted out as he ran the toy up and down the string.

"What's on it?" From where he sat, Stumpy leaned forward, hand on the top of his cane.

"Enough data to take down Fallen Comrades."

"Gimme." Stumpy's dark-green eyes glinted.

At Jake's growl right next to her ear, the hairs on her arm stood straight up.

When his hand curled into a fist on his hard thigh next to her, the air got stuck in her throat as she looked up at him.

"Kiera." It was amazing how the words made it through the tight clench of his jaw. "Those men from earlier today would have killed you for that piece of intelligence alone." Jake's gray stare bore into her. The mouth that had brought her pleasure earlier today now pressed into a hard, angry line.

Her neck and cheeks heated up. They would have killed Jake, too, if they thought he had the data. No one was safe with this information. Kiera had enough virtual blood on her hands.

Suddenly, six other men looked anywhere but at

her. The purple yo-yo's soft shush in the air stopped.

Big, muscle-bound chickens.

Hunt broke the stalemate by stepping forward and taking the drive from her shaking hand. "Stumpy will get to work on this. Thank you for bringing the information here. I know what it cost to get this."

Stupid tears pricked her eyes. Her head ached. Damn it, Brady's sister would not cry in front of his Special Forces squad.

Instead, she concentrated on the story. "So." She cleared her clogged throat and started again. "On our project, my job was to directly monitor Beau Lequire."

Gonzo made a face. "The asshole."

"Yeah, Beau was a real winner. He kept double books. In public audits, you'd never see how he diverted funds away from the vets and straight into his own pockets."

"Son of a bitch," Gonzo spat. "Begging your pardon, ma'am." His cheeks darkened.

"No offense taken. Besides, I agree. The company is supposed to be helping guys like my brother, but instead, they're financing yachts for their c-suite folks." She took another gulp of water and avoided making eye contact with Jake. If he didn't like how she had transported the thumb drive, then his hair was going to catch fire with this next tidbit. "What's worse, it looks like the donations are bankrolling Senator Lequire's re-election campaign. And we only have preliminary information, but there may be a connection to Bratva."

Indrawn breaths and rolled fists all around the room.

"The Russian mob's involved?" Jake exploded. "What the hell? You didn't tell me that part."

Tilting her head back over her shoulder, she studied his drawn brows. "You didn't ask."

Several coughs covered laughter. Barely.

Hunt rubbed his hand over what looked suspiciously like a smile. "Nice job." He pressed each fingertip to the end of his thumb, over and over. "However. Means we have a bigger problem."

"Bigger than this?" Kiera asked.

"Senator Lequire was involved in some of our … Special Forces activities," Hunt said.

"So? That was in the past."

"No. Not with the Senator. I'm going to—" The CO looked up at the ceiling then back to Kiera. "His involvement complicates everything from how we handle this information to what we risk by going public with it. If what you said about Bratva is true, then this goes way deeper than we can easily handle." He glanced at Doc. "We may want to sit on this…"

She leaned forward, head buzzing. "Wait. You're not going to use the files? After everything we've done? After what Brady sacrificed?"

Somehow, Hunt's shoulders became larger. "I said it's problematic."

No one moved.

No one breathed.

The silence roared in her ears. Her heartrate shot up by fifty percent. Another warm wave heated her cheeks.

"Christ," Rodeo breathed, his eyes narrowed into deadly, white slits in the shadow beneath his cowboy hat. "If we release the data, they could track us. We could be—"

Hunt shook his head. "Yeah. I know. Not to mention what would happen if Bratva gets involved." Another few seconds of painful silence passed. "Anything else we should know?" His words came out like hammer strikes on an anvil. He remained standing, thick arms crossed over a broad chest, studying her like a human calculator, adding up the pieces of her story over and over.

Because he must have realized by now that all of the pieces didn't quite fit.

"On top of cooking the books and being embroiled in U.S. politics and international mafias? That's not enough?" Her last few words came out too high, too pinched.

No answer.

She swallowed. "Well." In for a penny, as they said. "If you want more information to use, then you'll be interested to know that Beau's got some … interesting tastes. If people knew about them, it wouldn't help his father's re-election campaign."

Hunt prompted, "Such as?"

"You know. Weird stuff. With women." More silence. The commander wasn't going to make this easy. Clearing her throat, she said, "Beau had an interesting sexual appetite."

"Who doesn't?" Gonzo flexed his big biceps. "What's the big deal nowadays?"

Kiera almost giggled but stopped at Jake's dark glare at his teammate. "It's more than simple preferences and practices. Beau maintained a rotation of women in and out of his office for 'meetings' which his administrative assistant, yours truly, knew about. There were some, um, more aggressive, sexual-type activities."

Jake's voice came out hoarse. "You were exposed to this?" The rough tone dragged like the softest sandpaper over her sensitive nerves.

"Not quite the terminology I'd use. But yes, he propositioned me. I think it was his way of flirting."

"No," Jake said.

"Yes."

"And?" Like he couldn't help but ask.

She grinned. "Don't worry. His sexual charisma and fantasy stories didn't work on me, thanks for asking. I need flowers and chocolate first before moving on to whips and chains."

Gonzo choked on air, and Rodeo pounded him on the back with big, deep *whumps*.

She pursed her lips. "Kidding, guys."

"I like her." Rodeo started the purple disc up and down the string again.

"Seriously, though? People have all kinds of preferences, which is fine and good." She glanced around and smiled. A few of the men were studying the floor or the furniture like there was a final exam coming up. Interesting. "But there are supposed to be rules like consent and respecting safewords. Beau pretty much ignored all of those. Very few women returned for a second 'date' with him."

Hunt's smirk twisted into a scowl. "Bet Senator Lequire wouldn't approve of his son's extracurricular activities. Especially if it counts for assault."

"Why is this news?" Doc said. "Politics and sexual misconduct is nothing new."

"No doubt knowledge of these behaviors would play poorly with Senator Lequire's conservative voting base," she said. "And he really wants to be re-elected."

"He needs to be re-elected," Hunt muttered. "He's one of the puppet masters, in charge of pulling strings of government right now." He turned to the men. "How do you think a sex scandal involving his son and tainting his favorite stump topic, Fallen Comrades, with a dash of Russian mob involvement, would play out for Senator Lequire's re-election campaign?"

Gonzo raised his hand. "I know. It would play out poorly."

Rodeo rolled his eyes.

Rubbing his angular jaw, Hunt whistled low. "Son of a bitch, this is a mess."

Kiera blew out a slow breath. At least attention was focused somewhere else besides on her. She glanced up at Jake. Almost everyone's attention. Sweat prickled her upper chest. She shifted her legs, trying to find a comfortable angle for the throbbing injury.

Rodeo widened his stance, fingering a knife handle stowed at his hip with his free hand while he kept the rhythmic movement of the disk with the other. "Let's go back to the part about where the bastard killed Mateo. When do we get revenge for that?"

Low murmurs of agreement filled the room.

"Hold on, fellas." The CO held up his hands. "I'd love nothing more than to cram my fist through Lequire's entitled face for what he did. But we need to gather more information. Nail down a plan with a high chance of success. Unravel the layers of his company first. Figure out how it all connects with Senator Lequire. We have to do this mission right."

"You're going to help, right?" Kiera asked, chest not fully expanding. Her head swam. Had she wasted her time and theirs coming here?

Hunt gave a curt nod. "Eventually." He held up a hand at her protest. "We haven't forgotten about Brady and the sacrifice Mateo made. But we have to be careful."

"You mean do it in secret?" Stumpy asked from where he sat on the couch.

Hunt nodded. "Deep. We need to avoid any actions that could expose the squad." His gaze skimmed over the men and rested on Kiera. "For many reasons."

"Like what?" She studied each man in the room. Would this team be enough to stop Beau? What about a politically motivated senator? The Russian mob? Her gaze rested on Hunt, and his calculating stare turned her blood to ice.

If Hunt had a different agenda…

Any man in this room could be playing both sides and putting Kiera and her baby in more danger than she'd been in twenty-four hours earlier.

She couldn't get a solid lungful of air. Her headache intensified.

What if she had misjudged the entire situation? She glanced up at Jake. He remained next to her, a solid statue, tight lines etched on either side of his mouth.

Hunt smiled, the gesture not reassuring at all. "Our team does not exist. It needs to stay that way. That single fact complicates our little project."

Exposing a corrupt multi-billion-dollar organization and one of the highest-placed senators in government … a 'little project?'

"So, what are we waiting for?" Rodeo did a move where the toy whirred at the bottom of the string for a few seconds, then returned. Despite the superstar smile and the casual, quiet movements of his wrist, the tall cowboy vibrated with corded, dangerous power.

Everyone in this room gave off quiet, competent, utterly lethal vibes. She felt tiny and trapped on the couch.

"We're not ready. Not yet," Hunt snapped. "I believe we've got a far bigger problem here." He towered over Kiera. "So. Whose baby is this?"

Rearing back, she hesitated to answer his abrupt question. *Can you say,* 'not your business?' "Pardon? What?"

"Not me, sir." Jake didn't lift his head but nudged her in the back.

Good grief.

She swallowed sand. "Yes, it's Jake's."

Chapter Fifteen

"Fuck me," Gonzo spat, rearing back.

Rodeo's yo-yo clanked on the floor.

Hunt's face clouded over.

Jake's teammates looked like they had either sucked lemons or seen the portal to Hell.

His ears rang. How had he not figured it out?

Because denial wasn't a river in Egypt, idiot. Deep down, he knew.

Didn't want to speak the words.

Couldn't risk hoping and then being wrong.

At the curses of several men, Kiera wrapped her arms over her belly. His—her baby. Their baby. *Oh, shit.* He fought a wave of nausea. What a fucking time to get sympathy morning sickness.

Instead, Jake wanted to yank her into his embrace and fight anyone who dared question him for supporting her.

There wasn't enough air in this building, and Jake needed an oxygen tank, ASAP.

"Shit," spat Rodeo. "What can be done about it?"

"Is there still time to get rid of it?" Stumpy asked a blank-faced Doc.

More debate swirled. Options from people who had no right to an opinion.

His head buzzed like a swarm of hornets had taken up residence. Rubbing a hand on his head to try to clear it, he followed his buddies' lines of questioning. Logical, realistic conclusions.

Also totally unacceptable.

Heat blew out of the center of his chest and woke up the Morpheus Virus, zipping hot lines of rage through each muscle fiber. Taking care not to hurt Kiera, he dropped a hand on her shoulder. By God, he'd disallow anyone besides Kiera to move his hand.

Scooting forward, she waved a hand to get the guys' attention. "Whoa. What's the big deal? First of all, *it's* just a baby. And it's my baby."

And mine.

She continued, neck turning pink, but spine remaining straight. "These things happen. Welcome to the real world, guys. Second of all, there's nothing *to* do, other than I will deliver and care for this child when the time comes."

Jake's tongue stuck to the roof of his mouth. She had said *I* but no *we.*

Oh, shit. He kept his hand planted on her shoulder, maintaining a real and solid connection.

Shuffles of feet and unhappy-sounding rumbles came from the men. No one met his eyes.

When Kiera stood up, Hunt actually took a step back. Jake let his hand drop as he hovered right behind her. If anyone tried anything stupid, brothers-in-arms or not, Jake would stop them.

Lifting a hand, palm up, she said, "You guys. Have you never seen a pregnant woman? What's going on here? Really." She turned halfway around. "Jake?"

Her stricken grimace weakened his knees. She had no idea what she carried. No one knew what she carried. That was the problem.

Kiera patted her belly until she froze.

Jake curled a hand into a fist, wanting to punch every angry stare.

In a slow movement, she slid her hand down to rest at her side. When she glanced back, those wide, hazel eyes locked on to him like he'd become some kind of life preserver.

Damn him, but he wanted the job.

Hunt took control of the room with a slash of his hand. "Sit, ma'am. Please. Everyone, simmer down."

"I think I'll stand." Wincing, she remained on her feet.

"Kiera," Jake murmured. She had no idea what kind of virally enhanced bear she poked.

Crossing her arms, she shook her head. "No. What's the deal?" She wiggled a finger through the hole on her jacket. "Look, I've had a terrible last twenty-four hours, so someone had better tell me what's going on."

Jake was as proud of the way she stood up for herself as he was terrified of how the guys would react. He tensed.

"Ma'am, you really want to sit down." When she didn't move, Hunt lifted a massive shoulder. "Suit yourself."

His CO stared at her so long that Jake's back muscles twitched. The Morpheus Virus blasting through his veins desperately wanted him to get in between Hunt and Kiera. Ingrained military command structure kept him in his place. Barely.

Hunt took a barrel-chested breath. "The reason we can't simply take this information to a news outlet and blow the lid off of Fallen Comrades involves a couple of issues. Project Morpheus doesn't officially exist. *We* don't officially exist."

"Fine. Keep your work secret, then," she said. "I'll never rat you all out."

A chop of one meaty hand against the palm of the other riveted Jake's attention. "It's not that simple," Hunt said. "The short version? Each of us is a military biological experiment gone wrong, and if the government finds us, we'll be locked up and tested for life."

"Experiment? What?" The blood left her face. A fine sheen of sweat glistened on her skin.

The glare she shot Jake hit him like a slap. He should have mentioned something—anything—to her in the past few years. Wasn't like he never had an opportunity to tell her.

Her voice came out as a whisper. "Oh, God. Maybe I should take a seat, after all."

He wouldn't let her fall. Nothing was going to hurt Kiera or this baby. His baby. A brief stab of pain ice-picked his ribs before he grabbed her warm arms. She limped as he guided her back to sit on the couch. Damn everyone here, but he would protect Kiera and his child.

Hunt's piercing ice-blue gaze stayed locked on her. "While in Special Forces, each man here volunteered for a top-secret experiment. We were injected with the Morpheus Virus. It turned us into super-warriors … killing machines." He glanced at Doc.

The physician's mouth barely moved. "That's not entirely accurate on a biochemical level."

"Close enough." Hunt rubbed one muscled bicep.

****

Kiera didn't care about the exact explanation. These men had been altered by some military-grade virus, and here Kiera sat in the midst of these … machines. Her leg muscles tensed, ready to run.

But forget Lequire's goons coming after her. Forget the Russian mafia. The real threat stood mere feet away from her. She calculated the distance to the front door.

She wouldn't get far, would she? Her heart hammered away beneath her ribs. The baby kicked, probably amped up on her adrenaline.

She swallowed what felt like cardboard. Even her throat burned.

"Brady?" she asked, because she wasn't ready to ask the more pressing question about her child.

Hunt shook his head. "He was discharged with his injuries before we took the virus." He glanced around the room. "In some ways, Brady was one of the reasons we volunteered for the experiment. If stronger, faster soldiers existed, then what happened to him might not occur again. We could get in and out of conflicts more efficiently. Fewer casualties."

"By killing more people?" she asked.

Someone growled.

Okay, wrong question.

"If necessary," Hunt said. "Or by not getting ourselves killed because we possess a tactical and physical advantage. We complete missions at a much higher success rate, shortening the conflict."

In a bizarre way, his explanation made sense.

Jake had the virus? As she peered up at him, he gave her the briefest nod. Her heart pounded harder.

And. And? Oh, God, that meant the baby… Her face went numb.

Hunt continued, seemingly oblivious to her life-altering realization. "Factions within the government want to use the Morpheus Virus to create more soldiers. Maybe sell it to another nation-state, all buddy-buddy like. If they can run more tests on us first, they will make the next batch of soldiers easier to control. They want to refine the recipe, so to speak, and we're the guinea pigs. But first they need our bodies for all manner of testing. So far, we have remained hidden, and we're going to keep it that way."

Rodeo crossed his arms. "We're not giving them the satisfaction of our bodies." He scowled at Gonzo's snort. "Not in that way, dude. I meant scientifically."

"What does all this mean for me?" she said.

Hunt barked a laugh. "Besides the fact that in this room stand the best-trained weaponized humans in the world, and they all are protecting you?" He shot a nasty glare in the direction of someone's snicker. The snickering stopped. "That"—he pointed toward her midsection—"is a big unknown. What you carry contains the Morpheus Virus."

"What I carry? It's a human being." A baby. Her baby.

Jake's baby.

A curt nod. "No one knows what to expect. Will the child be like us? Will it be healthy? Who knows. But I guarantee this fact: if the government finds out there's a baby with the Morpheus Virus, they'll stop at nothing to get their hands on the kid. They will run tests on it, maybe for years. No one has any idea how the virus will affect an offspring of someone who had the virus."

"What about … will it—" She could barely creak out the word. "Survive?" Her lungs burned. She couldn't get enough air. Her head felt like it was floating away. Her pulse pounded a fast rhythm against her temples.

Doc blinked. "We simply don't know what to expect." His non-answer scared her more than a definite outcome.

Kiera froze. Then she dropped her damp forehead into her hands and fought the increasing number of stars as they invaded the edges of her vision. The baby. In danger. Might not even survive the birth. *Oh, God.*

Hunt said, "I'm still debating what to do with it."

Her head whipped up. A wave of anger smacked into her so hard, she lurched to her feet and yelped at the pain in her leg. "You're debating? You? Since when do you get to make these decisions?"

"Ah, I am the commanding officer of this group."

"You're not *my* commanding officer," she spat.

A few mumbles of *oh shit* filtered through the ringing in her ears.

She shrugged off Jake's hand on her shoulder. Damn, he had a hell of a grip. Oh, yeah, because he was somehow genetically modified or whatever the heck the stupid virus did to him.

She stepped forward, nose-to-nose with Hunt. It was more like nose-to-massive torso, but it would do. No one else in the room moved. "Look, you want me to spill all I know about Fallen Comrades and Beau Lequire? Fine. I'll do it. All of my information is yours to do with as you like. You want my best guesses on Senator Lequire and Bratva and how they connect to Beau? You got it. You want me to forget I know anything about you people? I can do that, too." Her index finger came within an inch of poking him in the chest. "But don't ever think about hurting this baby. Or taking this child away from me. Do I make myself clear?" Her legs quivered.

How the next words made it through the rock-solid clench of his jaw, she would never know. "Ma'am." His entire frame strained against the fabric of his shirt and pants. What in the world? He was growing bigger. Maybe fear made her imagine things. The guy *was* big and scary up close. His rock-tumble voice vibrated the air, raising the hairs on her arms. "I recommend that you step away."

"Why? Because you think I'll get the virus from you? I probably already have it. You can't harm me."

"Kiera." Jake appeared, inserting himself in between her and Hunt like a massive barrier slotting in front of a two-ton boulder about to roll downhill. He faced her. "You have to back down, now."

Staring at the strap across his chest, she sputtered, "Wait. You're asking *me* to back down from *him*?" She tried to sidestep Jake. "Are you joking?"

"Ma'am." Hunt's gaze darted to his men and then back to Kiera. "I'm trying to stay—" His thick Adam's apple bobbled. "Give me a second."

Rodeo and Gonzo planted themselves on either side of their CO.

"Not good, dude," Gonzo said, flexing his arms and shoulders as he eased the gun out of Hunt's thigh holster and handed the weapon to Curly.

Rodeo murmured, "Boss, you need some happy juice real quick."

The commander's ribs rose and fell quickly. He muttered numbers, over and over. His bloodshot eyes unfocused. Sweat beaded his lined forehead.

Jake remained planted in place, a wall of muscle in front of her.

Rodeo nodded to Doc, who ran to a table, cranked open a metal box, like what Jake had in the house, pulled liquid out of a vial with a syringe, and rushed back over.

"Little poke," Doc mumbled, jamming the needle straight into Hunt's upper arm.

Rodeo slung a corded arm around Hunt's neck, almost like a friend—if a friend wanted to place a chokehold on his buddy, that was. "Don't worry, ma'am. He'll be perfectly fine in a few seconds." His gleaming smile disappeared.

The CO roared like a rabid bear and lunged.

Chapter Sixteen

Kiera gasped as Jake turned, caught her by the shoulders, and pulled her forward into his broad torso. She was too stunned to protest as he wrapped his hands around her upper back and then walked her backward, well behind the couch. No piece of furniture would stop Hunt. That much was clear.

Jake's clenched grip digging into her skin hurt, but she didn't complain, given the alternative raging across the room. She peeked over his shoulder. She swallowed, her mouth dry, body burning up. Why was she having another hot flash?

Gonzo and Rodeo kept a firm hold on Hunt for a few minutes until the man's breathing had slowed and he returned to his previous stature.

What the heck? Imagine what would happen if…

Kiera wanted to throw up. Whatever caused the reaction in Hunt … somehow existed inside of her child. Air would not move through her chest.

Had she glimpsed her child's future?

If it survived.

Bile burned her throat.

She looked up at Jake. His gray stare narrowed. His nostrils flared and his shoulders flexed and broadened.

Oh, God, was he changing, too? Was everyone? She peeked around the room. Each team member was frozen in a state of tight readiness.

Jake clamped his hand on her arm. The pain brought tears to her eyes, but she didn't move. Didn't dare move. His rasping breaths next to her ear echoed Hunt's desperate heaves and muttered number repetitions on the other side of the room.

"Jake?" she whispered.

He squeezed his eyes closed as he moved his hand to rest on the back of the couch in a fist he clenched and unclenched over and over. "It'll be okay. A heightened need to protect or fight can trigger the virus activation. Give me a second." When he swallowed, the thick cords on his neck shifted. The wild expression calmed until his body finally relaxed. "I'll make sure you and the baby are safe. Mateo made me promise in his letter."

She bit the inside of her cheek, trying to regain her own control. No way would she go to pieces in front of these men.

While everyone was taking a moment, she stewed on that tidbit about Jake helping her because of a mandate from the grave. No sir. She squared her shoulders and raised her head. She was no one's burden. The baby wasn't an assignment. And they sure as hell wouldn't hang around here solely because of Jake's sense of duty.

Hunt took a deep breath. At his gravelly voice, she warily focused on him.

"Okay," he rasped.

Jake stepped to the side. As irritated as she was with Jake, she had to admit she felt a little safer with him standing next to her. But damn Mateo and his kind soul. He had no idea the situation he'd created for Jake and Kiera.

"I'm good now," Hunt said. It wasn't much of an apology but more of a status update. "Thanks, men." He shrugged off Rodeo and Gonzo. "As you can see, the Morpheus Virus is no joke. Your … situation puts all of us in a bind." His frame had gone from abnormally massive back down to normal. Which was to say, still huge. "Finish your story." He motioned to her, as if he hadn't tried to attack her a minute ago.

Jake rested his hand on her shoulder again.

As a shudder rattled through her, he gave her a gentle squeeze. But it didn't feel gentle anymore, given what she'd learned. What he was capable of—what they all were capable of—terrified her.

"Does this, um, change, happen to all of you?" She gestured toward the silent group.

"If we don't stay on top of the antidote doses or if certain buttons get … pushed. Yeah, we go over the edge pretty quickly." Hunt blinked. "It varies from man to man and also depends on the situation. Reactions become unpredictable. One of the many issues with the virus."

"Can't wait to hear about the rest of it." Later. She could only deal with so much awful information at one time. Her baby? A sob lodged in her throat, and she swallowed a hard lump. Soon. She'd deal with that fear soon. Damn it, she couldn't process everything right now.

She braced her hands and leaned against the back of the couch. "Okay. Here's the rest of the story." Anything to move this discussion along so she could get out of here. Anything to stay upright. "I mentioned about Beau's revolving door of women and how he didn't like to hear the word *no*?"

The men nodded.

"So, Beau wanted me to … participate," she said. Nothing like talking about sex practices in a room where every guy was a walking testosterone overdose.

Jake ground out, next to her ear, "I can't believe Mateo let you work there."

She craned her head back to scowl at him. "Hey, Mateo knew everything going on. If needed, he could have pulled me out of the situation immediately." Pointing at the dangerous statues in front of her, she added, "Now I know why he felt so confident. Actually, it wasn't until Beau started making serious moves on me recently that we got concerned."

"The fuck?" Stumpy spat. "He went for you while you were clearly pregnant?" He dropped a curled fist on his knee.

The other men grumbled.

"Yep. He's quite a piece." With more time to think about it, it was remarkable she'd gotten away unscathed. Tremors rolled through her body. During the mission, she had focused on revenge for Brady and making his death mean something. The risks hadn't seemed unreasonable. Then.

Jake planted his legs wide, supporting her with his massive frame. His thumb rubbed against her upper arm as he eased her back against his chest. As if he could absorb her fear. Transmute it.

Swallowing again, she finished the story, describing how she crawled through the exploding house's escape tunnel and how Mateo bought her freedom with his life.

After the chorus of curses and fists-in-palms calmed down, she piped up again. "Guys, Beau knows I saw the ledgers. What he doesn't know is that I have a nearly photographic memory. Also, I'm a CPA. I *understand* what I saw."

"The hell you say?" Hunt barked.

"I memorized key numbers. I saw the sham accounts linking to Senator Lequire and Bratva. The transactions. By now, Beau's probably figured out that I'm Brady's sister. He may have discovered Mateo's identity by now, which means he may find Mateo's connection to Morpheus Squad." Sucking in air, she said, "He already knows about Jake because Beau's men tracked us down at his cabin."

Silence.

She shoved damp hair behind an ear. "Guys. Don't you get it? It means you all are in danger. You need to protect yourselves. He might come for you. Here." Nothing. No response. "Your lives are at risk."

Gonzo gave a derisive bark. Additional deep chuckles followed from around the room.

With a couldn't-care-less shrug, Rodeo crossed his arms and propped his black cargo pants-clad hip against the foosball table. "You're worried about *us*? What about the pudknockers who are dumb enough to take on Morpheus Squad?"

Hunt snorted.

Blowing out an exasperated breath, she snapped, "Really? Okay, fine. You all think you're bulletproof and invincible because you're big, bad, super-duper experimental soldiers? Newsflash: you're not." She pointed at the men. "Recall that a so-called indestructible warrior exactly like you was recently killed."

All of a sudden, there was no posturing, no flexed muscles, and no swagger. Lots of studying the floor and ceiling.

That's what I thought.

Rodeo tapped his knuckles on the table. "Well? So what's the plan? We need to take down Fallen Comrades, expose a corrupt senator—yawn, take down the Russian mafia, and ruin Beau Lequire's life? Sounds like a good couple hours' work to me."

Other voices chimed in with enthusiastic agreement.

"More than that. We need to do it in such a way so no one can trace the outcome to us," Hunt added. "The U.S. military can*not* find out about Kiera or the baby, either."

Gonzo piped up. "Alrighty then, let's get to it."

Kiera groaned. These meatheads completely ignored the part where they were also in danger. She had entered an alternate reality, obviously. Her leg throbbed. Darn thing felt two sizes too big. She shifted her weight to the other foot.

"Not so fast." Hunt raised his meaty hands. "Guys, we need more intel first. We can't go into this one guns a-blazing and balls out."

Guys snickered.

Hunt's ears turned pink and his hard features twisted in a brief, wry smile. "Sorry for the language."

Bless their macho, boneheaded hearts. She burst out laughing. "You've met my brother. He could cuss any of you out of the room. He didn't save that language for his military buddies."

"Good point." The CO rubbed his angular jaw.

Gonzo scuffed the toe of his shoe on the floor. "So, boss. When do we get started? Patience isn't my strong suit."

"I hear you, but it's required for this op," Hunt countered. "Now, let's circle up and lay out some options." He turned his back on her, uncapped a marker, and unrolled a large piece of paper onto the big kitchen table as the men gathered around.

All Kiera wanted to do was relax against Jake's warm chest. They had so much to discuss. But there was much more at stake here needing to be addressed right now.

"Excuse me?" she said. All heads swiveled back to her. "There's another issue."

"What else?" Hunt's thick brows drew together.

She swiped at her damp upper lip. "Um, what about my sisters and my dad? If Beau knows who I am, and if he's as pissed as I think he is, then it's not a stretch to expect he'll come after my family."

A low whistle came from Rodeo as he pushed the brim of his hat up with his thumb.

"Protection is not a problem." Hunt turned toward Stumpy. "Start working on new identities and full mission files for"—he scanned the guys in the room and stared at the ceiling for a few seconds—"Rivera, Pele, and Red."

Stumpy settled in front of the banks of computers, already typing before he was fully in the chair. He lifted a radio and mumbled into it, and a muffled reply was undecipherable.

Hunt pointed at Curly and Gonzo. "You're on watch for the rest of the night while we get those boys out the door."

"Roger that," Gonzo said as he headed toward the door, a sullen Curly on his heels.

She breathed a sigh of relief and sagged into Jake's solid frame.

He leaned down to murmur, "Good job tonight." His voice next to her ear sent a frisson of excitement straight down to her toes, and she turned to face him.

When she looked up, Jake's dark scowl froze her in place.

She touched his upper arm. "Everything okay?"

"Fine. Just fine." His nostrils flared. "Realized I'm going to be a father of a..."

"It's a baby, Jake. You can say the word." She sighed. "We should talk. In private."

"Later."

Before she could say anything more, Doc strolled up, a brief flicker of emotion rippling his otherwise inscrutable expression. "How about we do a checkup of junior?"

"Sure."

He inhaled deeply, then studied her face for

several seconds. "We can also take care of that infection spreading up your leg."

Jake exploded. "What?"

All the strength left her body in a rush and her knees buckled.

Chapter Seventeen

Outside the exam room, Jake paced the hallway, stopping at the front door of the building and pivoting to return to the room where Doc examined Kiera. Was her leg okay? Why hadn't she told him it was getting worse? She had been burning up when he had carried her back here.

He needed to know what was going on behind that door. The infection. The pregnancy. Was the baby okay if she had an infection?

Hell, of course, the baby had an infection. The Morpheus Virus. Jake had given it to the child. It was part of the child.

He kept pacing. An outsider might look at him and see someone acting like a real live, goddamned expectant father.

Because he *was* an expectant father.

But life wasn't always simple.

He could blow up buildings and storm a nest of insurgents, but he hadn't been able to face the truth staring right at him with those big, beautiful hazel eyes.

He had known. Deep down. He hadn't let her say the words out loud, as if not speaking the truth would prevent him from facing his greatest hope and most paralyzing fear.

He took another ten-foot lap in the hallway.

Hell, he'd been in Special Forces. His whole existence involved taking risks, planting bombs, and taunting death. He'd signed up to be a human lab rat like it was no big deal. Nothing rattled him. Nothing.

Except for a pregnant woman who had taken his life's hope and his very identity and weaknesses and tied it all up in a messy knot.

It must be the antidote making him feel weird. It blunted his reaction time and his senses. That must be the problem.

Shoving his hand through his hair, he turned and stared at the door like he could manifest X-ray vision.

They were taking too much time. Was everything okay? How did he end up caring so damn much about a child that in the space of less than an hour, had become … his?

Shit. This whole situation was beyond fucked up, his mental state included.

When the door opened, he jumped like a rabbit bolting from a hide.

"Come on in, if you'd like." Damn Doc, the corner of his sphinxlike mouth quirked upward, as usual, giving little away. If the guy weren't the best field surgeon on the planet, Jake would permanently wipe that smirk off Doc's unflappable face. Or shake him by the lapels to make him talk.

Before stepping into the room, he grabbed Doc's arm and pulled him into the hall. In a whisper, he asked, "Did you check the wounds on her leg and back?"

His friend's mouth compressed into a thin line. "You did a good job getting the shrapnel out and cleaning the injuries. The one on the leg had become infected, so I opened it up, irrigated the area, and gave her a shot of Rocephin. We'll repeat the dose daily for five days."

"Will she be okay?"

"It's a strong antibiotic."

"You didn't answer my question."

"I operate in absolutes with Special Forces. Not in medicine. But yes, I believe we caught the infection before she became septic."

"Septic? The shrapnel. Injuries. Is the baby…?"

he asked. A tight vise wrapped around his chest. Damn it, he should have insisted on taking Kiera to a hospital. She would have refused, of course. But he should have done more to safeguard her.

"Could have been bad. They were both lucky."

Fuck. A couple of inches, and this conversation would be very different. The imaginary band beneath Jake's ribs loosened by a few turns.

"The virus?"

Doc said nothing.

"What?" Jake choked out the word.

"I'll do an ultrasound exam now, but it may not show us anything. We won't know the effects of the virus until after she delivers and I can examine the baby." He rested a rock-steady hand on Jake's shoulder, and Jake startled again. "If you don't mind me saying so, you need to chill. This woman has been through way too much, and more stress isn't going to help."

"Roger that."

After a few clench-and-releases of his fists in a feeble attempt to calm the fuck down, he followed Doc into the room.

As he stepped into the makeshift clinic room, his respect for Doc shot up several notches. The guy had created a compact, tiny, functioning hospital seemingly out of thin air. Racks of neatly labeled supplies in plastic bins covered one entire wall. The exam table looked like it could maneuver into almost any position imaginable, a thought that made Jake queasy. A light hung on a metal arm from the ceiling.

There was even an incubator thingy over in the corner. Like for a baby. His vision went gray around the edges for a second.

He pointed to the equipment. "How'd you know to have that … available?"

Doc blinked. "Mateo contacted me privately a few months ago, saying it was possible we'd be treating a pregnant patient or a newborn at some point. He didn't provide further information. Over the past few months, I've collected some extra pieces of equipment, just in case."

"Mateo thought of everything, didn't he?" Bitterness coated his tongue. Should have been Jake setting it all up. Should have been Jake going with her to appointments early on.

No. He should have prevented this from happening in the first place.

"Mateo tried to cover the bases to keep Kiera and the baby safe. I wonder if he meant to bring her here all along. He was good at probabilities. Maybe he anticipated what might happen." Doc motioned for Jake to precede him. "We'll never know."

Kiera rested on the exam table, head turned toward Jake, searching him with those soulful eyes. Her dark brown hair fanned out on a pillow. She had her clothes on, but the legging was scooted up on the one side. Red skin bloomed out from under the square bandage.

Doc indicated for her to pull the hem of her shirt up. Her rounded belly was too big for her delicate frame. Too small for how many weeks along she was in the pregnancy. The bandage on the side of her abdomen reminded him of how close she'd come to disaster.

The view of her lying up there made the muscles between Jake's shoulder blades crawl, like he wanted to throw his body over hers. Or rip the arms off of anyone who dared to touch her.

She grabbed Jake's hand with her smaller one, giving his protective urges something to focus on. "Doc's going to look at the baby." Fear moved over her features as her brows rose. Her cheeks seemed too flushed. Probably took a few hours for the antibiotic to kick in. "Will you watch with me?"

A lump in his throat made it hard to answer. But in this situation, there was only one correct response. "You bet." Not sure what to do, he stood next to her and patted her on the shoulder while twining her fingers in his. Gently, though. Even a small movement on his part could hurt her.

He would do this. He would stand beside her for as long as was needed.

Doc studied Jake. Then he turned on a small machine and flipped some switches. After a squirt of ice-blue gel, he placed a probe on Kiera's belly. A shifting black and white image filled the screen, and Doc played with the machine and clicked buttons, taking measurements. Jake stood completely still, knees locked, not wanting to disturb the exam, too terrified to ask any questions.

Because he didn't want the answers.

With a satisfied nod, Doc unfroze the last picture and finished jotting down some notes on a form next to the machine. "Okay, Kiera. Growth parameters are on the small side, but still within the bell curve of normal. Not sure where you're hiding this kid, but the baby is growing. Amniotic fluid level is also in normal range."

"The baby looks okay? Even with the…" Her chin quivered.

Jake vowed to do anything in the universe to make things okay for her. He forced the hand grasping Kiera's to relax. Every other part of his body went whipcord tense.

"You personally haven't gained much weight, but yes, this baby's growth is on track." Doc hadn't answered her question.

His teammate adjusted some settings on the machine. "Time for the fun part. Here's the nose and mouth profile." He pointed to the screen as he moved the probe around. "Here is one hand and … the second hand. And here are"—he slid the probe up over her stretched belly button—"two little feet."

Turning another knob, the rapid whooshing sound of the baby's heartbeat filled the room.

Jake felt that heartbeat in his own chest as an invisible connection clinked into place. His baby.

Then he looked again. It all became too real. His head throbbed. He was going to be a father. Not in the distant future, either.

Jake wanted to kiss her and then run away. The end of the earth would be a good place to start. Instead, he took in the sight of Kiera's glistening eyes, fought every instinct, and stayed put.

Doc twisted the probe and pressed it into Kiera's belly. "And here is … hmmm. Let's see. Yes. Looks like a hamburger."

"A what?" Jake spluttered.

She squeezed his hand, eyebrows raised and mouth open.

Doc raised a dark eyebrow. "Relax. A 'hamburger' describes the way the baby's genitalia look on ultrasound when it's a … girl." He smiled. "Could have been a turtle, and then it would have been a boy."

Kiera's expression was beautiful. "A baby girl? Oh, wow. They couldn't see gender on the twenty-week ultrasound. Uncooperative baby, go figure." She bit her lip. "I'd wondered. My sweet girl," she murmured, reaching out her free hand toward the screen.

Jake stood frozen, stupefied.

As Doc wiped gel from her belly and tugged down the hem of her shirt, he mouthed, "Give her a hug."

He exited, quietly closing the door.

And, in the absence of any other good ideas, that was exactly what Jake did, leaning down and wrapping his arms around Kiera's thin shoulders, the movement awkward on the exam table. How long he stood there, he had no idea.

Baby. Girl.

His.

His chest expanded with pride.

With the virus.

A wave of terror slammed into his gut, almost knocking him on his ass.

After a time, Jake pulled away. "Was it what you expected?" Damn, his voice sounded like sandpaper, like he had something stuck in his throat. He kept patting her shoulder, as if he couldn't bring himself to lose contact with her.

"I don't know, I mostly hoped it—she—would be healthy. Especially with all the stress and … everything with the pregnancy."

"So is everything else okay, um, physically?"

Despite the fatigue, she was even more beautiful than he could imagine. "Yes, Doc said I'm perfectly healthy for an almost thirty-six-week pregnant woman who's been shot at and exposed to toxic fumes and who has an infected leg. He checked my heart and lungs. Also, no dilation yet, and baby is in the proper position. Doc monitored for contractions and checked the baby's heart rate pattern. All good. No complications. I believe he called me 'large and in charge.'"

"Not so large, but yes, a good report." Damn it, he couldn't stop grinning. "Your leg okay?"

"It's numb right now, thanks to Doc. What a relief." She sighed. "Help me up?"

Like he'd been given permission to touch a

priceless glass sculpture, he took her hands and guided her to sit at the edge of the table, then helped her step onto the floor. No way was he going to think about how that tiny action of her placing hands in his and trusting his support made him feel a hundred feet tall.

Shoving his hands in his pockets, he said, "I'm really happy the baby is fine. It's one less thing for you to worry about."

"You've got that right. A big relief." She frowned. "With the virus, we'll have to wait and see, which is hard. But so far, everything seems good. So, another relief." She worried at her lower lip with her teeth.

As he shifted from foot to foot, black, creeping doubt wormed its way into his gut. Thank God her worry level had dropped.

Because Jake's fear level had just shot off the charts.

Chapter Eighteen

The next morning, Kiera shot awake with a gurgled scream.

Sweat chilled her forehead as her heart hammered inside her heaving ribs. She crumpled the blankets in her shaking fists. Brady. Mateo. The exploding house in Atlanta. The baby.

Beau's too-handsome face, twisting into an expression of sick lust and deep hatred.

Breathe.

Thin morning light straggled into the room and flung eerie shapes off unfamiliar furniture and plywood walls. Tree limbs swayed outside a small square window, casting shadowy claws on the walls.

The baby. The virus.

Another wave of terror hit her, and she gulped back a second scream.

The door flew open, crashing against the wall. A huge silhouette blocked light from the hallway.

Bicycling her feet on the sheets, she shoved herself back into the wall behind her.

The dark figure strode toward her.

She sucked air, drew her knees up, and wrapped her hands around her belly.

"Kiera?" That sleep-roughened tone sounded familiar.

Swallowing, she concentrated on the sound of his voice, even as nightmare and reality swirled together.

The figure took several deep breaths. "You're safe," came soothing words with a familiar southern accent. "Kiera. I'm here. You're in the compound. You're safe."

"Jake?" Even to her ears, her voice came out high

and tight, like a guitar wire stretched within a half turn of its breaking point.

Heat burned its way up her neck to her cheeks. Of course, she was at the Morpheus Squad headquarters. A breath shuddered out of her. She dropped her head forward onto her palms. Memories of the past two days tumbled through her mind.

Look around. The plain room they were in had a bureau in the corner. She cowered on a full-sized mattress on a bare bed frame. See? Normal, utilitarian items housed in one of the buildings on the compound. Nothing scary here.

"Hey, hey. It's okay." He took deliberate steps until he reached her side. The familiar masculine scent of aftershave and hickory she identified as uniquely Jake wafted over her. He stepped forward, and the morning light illuminated him in gray tones. She looked up.

And choked.

Boxers. That was all he wore. She locked her gaze on the floor, but she couldn't help herself when her line of sight rose. Good God, the cords in his muscled calves and thick thighs rippled right up to tight knit boxers. The night they had last summer … it was dark. She hadn't truly appreciated all of Jake 2.0.

He really *had* grown since she'd last seen any part of him unclothed. Was it the virus making him this large or was it simply Jake?

Who cared? Wow.

She took in the view of his rumpled hair. Somehow, he managed to be sexy and adorable at the same time. The hard line of his jaw was clamped tight while he scanned the room. He sported an aggressive, wide-spaced stance, as if he wanted to tackle something.

Realizing that her own bare legs were on display, she yanked the sheets up, but not before she caught the hitch in Jake's breathing.

The need to hide was strong. She dropped her forehead back into a palm and groaned. Once she'd settled her heart rate down, she took stock of the situation: one frazzled pregnant woman going to pieces and a perplexed former Special Forces soldier clad in nothing but boxers that fit his … service weapon … so well. The attire should be banned per Geneva Convention rules.

The wary way he sidled up to her, like a safari guide approaching a wounded and unpredictable water buffalo, made a giggle burst from her mouth. Poor guy probably didn't know if she was about to punch him or scream again.

Shoving her hair back behind her ears, she said, "Sorry. I'm fine now, thanks."

When he touched her shoulder, she yelped. Okay, not totally fine. Damn it.

This high level of sustained fear and stress could *not* be good for Little Bit. Under the blankets and over the borrowed t-shirt fabric, she smoothed a hand over the active baby.

The baby. The virus. Half of her brain needed to know her child would be okay. The other half couldn't deal with any alternatives. Right now? Nothing she could do except concentrate on staying healthy herself. Like she had done last night, once more she shoved all of her unrelenting terror regarding the virus and her baby into a mental box and shut the lid. She would deal with the unknown when she had the emotional bandwidth available. Not right now.

She took another big breath in and let it out, bit by bit, willing her tension to seep away.

When she peeked up at Jake, she stifled another bubble of laughter. Poor guy hadn't moved an inch. He stood there like a Roman statue. His damned muscled chest looked as hard as carved marble. Her fingers itched to trace the ridges and see if the skin was as velvety soft and taut as she remembered. Oh, God. The mere thought dumped out a truckload of inappropriate scenarios.

Concentrate.

Unfortunately, she did. Kiera studied his thick pecs dusted with light-brown hair and followed that line of hair lower, right down to his … boxers. She swallowed and pressed her thighs together. Anything to reduce the throbbing need building there. Damned hormones. All that prevented her superheated libido from spontaneously combusting was the presence of a small article of thin cloth covering the healthy bulge between his legs. Who the hell put stretchy material in boxers anyway?

Jake sure wasn't that guy from high school anymore.

She groaned as another pulse warmed her pelvis.

Clearing her throat, she tried to distract herself and unfreeze him. "Well, that was a heck of a wake-up call. I'm so sorry. You needed your sleep. I know you must be exhausted." She was babbling but couldn't help herself. Anything to fill the silence between them. Anything to distract from his presence.

"No more than you need the rest." His expression softened. "It was time for me to get up, anyway." The lightest touch of his hand on her shoulder didn't make her jump this time. "You have nothing to be sorry about. It's been a rough past thirty-six hours."

"Okay. Well, then…" Self-conscious in her t-shirt and underwear, she tucked the blankets around her hips, unwilling to get out from under the covers.

His eyes grazed her face and body, then back to lock onto her face. She squirmed. He leaned toward her.

"Are you okay? Leg doing better?" The boxer fabric strained above his corded legs.

Do not look down. Do not look down. "Oh, sure." The stupid quaver in her voice betrayed her.

"Can I—" He shoved his hair off his forehead. "Fuck it." Sitting on the bed, he hauled her onto his lap, moving her like she weighed nothing. The extra-soft mattress dipped under their combined weight. She clutched the blankets on the way to perching sideways on his warm, muscled thighs.

Good God, the heat pouring off his body warmed every inch of her. He cradled her head in his palm and eased her cheek to press against his upper chest. Warmth flowed from his skin to hers. Safe inside the circle of his arms.

"What happened?" His low voice vibrated through their connected bodies.

Ripples of happiness swirled right into her core. If she moved her head one inch, she would taste his skin. She inhaled faint aftershave and hickory again, and the spicy, vital scent of strong male: Jake.

"Besides the obvious?" She gave a weak laugh. "I think everything caught up with me."

"What can I do?"

No way could she answer that question with a real answer. Heck, she was sitting two inches away from his … Geneva Convention.

"Um, besides get a crystal ball?" When in doubt, deflect. Unfortunately, her laugh caught on a scary gulp. "You've done way more than anyone else would have. I've put you and the whole team at risk. My family, too. Oh, man. The virus and this baby." Air shuddered out as she exhaled. "This situation keeps getting worse and worse. What was I thinking?" The rat-a-tat of her heart sped up again.

"Hey." He tilted her chin up. "First of all, this is *our* situation now. Doc said the baby looks good on all the tests."

True. But the unknown. They wouldn't know everything until the baby arrived.

"Don't worry about the guys," he said. "They can take care of themselves and your family. They've been looking for a project."

"A project? Like knitting a sweater?"

The vibration of his low chuckle made her ribs tingle. "It's what we're trained to do. Helping other people gives meaning to everything we went through."

"Sure." She leaned back and studied his sincere expression.

"Seriously. No one's upset."

"You sure? Because I got some pretty angry vibes from some of the fellows last night."

"When it comes down to it, they'll do the right thing. They'll take care of your family, too." He leaned his head back on the wall and pinned her with those steady, gray eyes.

It sounded so simple. "What about Beau coming after me? Which means he's coming after you all, by the way."

He shot her a terrifying, tight-lipped smile, chilling her to the bone. "Any one of us would be honored to pulverize that bastard. And we'd sure enjoy helping him rearrange his priorities when it comes to vets. In addition, we'll gladly cut off … his participation in his father's senate races and snip his … ties to Bratva. As a bonus, it would be fun to remove his ability to walk and talk." He brushed his lips over her forehead, creating tiny tingles. "I'd love to render him incapable of harassing women ever again."

"All women or any in particular?" she asked,

pulling back.

The determined slash of his mouth triggered a quiver in her stomach.

It also made her want to taste his lips to see if they were as unyielding as they appeared and to find out if they would soften under her mouth.

"If he knows what's good for him, he'll never bother one particular woman. Ever. Again." The flash of a lethal smile came and went, like the quick blast of an acetylene torch.

"Good to know." Question was, did he care because of a sense of duty or did he care because he cared? His thigh muscles clenched under her butt. Next to her hip, his hardness pressed against her. Right now was probably not the time to parse motivations.

She swallowed.

"You're safe here," he murmured, brushing hair back from her shoulder.

She barely suppressed a shudder. "I know. But I am truly sorry to have turned your life upside-down."

He glanced at her belly. "You should have told me sooner." The hint of a growl made her shiver.

"Early on, I didn't know where you were."

He pulled a face. "That's valid."

"In my defense, I did try to tell you a few times."

"I know." His finger drifted down her cheek. "My life needed to be shaken up. You showing up in the middle of the night, with my baby on board, kicked me in the ass, gave me a purpose."

His mouth hovered an inch from hers.

Did they still have a connection?

Before she could test her theory, he closed the space, crushing his lips to hers as he held her in place with the iron bands of his arms. The tight grip was protective, not painful. Twisting on his lap, she reached as far around his back as she could. Velvet skin coated hard muscle. He roved over her mouth with ever-changing nips and licks until her head spun.

When she clutched at him to stay upright, he groaned against her mouth. Their harsh breaths rasped in the small room.

"Kiera," he gritted out. Angling her face up, he dropped kisses over her jaw and neck.

Under where her hip rested, he hardened even more. When she shifted, wanting to get closer, he took her lower lip between his teeth, and fireworks sparked in her vision.

"It's been so long, Jake. Too long," she breathed.

With another groan, he slid his hands down her back and sides, brushing against her breasts. Oh, God, his touch felt so good. He pulled her shirt up and ran a fingertip over a sensitive nipple. Her gasp rode on top of a moan.

Little Bit caught the excitement and kicked against his palm pressed against her side.

Jake froze. Then he snatched his hand away.

After kissing his hard jaw and mouth, she leaned back when he didn't respond. That blank stare made her eyelids sting.

"This is a mistake." His voice serrated the space between them.

"What?" Her brain was still lust-fogged.

"I shouldn't be right here."

"All right." No, it wasn't all right. There had to be a much bigger problem.

"Nothing about this situation is okay. We shouldn't have … done that. Now or last summer."

She flinched.

"You and me?" he said. "We're the poster children for why people are supposed to learn from their mistakes."

"Seriously, Jake?" She lightly smacked his hard chest, making her hand sting. He didn't even flinch. "What just happened here?" Seesawing emotions threatened to bring tears. She breathed through her mouth. No way would she give him the satisfaction of knowing how his words hurt.

His nostrils flared. His chest heaved. "This was another mistake."

"No. It was two normal people having a normal and enjoyable moment."

"I don't get normal moments." His voice came out hollow and flat. "Not anymore."

"But—"

"Please don't make it worse. This whole situation."

Like the baby? Deep in her chest, an ache stole her breath. "I haven't asked you for anything."

"I promise I will provide for you and this baby."

"This"—she waved a hand at herself—"isn't an obligation. It's a family, but only if you want it." She could imagine him as part of her family, pushing their daughter on a swing, going on drives in the Smokies during fall colors, and sitting down to dinners together.

"Not sure I'm the family kind of guy. This situation with my messed-up brain and uncertain lifespan won't allow me to be that kind of guy, even if I wanted to be. That's the problem."

"What?" Her head spun. She'd never considered … Jake … not being here.

"No one knows how long we'll survive."

The picture of her fantasy family shattered along with a piece of her heart. "Jake—" She bit her lip. How terrible had his life become after the experimental virus? It had taken so much more than his freedom. More than his humanity.

His defeated frown triggered tears threatening to spill.

"Don't," he said. "If you pull the sympathy card on me, I might say something un-gentlemanlike, Kiera."

Sliding her off his lap, he scooted over and stood next to the bed, his erection still stretching the boxer fabric. He didn't bother to cover himself, but instead rubbed both palms against his face. Every inch of him quivered with barely contained power. Sweat shone on his forehead.

She swallowed.

He did the same. Tight cords moved in his neck. "I'll meet you out front in ten minutes. We'll get to work collecting the information you have. Make a plan to take care of Lequire. Get this situation over with." Cold. Clinical. Like a switch flipped. Like nothing had happened between them. Had ever happened.

She had offered him a future only for him to remind her that, out of all the people on this Earth, he didn't get a choice.

Maybe she didn't understand his entire medical situation, but Kiera understood duty, and Jake was steeped in it. However, she and the baby wouldn't be another mission for him to complete or an obligation to fulfill.

But she couldn't push him. Wouldn't. She had too much leverage. No way would she abuse the situation.

"Okay," she managed. A sucking vacuum pulled at her ribs, threatening to cave her chest in with the pressure. She wanted to say more, but she couldn't get any words out.

He turned on his heel.

Damn him. The chiseled view as he exited the

room was as good if not better than his entry. As the door closed on the image of his toned butt, she curled up on the bed and with a groan, pulled the blankets over her head and pressed her palms to burning cheeks.

Shame, lust, and sadness. What a winning combination of feelings. Oh, and fear.

Rubbing her face as if she could swipe away all the bad things in her life, she sat up and squared her shoulders. No more wishing for something that didn't exist now and likely would never exist.

Time to get down to work.

Time to avenge her brother.

Chapter Nineteen

The front door of the plywood building slowly opened. Even though he anticipated the sight of Kiera, Jake's gut clenched where he stood in the cool morning air with fucking bucolic forest and chirpy woodland creatures all around him. Normally, the mountains provided him peace.

Not today.

What in the hell had made him think for a second he could have even a tiny piece of what he had always wanted? A family, a partner, a child. A normal life.

The door shut behind her with a muffled click.

A damned invisible knife twisted in his chest.

Back straight, chin up, she had her best armor wrapped around her. Classic Kiera. When things got tough, she stiffened the proverbial upper lip. It was good one of them had their shit together after a moment of weakness. Because he had been a heartbeat away from laying her out on the bed, stripping her down, and licking every inch of her body until he'd had her fill of her.

He'd never have enough when it came to Kiera.

"Ready to work?" He needed to keep their relationship on a business level. Needed to keep Kiera and her baby alive. So he would continue telling himself that "the mission" was why he had to emotionally disconnect from her.

Blinking in the mesh-diluted sunlight filtering down, she tugged the jacket closed. Whether she protected herself against the cold or his presence, he had no idea. He tried not to care too much about the rips in the legging fabric visible from where she'd fallen on her escape from Lequire. A hot angry wave flashed over him. *Stay in control.* He opened and closed his hands, willing his shoulder and arm muscles to relax already.

Unable to check the movement, he glanced again at the holes in the tunic from … yeah. Shrapnel.

"Sure. Let's go." Her perky tone was way too forced, but at least she played along with the nothing-happened charade. "This compound is bigger than I had thought."

As they walked down the two steps to the leaf-littered ground, he glommed onto the safe topic she had offered. "Six buildings. Gonzo was telling me last night they tried to make the buildings as comfortable as possible, since they knew they might have to spend extended time here one day."

"Like now?"

"Yeah."

"Where did the guys come from? Yesterday, when Hunt called the team together."

"Everyone lives in the southeast region, within a few hours of this location. They all have assumed identities. Even Doc, who works a few shifts per month in one of the Chattanooga emergency departments."

"Really?"

"Doc says civilian ER work keeps his skills sharp. Can't imagine he needs much help in that department. But working in a hospital also provides him access to medication and supplies, which is a bonus for us here."

"I thought the team wanted to stay hidden?"

"Yes and no. I'm the hermit of the bunch. Everyone else prefers hiding in plain sight."

"Because of the virus?"

"We were trained to blend into any group as part of standard Special Forces training. Then, after we took the virus, it enhanced all of our abilities, including being able to read a crowd and integrate seamlessly into any group of people we're with."

"That's wild."

"Comes in handy at times to blend into the background."

"I can't imagine you blending."

Huh. He took a few steps before answering and peered around the compound. "I'm impressed by the work the guys put into this place."

"Mateo would have loved to see what they've done."

He had little to add. Jake missed his friend.

"What's that?" Kiera stopped and cocked her head to the side, sunlight dappling her face in amazing shades of gold.

A high-pitched buzz filtered down to them. Shit. All of his senses focused on the possible threat.

But he didn't want to worry her. He had to focus, but do it casually. Great. Jake did nothing casually.

"Probably a drone." Using his nonexistent acting skills, he went for *nonchalant with a dash of we-got-this*.

"I thought they were silent."

"If they're low enough, it's not loud, but you hear them."

Her eyes went wide. "They found us?"

The muscles in his arms quivered with the need to pull her into his chest. "Might be part of a standard grid pattern, searching overhead."

"Shouldn't we do … something? Hide? Get out of here?" The vein at the base of her neck pulsed quickly.

"We're okay." Yes, they should do something, but damned if he was going to scare her. He prayed that Stumpy had the distraction system engaged. "Besides, the drone's camera is only seeing endless forest."

"What about the mesh in the trees? Won't they be able to tell that something different is here?"

"No. While the mesh muffles our on-ground heat and sound signatures, there is also a digital projection of bland woods over this location, providing even more proof there's nothing of interest here."

"Wow. What other secrets do you all have here?"

He motioned for her to precede him into the main building where she had met the team last night. Like last night, the moment she entered the front room, several heads swiveled around.

Four. Not the whole team of ten. Rivera, Pele, and Red were embedded by now. He scanned the room. That left Hunt and Doc out on compound patrol.

Everyone was protecting Kiera and her family from Lequire's revenge.

A wave of viral strength rushed through Jake's muscles, begging to be let out. Begging to rip, rend, and destroy anyone who would dare threaten Kiera or her child.

His child. Their child.

Shit.

The guys stared at her until Jake started to get twitchy again.

After a full minute where no one moved, Rodeo elbowed Gonzo, who glared at the cowboy and snapped back something in Spanish. Shoulders slumped, Gonzo shoved away from the table and picked up a large cardboard box. Jake tensed. As Gonzo stormed over, Kiera backpedaled into Jake's chest, and he instinctively cupped her shoulders.

Gonzo's expression twisted, like he had to deliver horrible news. Jake stopped breathing. Had something happened to one of her family members? Or worse?

What was in the box?

Gonzo held the box out to her. "Here."

"What's this?" she whispered.

His stocky teammate half-turned and snarled *shut up* when Rodeo snickered.

Jake spoke up from over her shoulder. "Man, what's going on?"

He offered the box to Kiera. "It's nothing."

With a shaking hand, she opened a cardboard flap and peered into the box. Jake looked over her shoulder as she gingerly touched the fabric.

Clothing? Why the drama?

He steadied the box while she held up items. The box was filled with colorful maternity tops, pregnancy jeans, stretchy sports bras, socks, and pregnancy panties. Even a new pair of sneakers and socks. His friends were amazing.

A sour taste in his mouth reminded him that deep down inside he should be the one to provide for her.

The men had expressions ranging from bland curiosity to anger to happiness. But Stumpy's hungry stare as various items of clothing were inspected struck Jake as especially out of place. Odd.

"How did…?" she stammered.

Another muffled cough and chuckle from the guys had Gonzo spinning around again and ripping off a line of Spanish so hard that Rodeo and Curly backed up. He might have been an inch or so shorter than his teammates, but Gonzo could tear the head off a mountain lion with his bare hands, and they all knew it.

Hunt entered through the front door, with his Sigs and knives strapped all over him. Probably plenty hidden, too. A twist of Jake's gut reminded him that he should be out there pulling his own weight. Now with more guys on missions to help Kiera's family, everyone here had extra shifts. With effort, he focused on what Kiera was saying.

She smiled. "Wow. Thank you. I'm not sure how

you got all of these things, but that's the nicest thing someone has done for me."

Jake swallowed bitterness. What about putting his life in danger to help her escape Lequire's men? Hell, he'd ditched his custom Jeep in favor of a shitty Taurus and even blown up a Waffle Palace for her. Didn't those actions beat Gonzo's discount clothes? *Quit it. Give her a moment of happiness within the hell she's been going through.*

She gave Gonzo an awkward hug around his thick neck, and Jake crammed his hands into his pockets to stop himself from yanking her away from his friend.

Gonzo's tanned cheeks flushed and he pointed his thumb back over his shoulder. "Uh, sure. I only did it because I drew the short straw. And so we're clear, I lost my man card last night, going shopping for women's clothing at the twenty-four-hour discount store. Looked like a freakin' moron, standing there in the middle of the store, holding up big-assed pink *chonies*." His neck even turned dark crimson as the men behind him snorted. He glared at them. "*Hostia*. Can we forget this all happened?"

Laughter burst from Kiera's lips. "That's hilarious. I can picture you picking through underwear." At the return of his black scowl, she quickly added, "I'm so glad you were willing to sacrifice your reputation for my comfort. You're obviously way braver than those other guys."

Jake, feeling like chopped liver, bit his tongue. Hard.

"Got that right." Gonzo puffed out his chest and strutted back to where the other men stood. "See? You all don't have stones like I do."

Jake set the box down near the door and followed her to what served as the dinner/strategy table. He said nothing as he pulled a chair out for her. Too many conflicts of personal and professional interest had come to light since Kiera's wake-up scream. Too much baggage and shit he had thought long packed away. New baggage he didn't even realize he was lugging around. He shook his head. *Deal with it all later.*

Hunt spoke up from where he stood, hip propped in a deceptively casual stance against the front doorjamb. "All right. Enough of this tearjerker, kumbaya shit with the fashion show. You all have work to do."

Jake growled deep in his throat. Next time, he would be the one to buy her a dozen pairs of pink panties, damn it.

Chapter Twenty

"Breakfast?" Hunt asked gruffly once the men left the room. The men had been there one minute, gone the next. Like real ghosts. Only Jake and Hunt remained behind.

Little Bit punted Kiera in the spleen, and she winced. "Apparently the answer is yes. Breakfast would be great. But first I have a question. The guys on the team seem super casual about this whole situation. If I so much as think about Lequire, my anxiety skyrockets and I want to take him on. Or run away. Is there something you know that I don't know? Is it all an act?"

Hunt settled into a chair across from her and studied her face until she squirmed. Finally, he said in a low, gravelly voice, "We're trained to be calm. In all situations."

Ironic statement, given his virally triggered implosion last night, but Kiera wasn't about to point that out now.

He rubbed his salt-and-pepper flat top. "Are you asking if my men have a fire lit under their asses about the problem they're facing?"

"Um…"

"You bet they have fires lit. Most folks can't see it."

"I didn't mean—" she sputtered, leaning away.

"Uh-oh," Jake breathed.

Moving a pen and pencil into parallel positions equidistant on either side of the notebook in front of him, Hunt said, "Because, ma'am, if you ever see one of us get sketchy, then you better believe that Armageddon is about to occur and there is zero hope for humanity's survival. Anything short of that? We're on it like the professionals we're trained to be, and we always have a plan." Another pencil was placed equidistant from the top of the notebook. "But yes, we're calm."

"Okay." Got it. So these guys were tense on the inside but freaky Zen Buddhists on the outside, always not-ready but ready for an attack. Good God. Next they'd be doing yoga while meditating about world domination. An image of Jake in athleisure attire popped up, and she covered a giggle with a cough.

At a sharp glance from Hunt, she folded her hands in front of her.

As Jake put together a quick breakfast, Hunt updated him on the compound operations. "The permanent security system will be in place soon."

"What's taking so long?" Jake asked.

"Glitch in the software. Stumpy's working on it. Won't affect anything since the temporary system is working well." He made a micro-adjustment on the notebook, lining it up perfectly flush with the table edge, and moved the pen and pencils to maintain their distances from the pad. "And we have a rotation of physical patrols and are monitoring audio and video feeds."

A muscle jumped in Jake's jaw as he popped four pieces of bread into the toaster. "What else?"

"Doc's got all the supplies he needs. For any contingency."

"Shit," Jake swore, making Kiera flinch.

"We're good," Hunt said.

The CO's level tone didn't reassure Kiera. Yeah, she knew what kind of supplies might be needed. A light twinge came and went through her lower abdomen.

"What about my family?" she said, desperate to deflect the conversation away from the all-too-real looming future.

"The men are already on the ground, soon to be embedded." The CO's icy stare swept her. "They won't let anyone hurt your family."

A chill skittered up her spine.

A few minutes later, Jake set plates down in front of Kiera and Hunt, then took a seat next to her, tucking into his own food.

After a few bites, Hunt used his fork to push bacon strips into parallel alignment with the toast edges on his plate. Then he leaned forward and opened the notebook with crisp, lined pages. He adjusted the book so the edge was parallel to the bacon.

Kiera would have laughed if the situation were any less serious.

He started, "I hope the information you provide will make it like Christmas here." The flash of his grin was nothing like jolly St. Nick. "I have wanted to take down Lequire for a long time."

"Why?" she asked before taking a bite of buttery toast. Despite the crappy situation, she still sighed as her hunger ebbed away.

At Hunt's tight, closed expression, her food turned to sand in her mouth. She felt safe enough here at the Morpheus Squad compound, but the team leader's every word, every decision, made it clear he was in charge and didn't appreciate her presence disrupting his tightly ordered world. She studied the determined glint in his eyes and the rolls of muscle on his neck and arms. He could probably destroy someone in five seconds flat without breaking a sweat.

Oddly enough, she didn't feel as uneasy around Jake.

The corners of the commanding officer's mouth rose again—like a cat right before it disembowels the mouse. "Mostly, I want to stop Lequire from stealing from our vets. With the new information you've brought me, I also don't want the guy who killed two of my men using a fake charity to buy power for his daddy. Punching holes in Bratva to keep its tentacles out of our country? That's a bonus."

She blinked.

"I have one more reason." Hunt's thick fist tightened around the pen, knuckles blanching. "It's personal. I flat-out hate the entitled prick and his power-hungry father."

Kiera picked up the fork again. "Jake said Beau didn't make the cut for one of your early teams."

A grunt. "The guy didn't get close. But he tried so he could impress his daddy. Always trying to make Senator Lequire proud." He tapped the notebook with the pen. "Beau fancies himself a Special Forces alum now. We've toyed with exposing him in one of those online forums, but the risk of being traced is too great. Hashtag asshole."

She choked on a piece of bacon. Hunt had a sense of humor, after all. "You know, I heard Beau mention something about the Green Berets," she said. "He was bragging about his missions and injuries he'd received on the team. But in reality, he washed out, didn't he?"

"People can say whatever they want. Truth is he lasted one day in Special Forces Assessment and Selection."

"What's that?" she asked.

"The preliminary phase of training. It's meant to weed out the weak." When Hunt barked what passed for a laugh, his eyes remained cold. Barren.

"So how can he claim he had been a Green Beret?"

"People lie. Yes, he did get injured in the service, but not as a Special Forces candidate or team member.

But he manipulated the media and spun quite a story. Jake knows the truth. We all do. I was one of the instructors for that class of Special Forces. I know precisely when he washed out. Some folks can't hack it. But he should own his shit, not hide it." He released the pen from his death grip and set it down on the table. Perfectly parallel to all other objects near it. "He got transferred to another base and ended up pushing paper in logistics until he got injured."

Jake said with a snort, "Injured, my ass."

Hunt grimaced. "Flag football, twisted his ankle. Then claimed 'chronic pain' and finally got discharged because he couldn't do PT. Ouchies."

She covered another giggle by dabbing her mouth with the napkin. Crunching the piece of crispy bacon, she thought back to all the times she'd seen Beau walking. "He never seemed to have a problem. No limp. Never sought treatment for an injury, to my knowledge."

"Of course not. But he was discharged because of it and got a service-connected disability designation. Then he used the GI Bill and his Senator daddy's money to obtain his MBA. Good for him. Serving in the military should come with some reward."

Kiera's chest ached. Brady never got a reward, did he? What about Mateo? All these guys who spent their lives in hiding now?

With a nasty smirk, Hunt continued. "After Lequire got his degree, his disabled veteran status attracted preferential government contracts, which helped him to create and fund Fallen Comrades. By that time, the story of his participation in Special Forces was woven into the fabric of the organization—icing on the cake to increase donations."

"Wow," she said, wanting to scrub off the invisible slime coating her skin from working with the creep for so many months.

Hunt rubbed his jaw. "There's more."

"Okay," Kiera said, sitting forward, like somehow proximity might produce more clues to keeping her family safe, finishing her mission, and getting on with her life.

"You know how his father's a big-shot senator?" Hunt said, drawing her back to the conversation.

Jake leaned back and crossed his arms.

"Senator Lequire is on the Committee on Veterans Affairs as well as the Senate Appropriations Committee." Hunt tapped a thick knuckle on the table. "Has access to everything regarding veterans. But more importantly, he has access to the entire budget of the Senate." His cruel smirk chilled her blood. "What organization do you think receives special funds from a line item in those budgets?"

Her heart sank. "His father is behind the government money getting pushed to Fallen Comrades?"

"Yep. Not to mention how he tugs the strings of a lot of puppets in the government, the president included. If he has any connection, direct or indirect, to funds being misused by this charity, it would be disastrous for his political career, wouldn't you say?"

"Not anymore," she said. "Politicians get away with bribery, extortion, misappropriation of funds, rape, and literal murder."

The CO shrugged. "We're going to use your information as a starting point to dig deeper." Nothing casual about how the cords of his shoulders and neck shifted and tensed. "There's always more. Like the Bratva angle. Guaranteed there's more than even the Russian mafia here. We'll find it. Deep state government stuff. False flag operations."

She took a bite of eggs and swallowed. "But you

can't make the connections public without exposing Morpheus Squad's secrets and risking your freedom. You all would be detained and used for more experiments, right?"

"Forever." Jake's grim smile congealed the breakfast in her gut. "Great Catch-22, huh?"

Jake, subjected to medical testing, trapped in a facility. She imagined his face, twisted in pain, as personnel collected specimens and ran tests on him.

How much could she ask these people to sacrifice for her? Mateo had given his life. Jake had torpedoed his entire existence to help her outrun Beau's men. The rest of the team had left their carefully crafted fake lives behind to help Kiera.

So, yes, she would do her part to protect the Morpheus Squad guys. Whatever it took.

And she would protect her child. Both goals were possible.

"Why are you all here, then? In the country?" she asked. "If you're at risk of being captured by the government."

"We have to stay close to our pipeline." Hunt didn't meet her eyes.

"It could be shipped," Jake offered.

What were they talking about?

"Too risky. Besides, this is the last place they'd look for us."

She pointed a thumb at Jake. "Apparently not."

"It's complicated," Hunt said with a growl. He drummed his fingers on the tabletop. "We don't have unlimited options."

A hot wave of anger made her hand shake, and she set the fork down. "So unless we do something, Beau will keep siphoning money designated for real heroes?"

"You got it."

"I assume you have a plan."

"Of course, I do, ma'am."

An image of her brother's earnest face appeared in her mind. "I hate Beau Lequire. What a loser."

"Damned straight. But he's a loser with a hell of a lot of power and money, which makes him a threat," Hunt said.

"No question there." She took a sip of orange juice.

He ran a hand over his flat-top hair. "Any public action by the Morpheus Squad means we risk re-capture. We haven't had a compelling reason to put our freedom at risk." He flashed a shockingly jovial smile, then it was replaced by a snarl full of pure vengeance. "Until now."

Jake pressed his mouth into a tight line. "Wait. Is Kiera in any danger by telling you what she knows?"

"Lequire killed Brady to keep him quiet, blew up Kiera's house, killed Mateo, and tried to capture and kill her in public. While she was pregnant. How much more risk are you talking about?" He turned to squarely face her. "Look, there's risk either way. Whether or not you share everything you know, you're in trouble."

Her breath caught in her throat. "But?"

"But you're safe here. You're surrounded by ex-Special Forces soldiers who train to fight at a moment's notice. They're in top shape." He smirked at Jake. "Well, most of them."

He lifted his hands. "Hey, even while sulking in the boonies, I stayed in form."

Kiera licked her dry lips, recalling his … form.

Hunt winked at her and said in a mock whisper, "That man is soft like a candy-eating kid. Out of shape and flabby. Don't let him lie to you."

She covered a chuckle with her hand. No one could ever claim Jake Zimmerman was unfit. She could personally attest to the cords of hard muscle covering every inch of his zero-fat body.

"So, yes, ma'am. Short of you disappearing completely into witness protection, which would be messy given"—Hunt waved his hand around the room—"the secrecy of this operation and how you're already involved with Morpheus Squad, we don't have a lot of choices. Frankly, I don't even know if witness protection would deter Lequire, with all of his connections. Also consider the fact that your baby will be highly sought-after by the government, and I don't mean for college scholarships. Your options are limited. But we *can* keep you safe here. Indefinitely."

She started. "Wait. I can't go back to my normal life?" A virtual vise gripped her chest. "That was never part of the plan."

"No."

"Like, no, it's not advisable, or no, you're not going to let me?"

"The second one. You can't leave. I won't risk my men's existence on a civilian's ability to keep her mouth shut."

A prickle at her temple turned into a pounding headache. "Hold on a minute."

"You can't leave. That's final."

Her ears rang. "I have a life to live, you know."

"So does your baby." Hunt's lips barely moved. "So do we."

Next to her, Jake's frame went ramrod straight. "Kiera, you have to listen to him. It's not all about you."

Oh, God. The baby. But her own future? Gone in the snap of two thick fingers.

"We'll keep you safe," Hunt said.

"I'm going to hold you to it, boss," Jake said, his mouth pressed into a grim line. Like he cared. Shocking, considering his reaction to her this morning.

She sucked in air, stunned. Did she seriously have to remain in hiding for the remainder of her life? She slumped as the weight of her decisions over the past year dropped onto her shoulders. Damn it.

First things first. Baby's safety. Father and sisters' safety next. Then Kiera would deal with her future later. She'd get her life back, one way or another. And no, she would never reveal anything about Morpheus Squad.

A frown forged lines across Hunt's weathered skin, aging him an extra five years. "I *will* ensure your safety and your baby's."

"I understand," she whispered. For now, she would stay. But later?

"Fair enough." Hunt's curt reply broke the thick tension in the room. "Now Jake, get your butt off to some training. The guys will knock the rust off. We'll start you on rotations tomorrow. Send Stumpy in so he can organize all of the information living in Ms. McNeill's noggin."

"Roger that." Before he spun, the flash of emotion in Jake's gray irises pinned Kiera to her seat. A combination of regret and longing shifted the features of his handsome face, right before he pasted on a bland expression. Damn her, but she couldn't stop staring as he walked out of the building and closed the front door.

Hunt's expression changed from in-command and harsh to almost … sympathetic?

After rearranging the perfectly aligned pen, he looked like he was about to speak. Then thought better of it and his mouth closed with a *clunk* of molars. A few seconds later, he muttered, "I'm no expert in emotional stuff, but Jake's a good guy."

She stammered, "I'm not. No, I—"

He folded his hands. "Don't get all squishy on me. It's just a comment." Watching her until she squirmed, he asked, "Speaking of comments, what do you think of him?"

She choked on her orange juice and coughed for a minute before she could respond. "What?"

"It's a reasonable question."

Not from a guy like Hunt. She'd bet her CPA degree he had never asked an innocent question in his life.

"Um." She shoved hair behind her ears. "Look, Jake and I dated years ago. We broke up ten years ago. No contact until last summer." Shifting on her seat, she stammered, "Pardon me, but is this information somehow critical to the data I have on Fallen Comrades?"

"Nope."

The skin over her chest heated up.

The damned interrogator merely stared at her. Then he leaned back in his seat.

Crossing her arms, she pursed her lips. "Aren't you supposed to be the grumpy commanding officer? Not a psychologist?"

That relaxed posture? Gone. In its place was the hard-nosed Special Forces CO. The guy sure could flip the switch on his personality. "Understand that I'm everything for these men. Father, commander, big brother, and counselor. Everything I do is to protect their best interests. It's my overriding goal. I only ask questions if I think the answers will help the team."

Oh, God, he had toyed with her. Like a cat with a naïve mouse.

Did Hunt have a separate agenda? If so, she and the baby might not be as safe as he claimed. She'd have to tread carefully.

She swallowed again. "Shouldn't we concentrate

on downloading my brain?"

He paused. Then, with a salute and a savage grin, he readjusted his notebook, setting it perfectly parallel to the table edge, and tapped the end of the pen on his angular jaw. She was surprised the writing implement didn't shatter. "Let's get to work."

Chapter Twenty-One

"How about a break?" Stumpy rolled his neck and lifted his hands from the keyboard, popping his knuckles and stretching his wrists. Puckered skin and scars shifted as the muscles on his left forearm tensed and relaxed.

Had he been injured along with Brady? Had Jake been there, too, in the line of fire?

She rubbed her arm surreptitiously and focused instead on the computer screen.

Images of the data danced in front of her eyes. Hunt had wanted details on Fallen Comrades, too: leadership, business structure, connections.

Then the CO had left her with Stumpy, whose job was to collect as much of the detailed information she could recall from her eidetic memory. Unfortunately, she couldn't simply plug in and download the data. All morning, the tech guy had worked tirelessly to transcribe the key portions of virtual Excel spreadsheets locked in her mind. Not exactly locked, but more accessible contextually.

They started by creating a fake spreadsheet similar to the one in Beau's office. Then she held portions of an image in her mind and dictated figures and text to Stumpy until his screen matched what she saw in her memory. It wasn't complete because her eidetic memory wasn't exactly photographic memory, but it was close enough to work with.

Then they went back and added specific account information from the thumb drive.

Hours later, her eyes burned and her head throbbed.

She stood up and pressed her hands into her lower

back, wincing when the wound pinched.

All her joints slowly loosened up as she walked around. The leg wound still ached, but thanks to another dose of the antibiotic this morning, the redness had receded. At least Little Bit had cooperated, limiting Kiera's bathroom breaks to a bare minimum.

Every muscle complained when she stretched. "A break sounds great," she agreed.

Stumpy pushed back from his chair and slowly rose to his feet. His stiffness seemed to have nothing to do with their work. With a rakish smile, he shrugged and wrapped a hand around the head of his ever-present black metal cane. If the Morpheus Squad guys were meant to be silent and efficient lethal operators, she had trouble visualizing a cold killer in the friendly computer whiz's body. The wave of his black hair, a precisely shaved goatee, and solid shoulders made him look more like an edgy barista than a soldier.

She tried not to stare but couldn't miss how he rubbed his left thigh. A rush of heat crawled up her neck when she met his determined stare. He had the eyes of a warrior who may have crawled through hell but came out alive on the other side. He'd served his country with honor.

She eyed the box on the couch. "I wouldn't mind changing into one of the new outfits Gonzo got for me."

"Yes, those clothes would be good to put on."

Odd statement. "Really? Do I smell bad? Jake laundered this outfit, you know. They're fairly fresh." How long ago had that meeting been? Less than two days ago, but it felt like they had packed a month of relationship into such a small space of time. Her chest ached.

"You smell like a daisy," he quipped, flashing a quick rakish grin. "But it might be nice not to have holes in your outfits." Something about his sideways glance made her skin itch.

"Sure."

"Anything else you need?" Stumpy picked up an alarm clock and fiddled with it, taking off the casing pieces. On breaks from entering data, he had systematically dismantled whatever mechanical object was within arm's reach.

Her stomach rumbled. Again. "Of course. More food."

"Can't let kiddo starve. Let me see what I can put together."

Kiddo. Hers and Jake's. "She's already eating me out of house and home."

After picking out an outfit, she stepped into the main building's bathroom. She took a few minutes to clean up. Then she donned fresh underwear, stretchy jeans, a long-sleeved red top that stopped mid-thigh, and a swingy black cardigan. New socks and clean shoes completed the outfit, and she nearly purred with happiness. The clothes with shrapnel holes in them? Trash can.

The night she had collected those holes … she and the baby had almost—

Mateo *had* died. She swallowed against a painful lump.

When she re-entered the main room, Stumpy clicked off a screen that had what looked like a diagram of a person on it. Weird. Pushing to the side the scattered pieces of the clock, he swiveled in the chair and gave her two thumbs-up.

"Looks great! Love that you're wearing the latest colors to dress your bump." The commentary was totally out of place for a tall, muscled ex-Special Forces soldier who ate danger for breakfast and sipped steaming cups of hacked data.

"Maybe later we can show Gonzo what good taste in clothing he has," she said, an odd quiver in her belly rising that had nothing to do with what Jake might think of her new outfit. She smoothed nonexistent wrinkles out of her outfit.

Stumpy's brows rose. "I'm a little scared of Gonzo's reaction." He screwed up his mouth and closed one eye. "No. Actually, he seemed to enjoy shopping way more than he's letting on."

The easy laughter relaxed her neck and shoulder muscles. "You know he's a big softie, deep down inside."

"Not exactly." His serious expression made her pause. "Gonzo—or any of the guys—could kill a person dead under five seconds flat."

"Jake?" The word left her mouth before she could stop it.

No mirth danced in his green eyes. "You don't want to know what he's capable of."

An icy shiver shot through her. "Any of you guys could take someone out in five seconds flat?"

"A top-secret soldier does not tell." He buffed his nails against his shirt. "It's four seconds for me."

"What?"

"Kidding." He rolled his lips, bringing the goatee together in the middle. "Not really."

Off-balance, she burst out laughing.

"For his part, though, Gonzo is still recovering from the psychic trauma of big box store shopping. Retail skills were not part of the competencies set by the Army."

"It's good practice for when he has a woman in his life."

"What, now you're playing matchmaker?" He

crossed his eyes, again so out of character compared with his demeanor around the other guys. "The poor lady. Actually, poor Gonzo. He'll never know what hit him if a woman gets hold of him."

Kiera smiled.

Stumpy rose and nodded toward the kitchen. "So, after a fancy lunch of sandwiches, would you like a grand tour of the compound?"

"Don't we need to keep going with the downloads? What about the data drive?"

"Ah." He swatted the air with his hand. "Rules are rules: no strenuous mental work on a full stomach. You'll get a brain cramp."

Chapter Twenty-Two

As Jake pressed up massive discs of metal in the open-air gym behind one of the buildings, he wanted to kill each guy nearby. Okay, maybe not Doc, since he had the redeeming quality of being able to save Kiera and her baby. But the rest of them? If Jake had to endure another insult from his worthless spotter, Rodeo … what he would give to knock that stupid cowboy hat off the guy's head. Or at minimum, wipe the smirk off his perfect smile. Permanently.

Lucky for Rodeo, a weighted, bent barbell currently crushed Jake's ribs as he attempted a bench press, making it impossible to breathe. Or attack. Or reply to snide comments.

Rodeo peered down at him upside-down, pulled out the goddamned purple yo-yo, and started doing tricks. Sure, the virus created some weird ticks and fixations, but for Pete's sake, Rodeo could walk the dog elsewhere. The whites of his eyes winked with every blink under his stupid hat. Damn him.

Even with the increased upper body strength the virus gave Jake, he still couldn't budge the 575-pound weight. 550? He could do it any day of the week ending in "y." 575? No go. Even his strength had limits.

If he didn't have the antidote on board and he released every last bit of control over the virus, he possibly could budge the weight. But then he'd be possessed by the damned Morpheus Virus, which would tip him all the way over into madness, or so the hypothesis went. No one ever wanted to beta test the theory. He'd come close enough to glimpse insanity.

If the virus took over one hundred percent, Jake would try to kill anyone—even his comrades.

Right as he started to fantasize in earnest about the various ways he could injure Rodeo, Gonzo's ugly mug entered Jake's field of vision from the side. Insult added to injury. *Please, if there is a God in heaven, let me get my hands on either of those morons and I'll never let go.*

"*Que pasa, princesa?*" Gonzo asked.

Jake gritted his teeth and wheezed. "You idiots are going to feel really bad when they find me dead beneath this weight while you two dumbbells stood by and did nothing."

"Nothing?" Gonzo's dark brows rose. "We're motivating your ass to get back in shape, aren't we, Rodeo?"

With a curt nod, Rodeo flipped his wrist and sent the yo-yo on a breakaway move, all while staring down at him. What Jake would give to hurl that stupid toy into the next county.

"By the way, you're welcome." Gonzo waggled a finger. "Hey, it's not our fault. If you had kept up with the program while you were playing emotionally wounded hermit out in the middle of nowhere, we wouldn't be having this conversation."

"Shit." Jake gritted his teeth as the bar dug into his chest, gripped the bar once again, and pushed. Nothing. "My ribs are breaking." The metal bit into his chest. No one moved. "Doc, don't you have a hypocritical oath or something to follow here?"

"Sorry, can't hear you," Doc said as he finished a set of dips. "Hippocratic oath and all."

Jake stared at the two talking heads in front of him. "You two suck," he gasped.

"In the best possible way, according to numerous beautiful ladies. All happy customers. Yelp reviews, all five stars." When Rodeo grinned, his goddamned perfect teeth gleamed in his goddamned perfect head.

"Yelp! Yelp!" Gonzo squealed and fanned himself.

Jake would rather hang out with a beautiful woman than these sweaty ass-clowns. A certain woman with soft curves and warm, hazel eyes came to mind.

"Weren't you gifted with superior upper body strength?" Rodeo winked and then turned and rocked the baby with a flick of his wrist. "Because I have to admit— I don't see it right now. Maybe the virus seeped out and you're back to being a puny normal guy."

"Damn you," Jake muttered. "I pushed out 550. What the hell do you want from me?"

"Ooh, 550. What do you want? A medal?" Rodeo grinned and continued the up and down rhythm of the lightly whirring toy.

"Could you quit playing with that thing!" Jake spat.

Rodeo concentrated on the purple orb's movement. "You know, if I had a dollar for every time I heard that line…"

"You'd have a dollar." Gonzo turned to Jake. "You should try thinking of something really positive. Like having amazing sex or ripping the heads off of bad guys."

Jake took a deep breath despite the heavy weight resting on his chest and let the good vibes from kissing Kiera wash over him. Hopefully his gym shorts hid any evidence of his interest because if these so-called friends noticed, Jake would never hear the end of it. Struggling to focus, he forced his burning arms to push out one more rep until Rodeo pocketed the toy, grabbed the bar, and lowered the barbell into the holders.

"Good job, hot shot." Gonzo batted his eyelashes. "I don't care what silly cowboy said, I always knew you could do it."

"With friends like this, who needs enemies?" Jake muttered as he sat up sideways on the bench and rested his elbows on his knees, hiding more obvious changes in his groin. Shit, the muscles in his arms and his pecs quivered like Jell-O in an earthquake.

"Our job is to make sure you're back in fighting shape now that you've rejoined the land of the living." Rodeo patted him on the back.

Land of the living. Jake's mind showed him a montage of his past: the empty seat at the table where his father should have been when Jake was a child, his ex-wife crying at their loss, the memories of Brady and Mateo, the uncertainty of his own life expectancy, and an imagined picture of his small family of three going up in flames.

His life was chock full of messy mistakes, like the way he'd gotten scared and defensive and then rejected the hell out of Kiera this morning. Not his best moment. Not by a country mile.

If he was being fair, he hadn't had time to explore what it meant to have Kiera back in his life. Actually, strike that. He'd explored her mouth pretty well when he took advantage of her half-awake and terrified state. Shit, those long legs got him going every single time. What he'd give to those silky limbs wrapped around him while he drove into her until they had mind-melting orgasms over and over.

Yeah, he'd jumped right back on the carnival ride of desire for Kiera.

Damn it, Jake wanted no part of exploring any fucking feelings. Been there, done that, got the t-shirt. Turned down the therapy session.

But seeing Kiera in bed this morning, vulnerable and scared, a horrible switch flipped inside of him. In an instant, he would have done literally anything to protect her. Would have killed anyone, destroyed anything. Friend or foe. Wouldn't have mattered. And the fact that his extreme reaction occurred even without the virus at full strength in his system made the whole situation even more terrifying. If he couldn't control himself when the virus was suppressed, what would happen if he ever let Mr. Hyde out to play?

The potential to lose control with Kiera scared the hell out of him.

The image of her surrounded by Jake's teammates last night and this morning should have comforted him, should have allowed him to relax his vigilance. Instead, the scene made him want to stand in front of her, mark her as his own, and scream at them to stop looking at her.

Only problem? Besides the knuckle-dragging Cro-Magnon reaction? He had no claim to Kiera.

The good thing that Jake and Kiera almost had ten years ago, he had ruined after the pregnancy scare then. Same as with his ex-wife. Good thing, *poof*, gone. Jake's fault because he freaked out and didn't know how to help. Then, when his ex had sent him packing, he'd gladly tucked tail and run.

What about now?

Speaking of shit he shouldn't think about, damned if Kiera didn't stroll up with that lucky bastard, Stumpy.

Jake's lungs seized up, and his hands rolled into joint-creaking fists. He tried to give the guy a warning glare—anything to wipe the big grin off Stumpy's face, but his teammate had eyes only for the lovely woman at his side who matched his slow pace.

Jake loved her pregnant hip-wiggle, the glow of her skin, and the way her hand drifted to her belly when she talked. Her body, in every iteration, revved the hell out of his engines. Always had.

Past tense. Had. As in, he *had* his chance with her and failed. Time to let those feelings go.

But that was before he tasted her lips again. Before he pulled her onto his lap on the bed and wrapped his arms around her, and it felt better than he remembered even in his dreams. It felt like a dream when she returned his kisses, right up until his fears short-circuited his brain and he said all the wrong things.

Right there in the crisp air of the woods—in front of him—stood the picture of everything Jake wanted.

He shook his head. He should concentrate on something simple for his brain to process, like how the red shirt material hugged her midsection and how the long-sleeve sweater thingy clung to her curved hips. He should think about how good her legs looked in the jean leggings. His mouth went dry.

Even normally glib Gonzo clammed up and stared at Kiera. So did Mr. Chatty, Rodeo.

"Hi," Kiera said. Damn it how her cheeks flushed pink in the brisk spring air.

God help him, but it sounded like she addressed him specifically. As her gaze met his for the space of a breath, a zing of attraction shot to his pelvis.

He shifted position. Desperate to regain control, he forced himself to run through a mundane mental packing list for a three-day assignment in a desert environment. By the time he'd reached MRE packets and sunscreen, he could stand up without embarrassing himself.

The guys around him remained stone-silent. Jake managed to put a few words together. "How's the data download going?"

Stumpy leaned on his cane, face shining as he

looked down at her. "Kiera's like a living camera. It's amazing! And with the accounting background, she's also interpreting the data as we write it down."

Kiera tugged at a strand of dark-brown hair. "It'll be another few days before I can get all the information out of my head. We haven't correlated everything from the thumb drive yet. The Bratva ties involve less concrete data and more connect-the-dots."

"At least we're on our way to nailing that Fallen Comrades dickhead in the keister," Rodeo spat.

Nothing but horrified, silent stares occurred for a full five seconds.

The giggle bursting from Kiera had a ripple effect on every man within a ten-foot radius. The bubble of tension popped. For the first time in forever, the rough and tough, on-edge, fucked-up group of soldiers actually relaxed and chuckled.

The air became lighter, easier to breathe.

Amazing.

She flicked the hem of her jacket and twirled. "Hey, thanks for the duds, Gonzo. What do you think?"

Jake curled his hands into fists as he fought a wave of pure fury. The guys needed to stop staring at her. Now.

Rational brain knew this was his viral brain talking.

Viral brain didn't give a shit about rational brain's opinion.

"Yeah, the outfit looks good," Gonzo said. "I meant, on the hanger. In the store." He scrubbed at his short, dark hair. "On you, too. Shit. Never mind."

Rodeo made a half-hearted attempt to cover his snicker with a cough. "Smooth move, there, Ex-lax." He palmed the yo-yo and sent it down the string a time or two.

Gonzo tried to glare the cowboy to death while the other men chuckled.

"So, you guys getting lots of work done?" she asked, eyes twinkling.

Rodeo pulled an offended pout and pocketed the toy. Then in a deliberate motion, he crossed his corded arms until they were on obvious flexed display for her. That fucker. Jake wanted to stand in front of him. Was this how it worked? Jealousy also triggered the virus?

No way would he go around taking a poll, on the off chance he was the only one who responded in such an extreme manner.

He struggled to focus on what Rodeo was saying.

The cowboy gave her one of those slow, seductive smiles.

Jake seethed.

Rodeo said, "You know, not all of us can be brainiacs like you and Stump-head there. Some of us have to rely on skills or brawn. But since Jake here has no skill, all we can do is try to pound him back into shape." He blew out an exaggerated sigh. "It's becoming a job and a half right about now."

In the background, Doc flashed a rare smile.

"Well, I can't think of anyone better qualified to do it." She laughed as Rodeo drew himself up to full height and preened like an overstuffed peacock. "Carry on, guys. Don't stop on my account."

Rodeo tipped his hat, and Gonzo mumbled goodbye.

She and Stumpy continued on a path toward the compound perimeter, and fuck if Jake didn't focus on the sway of her hips. Red fabric. Red vision. The entire image—Kiera, Stumpy, the forest—had gone red. Jake was in serious deep shit.

Once they were out of earshot, Gonzo whistled.

At the sound, Jake's temper went from baseline irritated to critical in a nanosecond. "What was that for, asshole?"

Gonzo's hands went up. "*Tranquilo*! Don't shoot! Only noticing how badly whipped you are, man. You have the disease."

"Disease?" Unable to stop himself, he looked over at Doc, who tilted his head in his usual paucity of extra movement. His irritating, calm countenance gave no hints.

Gonzo grinned and batted his eyelashes. "*Luuuv* sickness, of course."

"What the hell are you talking about?" Jake asked. The guys only knew the bare bones of his ancient history with Kiera. Those details had been courtesy of Brady's big mouth on downtime between missions.

Gonzo snickered. "Come on, lover boy, do another few reps. Then you can go take a cold shower."

Chapter Twenty-Three

"Pardon?" Kiera's neck heated up as she got caught daydreaming. She tried not to trip and fall on her own two feet.

Stumpy didn't deserve her inattention. But in her defense, her brain had locked up the moment she had seen Jake's shirtless torso, glistening with sweat, his flat nipples tight in the cool air. Every muscle in his massive chest and arms had been pumped up, ropey with veins, and hard. The way his muscled abdomen narrowed down to a peek of hair showing above his low-slung shorts. Her world had tilted, and her mouth had made the desert seem humid. She still hadn't regained her equilibrium.

"I was mentioning the sensitive perimeter protection we've got here, with the experimental mesh and the heat-detecting equipment layered outside of the compound." He paused at a small black box on a low post next to the mesh, opened the device, and punched in some numbers. Closing the cover, he stood back up with a low grunt. "Perhaps we should enjoy the walk in peace and quiet."

"I'm sorry. I appreciate you telling me about everything here. It's impressive what you've created. I feel safer just hearing about the different levels of security." Leaves crunched as she shuffled next to him. "The last two days have been beyond stressful." *Baby. Virus.* Her chest tightened.

No. Stop. She didn't have the bandwidth available to freak out. Not right now. Later. Doc had said everything looked good. Baby girl appeared healthy on ultrasound. That should reassure her. Her heart pounded. *Not now.* Kiera took a slow, deep breath in and out and compartmentalized her fear as best she could.

He was saying something. "… lots to process. Understandable."

"Yeah." She glanced at the thick foliage. "Um, you're certain we're okay here?"

The flash of his smile was blink-and-you-miss-it. "You bet."

A thwacking in the distance got her attention and over the next twenty seconds grew louder. "Stumpy?"

He went still, muscles and posture primed. Stumpy patted the gun in his thigh holster. "Stand next to a tree." It wasn't a suggestion.

He tapped on his cell phone as he glanced upward, mouth pressing into a hard line.

Her hands shook as she felt the rough bark behind her. She scanned the obscured sky. "Why?" she whispered.

A furrow formed between his brows as the helicopter noise increased above them. "Not that our heat signature would likely make it up to the sky, but by staying close to the tree, you'll be masked from anything else that might occur."

"Occur?" Sweat formed between her breasts.

"From above." He kept typing away, head bent over the phone as he leaned against her tree as well.

"I thought we were undetectable with your system."

More taps on the screen. He glanced at her. "Of course we are." Was that a bead of sweat on his brow?

The blades *whumped* above them, compressions of air loud, even despite the mesh muffling the sound. She pulled her shoulders forward, imagining Beau's too-calm face pressed against the passenger window as he scanned the landscape. Oh, God. This had all been a horrible idea. Coming to the compound. This little walk. The mission. All of it.

He squinted up toward the tree canopy and tapped on the phone. "Ah, there we go. Nothing to see here, folks," he muttered. "Nothing at all."

A black helicopter passed over their position, moving slowly. Kiera didn't move. "Someone's looking for us."

"Probably. Could also be a sightseeing flight over the Smokies, though it's early in the season for it."

"So, searching for us?"

"Likely." His grin was cold, calculating. "But thanks to my smoke and mirrors, they'll find nothing besides bland forest here."

She sagged against the peeling birch trunk. "Until they look again."

"With millions of other acres to cover? It'll be a long time before anyone returns to this tiny box on the giant search grid."

"There was a drone flying over this morning."

"It found nothing then, too."

She blew out a shaky breath. "It's okay. You don't have to sugarcoat anything for me. Shouldn't we get back to the building?"

"No need now." He beckoned her to follow him and spread his fingers over the top of the cane. "Let's continue our walk."

Like nothing had happened. The guy had nerves of steel. Catching up to him, she waited a minute for her heart rate to fall back to normal levels.

Shooting him a sheepish grin, she said, "You'd think I'd be used to being scared by now."

"No one ever gets used to it." Then his jaw clamped shut.

Another fifty feet, and Curly appeared, strolling toward them, rifle held across his chest.

The scowl and the deceptively casual grip of the

gun made her skin crawl.

"Eyes in the sky gone?" he asked.

"Not looking here," Stumpy said. "Anything interesting in your world?" Stumpy asked.

The bald man's gaze slid past Kiera. "Nothing." He didn't break stride.

Glancing back a few seconds later, she peered into the woods. He had disappeared. A shiver scudded through her gut.

They shuffled along for another few paces. She wet her lips. "Amazing how I have any adrenaline left, after the past two days."

"Understandable." After a few more steps, he stopped and leaned on his cane. "After losing Mateo and … everything."

"Well, yes."

He cocked his head to the side while he paused at another small box and punched in more numbers before continuing the walk. "You two were close. Right?"

"Mateo was a good friend. To Brady and to me." A prickle behind her eyelids reminded her there hadn't been time to properly mourn Mateo.

Stumpy's eyes cut to her belly and back. "Jake is acting like his guts are being ripped out when you're around."

She reared back. "Wow. Talk about a topic change."

"I figured you and Jake were working things out…"

"There's nothing between us," she said, too harshly. She winced.

"Disagree."

"We dated in high school. Then stopped. We had a lapse of judgment last summer." Holding her hands over her belly, she said, "Now I'm an obligation. That's all."

He snorted. "Was there something serious once upon a time?" he asked.

"Yes. Long time ago. Ancient history."

"Not so sure."

She stopped and rested a hand on her hip. "Trying to become the next Dear Abby?"

"No, but I have sisters and they explained to me the multiple ways men can be idiots." A flash of sadness drew his brows together, then it was gone. "I've made my fair share of mistakes in the relationship department over the years." He rubbed his goatee. "Also, I'm not blind."

"I'm not sure how to answer."

"You don't have to." He stopped and crouched at another box, performing the same check on it.

"Everything working okay?" She motioned toward the mesh and the box.

"Why wouldn't it be?" He presented a bland expression as he stood and began walking again.

"That's not an answer."

"Double-checking the hardware since we're out here anyway."

Stumpy's shoe with the prosthetic foot in it scuffed against a root, and she slowed down to match his change in stride. Her injured calf muscle welcomed the slow pace.

He planted the cane with each step. "Jake's a good guy. He's given his all on the battlefield and tries to do the right things, even when it hurts him to do so."

"What are you saying?"

The dull crunch of damp and decomposing leaves filled the silence. "That it's obvious why he's having issues with you, pregnant and all. At risk. With his past and with a virus which might cause … issues."

Nausea swirled, and for once, the baby kicks didn't reassure her. "I'm not feeling great about things right now, either."

Holding up a hand, he said, "My bad. Sometimes my mouth gets in the way of good sense. So my sisters tell me."

"You can say whatever you need to. Not like I haven't had the thoughts." She pinched the bridge of her nose. Her laugh came out thin, forced. "Nothing like something unknown growing inside of me." Nothing funny about it at all. She had to force her weak legs to hold her up.

"I don't…" He peered away, into the forest. A few crunches echoed in the trees. "What's that?" He stepped in front of her. "Don't move for a second." Pushing a recessed button on his cane, he stabbed it into the ground so it stood upright. He then pulled out a cell phone and tapped on the screen.

Kiera sucked in a lungful of air and held it as she studied the thick forest, looking for a place to hide. Behind a mountain laurel? Or in a nearby rock-filled dry draw? Next to a tree again? Her heart pounded a drum beat against her ribs.

Another crunch made her jump. How many frights could a pregnant woman take before she became unglued?

A rustle of leaves answered her.

Chapter Twenty-Four

Jake switched monitors to a different security camera view at Stumpy's command center in the main compound building. He wiped the cooling sweat from his brow and pulled on a t-shirt with still-quivering arms. An image of Kiera and Stumpy happily strolling along the compound perimeter filled a screen. He was being merely watchful. Not fixated on her safety at all.

Not fixated on *her* at all.

It was at times like this he wondered if rationalizing his bullshit was another quirk the virus had given him.

Her smile as she looked around the forest caused a sad mimic in the corners of his mouth.

Of all people, he understood why Kiera wanted space and air and things normal humans needed to not feel trapped. A nasty twist in his gut reminded him that the act of bringing her here might have saved her life but also had limited her future.

Damn it, he had overreacted this morning. Been a jerk, thanks to his own guilt and insecurities. He could have at least been more understanding of her situation.

Their situation.

Maybe he still had a chance to at least try to recapture some of the friendship they once had years ago. What if the possibility still existed that there could be more than friendship?

Dare he think about things like *relationship* and *family*?

Well, then. To regain her trust, he shouldn't invade her privacy. He stepped back and deliberately looked away from the screen.

Nope, couldn't do it. His head swiveled back. He

was riveted to the images on the monitors. Damn it, the temporary security system didn't have sound yet, or he would have eavesdropped.

The door slammed open, startling Jake, and he spun around as Hunt stalked across the room, phone crammed to his ear. Curses flowed from his snarling mouth. After a pause and a glare, his CO muttered, "Thanks for the intel. I guess now I owe you one." He ended the call. "Well, shit."

"Who was that?"

"Someone who knows things."

Jake took a stab at the obvious. "Something wrong?"

Phone stowed, Hunt didn't answer but turned his attention to the screens behind Jake. He peered at the images of Kiera and Stumpy walking the compound's perimeter and snorted. "I should ask you that."

"Sir," Jake growled, his internal temperature spiking, muscles expanding. Damn it, it would be no good unleashing on his CO. He curled his hands into fists and released.

Hunt clapped him on the shoulder. "Stand down, soldier."

With effort, Jake's red-tinged vision faded to normal color. "Yes, sir." He dragged his gaze away from the screen once again. Motioning toward the phone in his CO's hand, he asked, "Do we have a problem?"

A weird flush crept up Hunt's neck and he looked down. A response Jake had never seen before. "More than you know." He ran a palm over his high-and-tight and blew out a big breath. "There's activity on a supposedly secure server containing the main Project Morpheus files. Records buried so deep within other files, even the government doesn't know about them."

"Someone knows."

"Yes."

Jake pulled his head back. "Beau Lequire has access to files on the team?"

"Not him. His daddy. Senator Lequire has deep ties into the military going years back. He had … involvement in the project from the beginning."

"What if whoever is accessing the information isn't connected to Beau Lequire or his senator dad?"

"Then it may be an attempt by the Army to determine our current status and whereabouts."

"How do we find out which it is?"

"Good question. My … source isn't certain."

"Who is your source?"

"Need to know," he snapped.

Okay, then. "If Senator Lequire is snooping into our existence, shouldn't we do something?"

Hunt paced the room with long, heavy thuds. "No. No, we don't disrupt our plans. Yet. But we have our contingencies ready to go. The security tech is solid, and we've got physical patrols in place. By the way, you're up in an hour for the afternoon shift, so plan your life accordingly."

"Roger that."

Hunt stopped, and a terrifying grin warped his hard face. The deep pops of his knuckles ricocheted off the walls of the room. "Between you and me, I'd love for someone to try us. Dust off our skills in actual combat and rearrange some people's … priorities."

"Here I thought you were the voice of reason."

"Most days. Hey, don't worry, if I ever unleash the full force of the Morpheus Squad, you'd better believe I'll keep things discreet. No one will ever find the bodies." His CO wasn't making a joke.

"So, does your connection on the outside put us at risk?"

Hunt turned and faced Jake. "They can call me but not track me. Stumpy's got our location and communications data so scrambled that any spy satellites will run into each other and talk pig Latin if they try to locate us."

Jake glanced back over his shoulder at the monitors. Kiera and Stumpy had stopped walking and were pointing into the forest.

Stumpy moved in front of Kiera as he pulled his Sig out of the thigh holster.

Chapter Twenty-Five

"Got it." Stumpy shifted to one side as Kiera stepped up next to him and peered around his shoulder. He stowed the gun he'd briefly drawn. A black and white image flashed over the phone screen. Big, innocent eyes stared back at her. "Just a doe having an afternoon snack." He pointed. "About fifty yards thataway."

"Shouldn't we be able to see it?"

"Normally, yes. But the mesh makes it hard for us to see. That's what the perimeter cameras are for."

"We're okay?" The tension in her back loosened by a few degrees.

"You're safe here. I swear. That's what the system is for."

"It's the backup system." She crossed her arms over her chest. "Why are you sweating?"

"Lady, I don't sweat, I glisten. Besides, the backup works well." His smile went from rakish to hungry. "If anything tries to come through the barrier," he said and pointed, "the intruder will literally get lit up."

"What?"

"Touch mesh and *bzzz*—couple thousand volts of no-thank-you."

She took a step back. "Would have been nice to know about the risk of electrocution before this little hike."

"You're right. Should have been on the safety brief."

"What about the deer? Won't it get zapped?"

"That's why the system didn't fully alarm. It's programmed to know the difference between Bambi and a bad guy." He scrolled through other surveillance screens and showed her images of swaying hemlock branches and rhododendron leaves. "These digital feeds are of the immediate perimeter"—he swiped again—"and these are from a quarter-mile into the woods on all sides. All we see is Bambi and woodland friends." Putting the phone in his back pocket, he pulled up the cane, moved his fingers over the top of the support, and they began walking again.

Thick, uncomfortable silence settled between them. Finally, she cleared her throat. "Not to bring up a taboo subject, but don't you worry about the government finding you guys?"

"You know the whole story? How the squad got to this place—literally and metaphorically?"

"Some of it."

He nodded. "At first, the government was our biggest fan. We were good little soldiers, taking part in the experiment. Things went great. We were unstoppable. The Army flat-out loved what we could do. And to whom." His step faltered. "It wasn't until the changes emerged in each of us that the brass realized the project wasn't as fabulous as they had hoped. We couldn't be controlled. So they told us we were going home for an honorable discharge from the military."

"No?"

"Not even close. When we realized the truth, that's when we all exited the service early."

"Exited?"

"The Morpheus Squad escaped a maximum-security military testing facility. Together. Unscathed. Which is more than I can say for our jailors." A grim smile flashed. "We were on the same side as those people … until we weren't." His gaze hit somewhere a mile behind her. "Then our team all went AWOL. No other choice."

"But wait." She planted her feet and faced him.

"What about Jake? Hadn't he left before the rest of the team?"

He leaned on his cane. "Yes, then no. We all received the virus at the same time and performed missions together. A few months prior to the time when all the … stuff happened in his personal life. He rejoined the team in Afghanistan a month later. So … a little less than two years ago. Shortly after he returned to fight with us, the Army pulled the plug and brought us all home." His barked laugh came out hard.

"You volunteered for a dangerous mission to serve your country and they put you in jail?"

"Well, they said it was for testing, but it was against our will. And painful. Therefore, prison. This little virus of ours made us prime experiments for good old Uncle Sam. Too valuable to let go."

"How could they?" She conjured a picture of Jake, alone in a dark cell, escorted out to have horrible tests run and then returned to the isolation. She rubbed her aching chest.

"We were government property. They could do whatever they wanted." He flashed a tight grimace. "And they did."

That wince had nothing to do with his limp, did it? Oh, God. They had been through hell. All of them.

"You all really did escape military prison?" she asked.

"*Top-security* military prison." At a right angle in the mesh perimeter, he stopped at another security black box for a minute. Now that she knew the secret, it was clear how he avoided touching the electrified mesh.

"Wow." She studied his closed expression. "Including Jake?"

"Yes. After escaping, most of us kept in touch, worked together, and eventually created something useful from the ashes of our lives. We're good at maintaining low profiles so most of us literally hid in plain sight. But Jake? He didn't just leave. He disappeared." They turned at the back property line and headed toward the main buildings.

She rubbed the bridge of her nose. "I had no idea. But then again, Mateo never mentioned it. Other than what Brady shared, I haven't known details about Jake's life for years…"

"Brady. That's another story. He got injured and discharged from the Army several months before Jake had to take leave with his wife and all. Man, that was a really bad year for Jake. He blamed himself for your brother's injuries, too."

They started walking again. Kiera sniffed. "I blamed Jake, too, for a while. It wasn't fair of me."

The words came slowly. "Your brother was a good soldier. Strong and eager. He wanted to prove himself on a mission. He took … a calculated risk to try to accomplish the mission objective."

"Brady never got the virus."

"You're correct. Brady was injured and discharged right before we were inoculated." He looked up at the trees again, then back to her. "It's not to say he wasn't an excellent soldier and a valued member of the team."

"Of course. But you said he took a calculated risk?" Her eyes stung. God, she missed her headstrong brother.

Stumpy leaned on the handle of his cane, knuckles blanching. "Brady calculated wrong. His decision had a ripple effect."

Something in the way he rubbed his leg and stared into space made her pause.

Before she could stop herself, she blurted, "Did

that have to do…"

"With my nickname?" he interjected, way too fast. He held up a hand when she tried to take back her words. "No. I've been called 'Stumpy' since high school. I was a late bloomer in the, uh, height department."

"You sure made up for lost time." She leaned back and smiled up at him.

"True." His cheeks went scarlet. "Anyway, my nickname became much more fitting later on in life, as it turned out." He knocked the cane against his leg.

They followed the perimeter, the afternoon light shifting as a cool breeze moved tree branches in the forest. The rustling sounds remained muffled. Shadows danced all around them, hinting at hidden threats in the woods. She didn't care how good Stumpy's security system worked and how Bambi wouldn't hurt anyone, the creepy-crawly feeling remained. She tugged her cardigan closed.

He finally spoke. "When Brady took the risk, damn it all if Jake didn't try to stop him. Ran in after your brother. We all did." His Adam's apple bobbed. "But it was too late. The bomb had gone off." Pausing, he thunked the butt of the cane into the ground in a rough circle. "Several bombs, actually. We all walked right into a trap."

Through a dry mouth, she managed to respond. "I had no idea."

"Classified."

She had to clear her throat to let the words out. "So, my brother made a bonehead move and Jake tried to bail him out, but failed. And you got hurt as well?"

"Not this." He gestured. "I didn't lose my leg until after I'd taken the virus. Apparently, the Morpheus Virus does not regenerate limbs when they go missing. Or heal preexisting scars. See these?" He held up his striped arm. "They're from moving burning wood to get to Brady." He raised his hand. "We all knew what we were getting into when we signed on as Special Forces."

"I understand."

"It's also why we volunteered to take the virus. We knew that risk was part of the job. If we could become more effective and help to shut down the fighting over there and if it meant other lives would be saved? Hell yeah, we would take that chance all over again."

"I've got a good picture of what happened." They had all sacrificed so much.

"See, I'm not sure you do." He went from friendly to fierce in a split second. She sucked in a breath.

"At least, not about Jake," he continued. "He volunteered to take the damned virus partly because of what happened to Brady. Said if he'd been faster or stronger, maybe your brother wouldn't have been injured." He leaned more heavily on the cane.

Each slow step drove a nail of guilt into her chest.

Stumpy continued. "Now you're here, and the stakes are higher than ever."

"Stakes?"

"Stakes. Also known as our freedom from a government facility, your life, and your baby's life. Also known as Jake's sanity. Even more pressure for him not to fail."

"Okay, look. You don't need to remind me what's at risk, thanks." She blew out a lungful of air and then softened her tone. "Jake doesn't owe me anything. I willingly worked with Mateo to get information on Fallen Comrades. I felt the risk was manageable. And yes. I take responsibility for the consequences of my own decisions. Every minute of the day."

Rubbing his goatee, he said, "That's not how Jake sees it. I believe when he looks at you, he sees all of his past failures."

A sour taste in her mouth made her swallow hard. "Thanks."

He tilted his head. "But then he looks at you and sees future opportunities to screw up. His paranoia goes off the charts. Most guys would be paralyzed stupid."

She crossed her arms over her midsection again, taking a moment to rest. The stroll was wonderful for getting fresh air and clearing her mind, but it was hell on her hips. "I'm not putting any pressure on him."

He dropped his hand, gaze intent, assessing. "I didn't say you were."

Chapter Twenty-Six

The scene at dinnertime made Kiera laugh out loud.

It was like 'Kiera and the Seven Dwarves,' except the dwarves were hulking giants. Worn out from her afternoon of yet another brain download, courtesy of Stumpy and his darned computer, she sighed and stretched her legs out on the couch cushions while activity swirled around her.

Not exactly swirled. The way these guys moved, they'd hang out at Point A. Then they would suddenly appear at Point B. Every action in between was performed with smooth, noiseless efficiency.

When Rodeo arrived after his afternoon patrol, she asked about the stealthy movements. He dropped into an oversized leather recliner across from her. His body language projected casual ease, but his gaze tracked every movement in the room. Thumbing the brim of his hat up, he said, "Green Berets are known as the Silent Professionals. We're stealthy to begin with. But now, thanks to the virus, we're even more dangerous. Soundless, too."

She jumped at a loud crash in the kitchen.

"My bad!" Gonzo yelped as he waved his hand in the air and galloped in place until he thrust his hand under the cold water tap.

"Soundless. Check." She grinned.

Rodeo pulled a face and drew out the yo-yo, turning it over and over in a palm. "Uh, except for mealtime. Iron Chef over there is the current gourmand, and he only has the title because expertise is relative around here. Now Pele. He's the true culinary expert. Amazing skills." Rodeo patted his flat belly. "But he's out on assignment watching your sister, Reagan." He leaned forward and whispered behind a hand. "If it was up to my cooking abilities, we'd eat frank and beans out of the can." He leaned back, propping an ankle on the opposite knee. "So, the best of the worst is Gonzo. Oh, he always makes a ruckus in the kitchen." He called over his shoulder. "It's so we will notice and appreciate his hard work, right, George Alonzo?"

Gonzo spouted a line of Spanish, punctuated by a flap of his unburned hand.

"What did he say?" she asked.

Rodeo waved his fingers in the general direction of the kitchen. "He thanks us for the support and kind words and promises to follow military protocol in his food preparations."

Another spurt of Spanish emanated from the kitchen.

The cowboy pressed both palms against the purple toy. "More or less."

She touched her mouth, holding back a laugh. "Um, you didn't happen to be one of those little brothers who constantly irritated their older siblings?"

He lifted his big hands in a gesture of innocence negated by the impish glint in his dark eyes.

"Exactly. Hey, I am a younger sister. I know how things work. A little poke here, a little poke there. Older brother or sister explodes. No idea why. Hey, I'm innocent." A warm blanket-like sense of family love was quickly swept away by the sharp pinch of guilt for the risk she'd created for her family.

Rodeo opened his mouth to comment.

"And, that's enough for tonight, Casanova." Jake inserted himself into her field of vision. He had on his ever-present tight t-shirt and shoulder holster.

Her heart skidded as she inhaled his hickory and

outdoorsy scent. He must have come in from a patrol shift as well.

Jake pointed at Rodeo. "Stumpy needs help laying out wire."

"No, he doesn't."

"Then keep an eye on Gonzo before he blows up the stove with his terrifying 'salute to Asian cuisine' he's fixing." He cringed as the chef brandished a wooden spoon while mumbling to himself. A puff of steam burst from a clattering lid.

Rodeo's eyes narrowed to slits as he studied Jake. "Roger." The cowboy pushed up, uncoiling in a fluid movement. Then, in a blink, he was in the kitchen.

Jake sat on the other end of the couch and let out a groan as he sank into the cushions. Similar to Rodeo, though, Jake visually swept the room, over and over. She drew her feet back, but he patted his thighs. "It's okay, you can stretch out."

He wrapped his hands around each ankle and gently tugged her legs onto his lap. Several conflicting thoughts crashed into each other. One, she could get used to the feel of his palms on her lower leg. Two, they'd done this exact activity years before, sitting together on a couch, enjoying each other's company. A painful bubble formed in her chest.

At the end of the day, she was still an obligation for Jake to fulfill.

Unfortunately, Kiera The Obligation noticed too acutely that her calves were heating up thanks to the toasty warmth of his hard thighs. As a matter of fact, her legs rested inches away from … places she had no business thinking about.

She knew where things stood. She was a mission for Jake—a mechanism for him to atone for Brady's fate, a do-over of his childhood, and a way for him to complete Mateo's mission. With a dash of paternal duty thrown into the mix.

With all that baggage in mind, she vowed not to get sucked into the emotions stirred up from her proximity to Jake. Vowed. She mentally pushed the 'firm resolution' button. For good. Mentally brushed off her hands.

"How did the afternoon go?" he asked, rolling his massive shoulders and turning his head toward her. The weight of his steel gaze knocked the breath out of her. The resolution button hadn't been enough. *Come on.*

By God, she'd keep things friendly and professional. "It went well. Slow going, but we'll eventually have a complete database of information. What I recall plus the data on the thumb drive should be more than enough to bury Beau. The details about the connection with Senator Lequire and Bratva are slower going, but we'll get it fleshed out as well."

A muscle jumped on his jaw. "I don't like that you're tangled up in this mess."

"What's done is done."

"I'll say." He stared at her until she began to sweat. A blink. He muttered, "It's too dangerous, you having this knowledge. Too many people will want your silence. The reporter died because of this information."

A cold shiver got her attention. "I can't un-ring that bell. At least if Morpheus Squad has the data, then I'm less of a liability, right? Multiple targets. They can't silence all of us."

She froze.

Oh, God.

"I don't like that you're involved." He patted her leg. "I want you and the baby safe. My baby," he whispered.

Her resolution, and a piece of her heart, melted.

"Jake."

He blinked and pressed the slash of his mouth into a hard line. "New topic."

"But—"

His eyes took on the color of a thunderstorm. "Move on."

She rubbed her arms. Later, always later.

The tight lines around his mouth softened. "Stumpy's not working you too hard, is he?"

"No." She sighed. "He makes me take breaks and drink lots of water. Thinks it's better for the baby."

"Good." His lost, empty expression gutted her.

What she'd give to see the lighter, laughing Jake again.

She shoved the hair behind her ears and pretended to pay attention to the cooking show happening in the kitchen.

Hunt entered the building, and the atmosphere became charged, like the men unconsciously homed in on him.

With a businesslike nod to everyone, he strode over to Stumpy, who sat at the desk, surrounded by computer consoles. Murmurs from the two men filtered over to her. After a few minutes, Hunt walked over to Kiera. Even from a seated position, Jake sat up straight as he tightened the grip on her ankle.

"How are my sisters and dad?" she asked the CO.

One curt nod. "Safe. The men are in place and have begun surveillance on your family members. They will have fully infiltrated their targets' lives by Tuesday."

"Infiltrated?"

His calm smile? Scary. "It's easier if we hide in plain sight. Each team member will get close to their target by any means necessary."

"Target?"

"Your family member."

"How, exactly?"

Hunt winked. Really? A wink?

"For example," he said "an assistant postmaster position has been available for some time in your dad's office. Well, what do you know, turns out Rivera was the best qualified applicant for this job. Funny how stuff works out. His application must have gotten stuck in the system for a while until it happened to pop into your dad's email inbox today. Coincidence. Right, Stumpy?"

Without turning around, Stumpy lifted a hand and gave a thumbs-up, then returned to tapping away on the keyboard.

"How—?" Kiera sputtered.

Jake smiled.

"Amazing how a computer genius can infiltrate even USPS jobs website. Stumpy made it look like Rivera's application had gone through all the preliminary review and background checks with the regional office." With a calculating glint in his eye, Hunt continued. "Of course, Rivera has an airtight but completely bogus identity, complete with a stellar work history and superb references from previous supervisors." Hunt tapped his cell phone attached to his belt. "Since they were desperate for an assistant postmaster, your dad did the on-site interview today and offered Rivera the job. No surprise, since he and Rivera got along like old friends."

"Old friends?"

Even Jake sat forward, hand remaining on her ankle.

"But of course." His smile didn't make her feel warm or comfortable. "It's how we infiltrate. Each team member receives a file on their target—each of your family members—and adjusts their approach to fit the target's personality accordingly."

Her gut clenched. "Do I want to know how you got all this information?"

Hunt barked out a laugh. "No, you do not."

"So, someone's working up at the environmental education camp in the mountains?"

He nodded. "Pele. Here's his chance to get away from it all."

"You know my sister Reagan has survival skills, right? She could probably take care of herself and Pele."

A corner of Jake's mouth rose. "He'll be overqualified window dressing, then."

She thought for a moment, then squinted at Hunt. "Who gets to attend art school?"

Jake snickered, a sound she didn't hear nearly enough. "With Britt?" Jake's thumb rubbed her skin.

"Yeah. Good luck whoever keeps track of her."

"Ah, yes," Hunt said. "Red. It's almost impossible to wear him out."

Catching Jake's eye, she exchanged a grin. "Red hasn't met my baby sister."

Hunt crossed his big arms. "It's okay. Red can handle any hostile environment."

"Like art school? With a budding fashionista who is part Energizer bunny?"

"Exactly."

She relaxed into the cushion and adjusted her legs, so comfortable with Jake's hand still on her ankle, yet careful not to bump the holstered gun on the side of his chest. "I'd love to see it."

The kitchen sounds, conversation, and laughter swirled around her, almost like she sat in a normal living room with normal people whose lives weren't in perpetual danger.

Almost.

Chapter Twenty-Seven

Too perfect, this cozy living room scene. Too easy. Like a calm moment in Afghanistan, with the warm sun baking the dun-colored hills, all the while knowing that insurgents massed and waited in hiding for the perfect moment to strike.

The skin between Jake's shoulder blades twitched as his heightened paranoia, a bonus quirk courtesy of the virus, went into overdrive. Without looking, he knew precisely where each team member stood and what they were doing. He calculated the distance and time to all exits, factoring in Kiera's abilities and limitations. He filtered all images and sounds and compared them to normal variants, monitoring for outliers. A *clang* of metal that didn't fit with cooking sounds. An abnormal flash of light or shadow. A *whoosh* of a rope and a light *thud* on the roof.

He was ready for all of it.

The soft curves of Kiera's delicate body, relaxed against the couch cushions as she napped, didn't fully distract him from his worries. This might be a nice moment in time, but nothing good in his life ever lasted.

Including Kiera. He'd already burned that bridge to the ground years ago, poured gasoline on the smoking beams last summer, and then dynamited the concrete foundation this morning.

This evening felt comfortable, but like every other thing in his life that was decent and good, at some point, the other shoe would fall and his world would go up in flames again. The fact scared him even more than a live grenade.

What was the worst that could happen to Kiera?

His brain went to the darkest place imaginable.

That. But with his baby.

He turned his face away from her and ran a hand over the skin, like he could rub away the horrible image.

Shit. If Beau came for her?

If?

When.

With the guy's money and resources and whatever the hell was going on with his daddy's political aspirations and Russian connections? No question Beau and Senator Lequire had a vested interest in permanently eliminating any threat to Fallen Comrades' reputation and their political futures

He brushed his fingertip over Kiera's jeans legging-clad shin, taking care to keep the contact light and gentle.

If she ever got hurt, or worse, what would be left of Jake's life?

Nothing. There would be nothing left.

Jake would go right back to the mental black hole. Back to playing games with the limits of his viral control. Except this time, he would let the virus run unchecked in a final act of human supernova and give those damned researchers some experimental data to analyze.

Kiera's sigh whispered like filmy and smooth nylon parachute fabric, instantly calming his riled nerves. God help him but he wanted to listen to her soft murmuring breath for much longer than this short period of time.

"Hey, daydreamers, soup's on," Gonzo called out from the kitchen.

Jake patted Kiera's leg. The image of her eyes flickering open was like witnessing a perfect mountain sunrise. Peace and light centered him as she smiled.

Peace and light? What the fuck was he smoking?

The cool emptiness when she moved her legs away was replaced by the connection of her hand in his. He went on some sort of automatic pilot, stood, and helped her to her feet. Scanning the room, he fought another urge to loom over her and shield her.

On instinct, Jake shifted so he was positioned between Kiera and his friends. His arms tensed up again, muscles primed.

What the hell? He'd taken the antidote less than two days ago.

Cold sweat chilled on his forehead. Had the antidote stopped working? Had his experimentation with the boundaries of his control already unhinged him? He gritted his teeth, clamped down on what little self-control remained, and did his clench-and-release move with his free hand until he had pushed the damned virus back into the mental box and shut the lid. Good for now.

Then, like he wasn't actively losing his mind, Jake led Kiera to the dining area.

Around the table, none of the men sat before she did. With a dramatic flourish, Gonzo presented egg rolls, an obscure noodle dish with vegetables, and blobs vaguely resembling dumplings. Kiera smiled and praised Gonzo like the guy had won one of those TV cooking shows.

Everyone laughed.

Except for Jake.

Shit, he had nothing to offer her as a man. Deep down in his soul, he was a damaged man with a shortened life, and even his virally enhanced body couldn't change that fact.

Her eyes twinkled as she ate the hearty meal, easily drawing the men into conversation. It was obvious the guys remained on their best behavior, using their most careful manners. She didn't make anyone feel self-conscious about their limitations, their jobs, or the obvious—the virus hanging like a guillotine blade over each team member. Kiera treated each man with kindness and humor.

What would it be like for Jake to have someone in his life like her, every single day?

She had offered. He had rejected her.

He pushed food around on his plate, eating little and tasting less.

Maybe he could try. They could try. Together. He could keep the virus at bay.

He'd keep Kiera and the baby safe. They could become a family.

Could he drop his defenses and expose his soul completely, knowing his sanity hinged on whether she accepted him?

"Don't you like it? You're not eating, man," Gonzo whined, breaking into his dark thoughts.

"No appetite."

****

The meal and company warmed Kiera as she leaned back on the chair.

Gonzo and Rodeo were busy one-upping each other with stories about their heroics on the battlefield, each tale more animated and amazing than the last one.

Stumpy rolled his eyes before pushing back from the table and departing for patrol rounds.

Hunt and Curly had stepped out a while ago.

Doc sat with an almost-smile on his immeasurably calm face.

"… and I took out those ten fighters singlehanded before the virus even kicked in." Gonzo jutted out his chin.

Rodeo snorted. "I could do that before I was out of high school, man. After I got the virus, shoo-wee—

game on!"

Before she fully thought about her question, she said, "How are you all so casual about the virus?"

"What?" Jake whipped his head around. It was the first word he had spoken in the past hour.

Her face warmed. Maybe this conversation was too taboo. "Um. This experiment changed your lives. In some bad ways—"

Rodeo interrupted with a flex of a corded arm. "In good ways, too."

"Does your ability make up for it?"

No one answered for a full minute.

"I don't even understand how the virus works," she mumbled.

Gonzo inclined his head. "Doc can explain it better than we can."

For a few seconds, she didn't think Doc was going to answer. Finally, he leaned forward in a whisper of conserved movement. "It's not exactly a virus."

"Okay?" she said.

"We call it a virus, because it's an easy way to visualize what it is and what it does. But the reality is more complex." The guy's solemn eyes made him look like he carried the world's weight on his shoulders. "It's actually quite interesting how Morpheus came about."

"Interesting?" She wouldn't call an unstable human experiment *interesting*.

"Let's go back to the basics." He smiled, steepling his hands.

"Uh-oh," Gonzo said. "Professor mode activated. Be sure to take notes for the test later."

A flash of a scowl was all the emotion Doc wasted. "The Morpheus Virus was created by using the science behind recently developed cancer treatments. In our bodies, we have human endogenous retroviruses. We call them HERVs. Normally, they lay dormant in our DNA. In oncology trials, a particular HERV is activated, finds and sticks to cancer cells, and then expresses a new antigen so the body has something to fight. That's great. It means our body can attack the cancer. Like a big bull's eye."

"Antigen?" she asked, shaking her head. She knew the word but not the full medical meaning behind it.

"An antigen is a protein found on the surface of a disease, say whooping cough or the flu. Or cancer. The antigen then triggers our immune system to create a response to fight the disease."

"So it's like you all got the flu virus?"

"Not exactly. The researchers created a drug that activated a latent HERV in each of our DNA." He paused, as if letting her absorb the information. "This particular HERV didn't attach to cancer cells and create cancer antigens. This HERV sticks to different cells, making new antigens and triggering biochemical reactions. In animal experiments, the subjects required little sleep because of changes in melatonin and cortisol levels. There were faster reaction times occurring at the level of the nerve cells."

Gonzo's eyes narrowed. "Sounds like a good deal, right?"

"Obviously not," Kiera said. "No one is happy." She took a big breath. "So, your DNA got triggered and your body chemistry changed."

"In broad brush strokes, yes."

"But it didn't work like it was supposed to." She wasn't asking a question.

"Worked too well, depending on how you look at it."

"That means…"

Rodeo clunked the purple toy on the tabletop. "We're superheroes." He grimaced. "Sort of."

Jake leaned forward. "We're ticking time bombs."

"The antidote?" She exhaled, hand drifting over her abdomen like she could somehow detect the virus in the baby by touch alone. "Wait. This doesn't make sense. Once I get the flu and the immune reaction finishes, that's it. No more flu. It doesn't keep going and going for years. Right?"

Doc nodded.

"So what's different about the Morpheus Virus?"

He paused. "Once the HERV is activated, it can't be turned off."

"Which means…" Like an awful jigsaw puzzle, the pieces started falling into place. And the picture wasn't pretty. Jake. The relentless activity of the virus. Tears stung her eyes. Where was the endpoint?

"Once someone gets the HERV-activating drug, the reaction has no stopping point." He pressed his steepled fingers against his mouth.

Death. Death was a stopping point when an immune system went into overdrive. Her heart banged against her ribcage. The baby jiggled inside of her. Oh, God. The baby. She gripped the table edge. "So the reaction is still going? Right now?"

"Yes. If we don't blunt how quickly the mutated HERV creates biochemical reactions, then our immune systems will keep responding with all of these chemicals and abilities."

"Which will do what?"

Gonzo shrugged. "No one knows the answer."

It amazed her how casual the guys were about their immune system essentially attacking them every minute of every day. "Why not take a ton of antidote and kill the HERV?" She couldn't be the first person to consider that solution. Heck, if she had the idea, then it must have been tested already.

Yet they were still here. With the virus churning away inside of them.

"First of all," Doc said, "taking a massive dose of antidote would create an intense immune system cascade that will kill us." He tilted his head to the side. "The more nuanced answer? We like our abilities—our strength and reactions. However. If we lose control of the chemicals being produced, then we won't be able to overcome the imbalance in brain chemistry."

That meant… "You would lose your minds."

"Yes."

She sucked in air. "Therefore, you have figured out how to titrate the antidote." The shots. The terrifying edge of the cliff they all skirted every day. Her skin itched as she considered the virus was inside of her, too.

"More or less." Rodeo spoke up. "Turns out, nothing about our situation was an exact science. Or exactly legal."

"Or ethical," Doc muttered.

Sweat prickled her lower back. Viruses. Antidotes. Immune system. "Did the research say whether this can be transmitted?"

Doc's dark eyes locked onto her. "Million-dollar question."

Chapter Twenty-Eight

After a nice, warm shower that evening that did not relax Kiera one bit, she wandered around the living room of the building she and Jake shared.

Hot water. The guys' ingenuity amazed her. The water heater ran on power generated from a small creek on the property. One of the squad's engineer sergeants had set it up.

The *only* engineer sergeant remaining, actually, now that Mateo had died.

Mateo.

An imaginary fist clenched inside of her chest, and she had to grab the back of the straight-backed chair. She missed her trusted friend. She missed the normal life she'd given up the minute they'd agreed to avenge Brady's death.

She studied the utilitarian furniture in the small dwelling where she had slept last night.

She needed to get out of this situation.

More importantly, she needed to get her baby out of this mess. She rubbed her throbbing temples.

Her baby had been exposed.

No, her baby had been *made from* DNA altered by the Morpheus Virus.

Acid burned the back of her mouth. What did that mean for her child?

Unable to stand still, Kiera paced while the sounds of Jake now washing up drifted through the building. Unbidden, images of water rivulets over his sculpted chest and abdomen, streaming lower over his powerful—

Damn it. Jake.

Her past. Her reluctant present.

What about her future?

If she figured a way out of this mess and if her baby survived the—a hard knot lodged in her throat. No way would she ever rope a guy into being with her solely because of a baby.

What else did her future hold? Once she left the team's protection, that would be it. The guys needed to stay hidden.

Would she meet someone else, create a family together?

Her eyelids burned.

She touched her lips, remembering the velvet-on-steel of his kisses and the way Jake surrounded her with his scent and his body. The security in his strong arms. How he looked at her, like a man wandering in the desert who glimpsed an oasis for the first time in weeks. She pressed her legs together to reduce the throb deep in her pelvis.

Stop it. They weren't in the Sahara, and she wasn't a glass of water. A few kisses didn't indicate lifetime commitment. Neither did one night of passion. She patted her belly. Obviously.

She shook out her tense arms and shoulders. Time to break this problem down into easy steps. First of all, she needed to get out of this mess. Where could she go?

Nowhere. Nowhere was safe.

Step two didn't matter if she couldn't get past step one. Damn.

"Penny for your thoughts?" Jake startled her out of her churning worries.

She spun around. The two tan lamps in the combined living room and kitchenette gave off a warm glow. He prowled from the second bedroom to where she stood.

His damp hair glinted. He'd changed into yet

another pair of jeans and a fresh t-shirt. No chest holster this time. Good God, every piece of clothing he owned fit him perfectly, making each hard ridge of muscle visible. Would it be too much to ask he wear something a little baggier, like a burlap sack or a thick winter coat?

She stifled a frustrated groan.

He merely stood there, his non-action riling her tense nerves. His clean soap and mild hickory scent wafted over her.

She blurted, "Just thinking about the virus."

His brows pulled together. "Me too. Every single damn day."

"Sorry, it's—"

"Weird?"

She looked up at him. "That's a word for it."

"Wondering what's going to happen to you? To the baby? To…"

"And to you."

Rearing back, he searched her. "Not only me. It's all of us." He bared his teeth briefly. "You heard Doc. No one knows what the virus will do, now or down the road." Glancing downward, he said, "No one knows how it will affect a baby." His gray gaze slammed into hers once more, rocking her back on her heels. "But as long as you're here, you will be safe. We'll see to it."

"What about you, Jake? What's your life going to be like?" *Who are you going to spend it with*, remained unsaid.

"All I know for certain is if the military gets hold of any of us again, we're done. We were the test batch." He pointed a thick thumb at his chest. "Once they improve the recipe and create Morpheus Squad 2.0, we won't be needed."

"What if the military never finds you? What then?"

"After this Lequire mess is over? I don't know. This shit is never over. Might go back into hiding and lay low. Might help the guys out." He barked out a harsh laugh. "Life is funny."

"Funny, but not funny?"

"Yeah. Sometimes it gives us exactly what we need, but not what we want." He paused, his gaze like a palpable caress as he searched her face.

Her cheeks warmed as his gray eyes darkened almost to black. A flutter in her chest triggered a few short breaths. The room had become far too warm.

The moment stretched too far for comfort, but she didn't want it to end.

Finally breaking the tight silence, she cleared her throat. "True. But I've learned through trial and error—mostly error—that life is also what we make of it."

"Yeah?"

"You ever want a do-over?" she whispered, shocked that she had spoken the words.

"Regarding?" He wet his lips.

"Like, a do-over from this morning."

He closed the gap between them in three strides. "You have no idea." His voice abraded her nerves.

Skin prickling, she stepped back, bumping into the chair.

His broad frame took up all available space and light in front of her. "Life is all about decisions," he murmured. "Sometimes we get a second chance."

She rubbed the bridge of her nose. "Depends. If the person learns from their choices." At what point had she become out of breath?

"I can learn." He was too much, too present, too intense.

Tightening her grip on the back of the chair, Kiera tried to change the subject. Being so close to Jake made it hard to think. "So, was Hunt telling the truth? Will my dad and sisters be okay?"

He gave a knowing grimace and backed up a step. The air cooled a few degrees. With nothing but a confident nod, he knocked her anxiety down several notches. "Yes. The guys are experts at covert security. Your family won't even know they're being watched. No matter what activities they do." Taking another half step closer, he rested his hand on hers.

His warm strength flowed through her. Everything she wanted.

She swallowed. "Not sure I like the idea of my dad and sisters being spied on. Loss of privacy, and all. Although I can't imagine Dad having a secret life as a pole dancer, where we need to keep the information hidden."

Jake chuckled with a rare twinkle lighting up his gray eyes. "That's a terrible image: your dad with a G-string, gyrating around a ... my eyes, they're burning!" He made a show of cringing and throwing an arm up over his face.

It felt so good to laugh. The tension in her entire body faded away.

Reaching out, he trailed his thumb over the back of her hand until she let go of the chair. Then he held her hand in his. Such a simple action. This man was capable of deadly force. Heck, he *was* the deadly force. Yet with his thick, rough hand, he held her like a piece of delicate crystal. The contradiction made the world shift under her feet.

The crooked tilt of his mouth made her heart lurch. He murmured, "It's a good thing the guys are discreet. Don't worry—your dad's exotic dancing habit will remain a secret." His earnest tone lowered her blood pressure even more. "In all seriousness, your dad will be fine. Our second-in-command, Rivera, is watching out for him. Rivera's solid."

Despite her pulse pounding with him so close, she laughed. "It's not Dad I'm worried about, come to think of it. Britt is the wild child."

"She'll be safe."

"But she's in Atlanta. Too close to Beau—" Her words choked off.

He squeezed her hand once more then let go. "Red will take care of Britt."

"Yeah, but who's going to take care of your lethal squad member?" Her hollow laugh didn't help. "Britt's a whirling dervish."

"Red doesn't need to sleep."

"Really?"

"Yes. All of us can stay awake for days on end. He's the best when it comes to operational insomnia."

"Because of the virus or your Special Forces training?"

He tilted his head to the side. "Both."

"How long can you guys go without sleep?"

The warmth in his expression fled. "As long as it takes to get the mission done."

A finger of ice melted down her spine. *Mission.* He was talking about her family. The same people Kiera had placed in danger with her misguided attempt for revenge.

She kept talking, if only to keep from crying. "Well, good luck to the guy following Reagan through the woods. Seriously, if someone would explain the situation, she can create her own covert operation with those crazy outdoor survival skills. Heck, if she's in the forest, Reagan can protect *him.*"

Jake's crooked smile triggered a flood of warmth in her chest. "Pele's adaptable and professional." His low, reassuring voice calmed her nerves.

"What's his background?"

"He's the big Samoan guy you met last night. Hates the cold. Also not a fan of poison ivy or hiking. Or crafts. Or kids." He grinned. "It's good for him, getting out of his comfort zone."

Condolences in advance for Pele.

After another long silence, she blew out a breath. Well. "So, I've been thinking about this all day today. I've made a decision: it's time for me to go."

"Go?" He crossed his big arms over his even bigger chest and scowled. *Uh-oh.*

"After I give Stumpy all of the data and interpret the spreadsheets, of course. It's best if I get out of Morpheus Squad's collective hair. You all have a lot of work to do, and my presence distracts from the team's mission. Also, my being here exposes you guys. If I'm not here, it might draw Beau away from my family and from your team." She laid a hand on his corded forearm.

He tucked her hand under his palm and didn't let go. "No." His gray stare pinned her in place.

Her heart rapped a beat on her ribs. "No?"

"Uh, you can't leave. Because it's not safe for you yet."

Ah, there it was. Duty. She brushed a hand over her eyes, praying she wouldn't cry in front of him. "I'm sure there's someplace I can go. I'll find a small hospital, have this baby safely, and lay low afterward."

"If Beau wants to get to you, then there's nowhere else to go that will be as safe."

"You're only concerned about my safety?" She yanked her hand away from him. Unfortunately, he didn't take a step back. He stood there, leaving her with zero personal space remaining between his massive frame and the chair behind her. "Duty, right?"

Oh, goody, unwanted emotions. A tiny ember of irritation appeared, something she hadn't experienced in a long time.

If she rubbed her raw feelings against his bland, objective steel wool talk about 'duty', would the friction cause a spark?

His voice hit somewhere between a whisper and a growl. "I ran ten years ago, Kiera. I won't make that mistake again."

"But—"

"I won't let anything happen to you. Not after—"

Crossing her arms, she leaned back and looked up at him. "Jake, stop. I'm not a mission to complete or a promise to fulfill. Not then and not now."

"What about—"

She stopped him with a chop of her hand, the movement limited by the close quarters. "No. I will not be with someone out of guilt."

"Who's guilty?"

Raising an eyebrow, she glared at him until he broke eye contact.

"Damn it," he said from a clenched jaw. "There are solutions to all of this—"

Little pops of hot irritation formed inside and bubbled up, threatening to upend her tight control of her emotions. "Now you're bringing the can-do soldier mentality to this discussion. Like this situation is a challenging problem to solve? Or maybe I'm only a mission op to you."

"That's not what I'm saying. This is my child, too." He stood tall.

He didn't scare her. "Then what? Be clear," she said. "Do you really want to be mixed up in this screwy situation? Because most normal folks would not wade into this mess." She pressed her sternum with her palm.

"Perhaps I'm asking the wrong question. What do *you* want, Jake?"

"I—" He shoved a hand through his hair, making it stand up on end. "I want to—"

"Don't you dare follow up that statement with the words *be responsible* or *take care of me and the baby* because anyone here can do that."

His head jerked back. Nostrils flared.

Point to her. Good.

Would it be too much to ask for him to want her for who she was, instead of using her as a way to assuage deep-seated remorse?

"Kiera." The word barely escaped, like it hurt to speak her name.

"What, Jake? Solve this puzzle. What solution do you have to this crappy situation?"

For a second, every muscle in his body tensed as he turned into a linebacker about to tackle someone. Then he scraped fingers through his hair as his chest rose and fell once, twice. His big shoulders slumped. "Nothing. I have nothing to fix it. I have nothing." His rough, broken voice sliced like a shard of glass across her nerve endings. "With the virus on board, my only value to society is the ability to keep this damned monster under control. Even with the antidote, it's no guarantee of success. That's it. It's all I am to the world. To anyone. A risk."

Not to me. But she couldn't speak the phrase, so Kiera picked something neutral to say. "How often do you take the antidote?"

"Roughly every two weeks if I'm alone and calm. With you around and the increased stress, I'll need another dose in the next few days."

The guy had to inject himself with a drug just to handle being around her. Fabulous. "Are all the guys similar?"

"More or less. We all react in different ways to the virus. We're each on our own schedule for the shot. What worries me the most is if the damned antidote stops working."

"Who supplies it?" *Stick with a safe topic. Anything to avoid dealing with stuff like feelings and hope and futures.*

"It used to come from a secret source of Hunt's, but Doc can synthesize it now."

"Secret source?"

"Hunt keeps some irons in the fire he won't tell us about. Connections going way deep—deeper than black ops."

"Which means?"

"The experiment group before we took the shots turned into mindless monsters. Our own government executed those men rather than risk having them out in the world. Hunt's got evidence. He was there. If he ever goes public with Project Morpheus, he has enough names to take down large chunks of the military, the Ways and Means Committee, Senate Appropriations, and probably a few random sub-committees, senators, and congress members."

"Wow. That would be something to see." She pressed her lips together, but still, the words came out. "You didn't answer my question."

Curling a hand into a hammer-like fist and releasing it, he finally said, "You asked what I wanted."

"Yes."

"I want the virus out of my body." He spoke on a hard breath of air. "I want to touch you without fear that I will hurt you. I want to go back in time and save Brady. And Mateo. I want to protect this baby. I want to go back and be the man I should have been."

A tiny ray of hope lit up the dark room. "What?"

"I-I need to be a better man. For you."

"Jake, you're—"

He shook his head. "Shit, Kiera. You scramble my brain and give me stupid hope. Please. I need—"

She stood at the edge of a flood-stage dam, concrete shaking beneath her feet as the structure held back millions of gallons of pain.

Their past. The virus. The future. All those doubts and fears. Nothing mattered in this small moment in time except for Jake and Kiera.

"I need it too, Jake."

Like the dam breaking under a crush of water, he surged forward.

Chapter Twenty-Nine

Jake grabbed Kiera's upper arms and yanked her to his heated chest, meeting her lips in a bruising kiss. After a moment, he eased up, flicking his tongue over her mouth as he feathered kisses over her lips and jaw, sending delicious sparks deep into her body.

Her earlier irritation flipped over to desire in about two seconds flat. Way to diffuse a tense situation. Her knees wobbled in response to his sure touch. But he wouldn't let her fall.

Zips of delicious sensation flowed through her body with each kiss.

Then something shifted in him, like a car going into a higher gear. Every muscle in his body tensed, but the turbulent shaking in his frame smoothed out to more of a rumble. He surrounded her with his physical presence but remained gentle. He took the kiss deeper, became more demanding. The air warmed as their lips slid against each other, heat against heat. His grip on her arms tightened.

No rasp of stubble on her jaw. He had shaved. Which meant—she inhaled—that wonderful scent of aftershave.

Her toes tingled.

Relaxing his hands, he swept thick, rough fingers up her arms over her shoulders and neck, and then buried his hands in her hair. He tugged her head back and nudged her mouth open with his until he could kiss her at will. An arm snaked around her shoulders, keeping her close, nestling her body against his.

She slid her palms up his broad chest and around his corded neck. Jake was so familiar, but changed. Harder, decisive, bigger, just … more … than he'd been in the past. He wasn't her eighteen-year-old high-school flame anymore. She pressed her hip against the hardness growing below his waistband.

Kiera was no longer a sixteen-year-old girl, trying to figure out who she was and what she liked from a partner. No more. She knew what she wanted. To prove the point, she ran her tongue over his front teeth until he groaned and tightened his hand against her scalp. The tingle of his fist wrapped in her hair shot delicious sensations down her spine.

That night last summer had been a small taste. Tonight, Kiera wanted the feast.

He slid a hand down to caress her breast. At the brush of his rough thumb over her fabric-covered nipple, she bit her lip. Then he gave gentle flicks to the hard, sensitive tip until she moaned.

He moved until he stood flush against her back. Heat poured from his muscled torso into her body as he ran his hands over her shoulders and chest. Tilting her head back and to the side, he pushed her hair away and kissed her neck until wonderful liquid pleasure melted deep in her core. The warm air from his mouth tickled fine hairs at her hairline.

She reached up for him, but he eased her hands to rest back on his thighs, where she hooked a finger in the jeans pocket and kept him snugged up close.

A gasp escaped her lips, and when he cupped both her breasts, she leaned back into him with a sigh, resting her head against his shoulder.

Against her backside, his erection hardened. An answering ache between her legs had her pushing back in response, anything to get closer to him, to feel more of Jake against her body. What had she been irritated about earlier this evening? No idea.

"Shit." He spun her back around to face him, his

sand-on-rock voice making her shiver. "Damn, Kiera. I want you. Now." Thick cords moved as he swallowed. "I have no right to touch you. I have no right to any of this…"

His shoulders and arms had grown in size. Hell, his entire frame had expanded. But Jake was still there. Waiting.

He bit his thumb as she drowned in his intense gaze.

Like a whirring calculator, she processed a million pieces of data in a split second.

So what if she and Jake didn't have a forever kind of thing here? They were both adults. They could make choices. They could still provide each other comfort and more. Danger dogged her no matter what choice she made tonight.

She might not have a certain future. She took in the rapid rise and fall of his muscled chest.

But she sure as hell had a certain present. And a choice.

She wanted his hands all over her, wanted the connection.

Wanted Jake. Not the guy from high school who played with her hair while they looked at the stars. Not the man from their desperate, grief-driven coupling from last summer. She wanted the man in front of her now.

"Jake," she whispered, going up on tiptoes and kissing him as hard as she could.

He didn't pull away.

With one hand still stroking the nape of her neck, he turned backward and walked with her into the bedroom. Not breaking contact, he kicked the door closed and flipped on the utilitarian bedside lamp. Then he wrapped his arms around her again and sensations flowed, hot and insistent. She couldn't get close enough to him. He whipped his t-shirt off and flung it to a corner of the room. His disheveled sandy hair made her fingers itch to comb through the strands.

Ridges of muscle rippled over his broad torso down to where a line of light-brown hair disappeared below the waistband of his jeans. She licked her lips.

He had her undivided attention.

In a whisper of movement and sleight of hand, he had her top and bra off. Self-conscious of her pregnant body, she tried to cover herself.

"God, no. Please." He gently drew her hands away. "Kiera, you are beautiful."

He lifted a heavy, tight breast in his massive hand and carefully, like she was made of china, dropped light kisses on it. When he did the same with the other breast, she lost the ability to see straight.

Then he gave her breast a tiny nip and her toes curled.

His possessive, wicked grin had her moaning in response as he licked and nipped his way over her neck and chest.

He reached for the button on his jeans and eased them along with his boxers down over his narrow hips until his erection sprang free. Hot, liquid anticipation dampened her panties.

Scooting her back to lie on the soft mattress, he hooked his fingers under the waistband of her pants. Then he hesitated.

She reached out and touched his forearm. "What?" Oh, God, he going to bail. He had changed his mind. "Jake?"

He swallowed. His pupils had dilated. He bit the tip of his thumb, looked at her belly, then up to meet her gaze. "Is this safe?"

"Oh. With the baby?" Doc had said there was no

indication of preterm labor or any complications. According to him, she was cleared for 'regular activities,' though technically she wasn't having regular sex on a regular basis, on account of the mission and… "Yes."

"What about with my, uh, the virus. Are you sure you want us to——?"

"Pretty sure that train has left the station." A wave of heat flooded her cheeks. She covered her breasts. "But if you don't want to … because I'm …?" Why yes, she would be the first person to actually die of embarrassment mid-seduction. She reached for the blanket edge and pulled it toward her as she half sat up.

He stilled her hand with a light stroke of his finger on her sternum, even as he stood over her. "You think I don't want you? Is it not obvious?"

He had a very good—and very obvious—point there.

Sweat glistened on his forehead. "I want to taste every inch of you. God, Kiera, you're sexy as hell."

The corners of his mouth tilted upward. Not exactly happy, though. More like … hungry. Anticipating. Possessive. He eased her further onto the bed and knelt over her. With their combined weight, her torso sank into the too-squishy mattress. He eased her arms out wide, lacing his fingers in hers, then trailed a line of kisses from her lips down her neck and over her breasts. Sitting up, he skimmed his rough fingertips over her rounded belly, and then drew her leggings off, along with her panties. *Well, no more mysteries tonight.*

The track of his fingers down her legs drew goose bumps. Her thighs quivered.

More. She needed so much more.

He slid his palms over her sensitive skin, down to her pulsing heat.

Nudging her legs open, he stroked her along the swollen, sensitive tissue, and she squirmed.

He panted as his pupils dilated. "I want you. I've wanted you since you showed up at my house the other day. It was like a miracle, seeing you again."

When he traced her superheated skin, she whimpered. "Please, Jake." She reached for him, brushing his pulsing erection. Wanting to touch him even more.

"I need to be inside of you." Pulling away, he bit out, "Only if you're safe."

Dodging away from her, he leapt off the bed, making the soft mattress bounce, grabbed his jeans, and fished out a foil packet. With a tear and a quick movement, he had himself sheathed.

Jake protecting her again. Not that it mattered, given she had already been exposed. But he took the precaution.

Kneeling over her again, he eased her knees apart. The bed sank under their combined weight once more. His hard erection slid over the skin on her thigh, sparking anticipation deep between her legs. God, she ached to have him inside her. She swiveled her hips, encouraging him.

Another nudge of his erection against her leg.

A grunt. He crouched and repositioned. The bed dipped down further.

Yet another nudge on her thigh. Then her hip.

Then nothing. Silence.

Why had he stopped?

She opened one eye, then another.

The sour purse of his lips looked like a man trying to perform a calculus problem.

"What's wrong?" she asked.

"No go. Mission failure." His brow furrowed as

he leaned over her again. The bed sagged beneath his considerable weight. Each time he pressed his pelvis forward again, her hips dipped into the mattress. He sniffed and raised an eyebrow. Blocked by her belly, gravity, and an extra-soft mattress.

Dear lord, if he didn't get inside of her right this minute, she would spontaneously combust. "What seems to be the problem?"

"Laws of physics aren't working." With another perplexed frown, he shrugged and motioned in the general vicinity of both their groins.

She had to prop herself up on an elbow to see over her abdomen and view his dilemma.

He had his hard erection in hand, but it had nowhere to go. Their collective weight and some bad angles thanks to the dip in the soft bed interfered with their fun.

Ah, yes, sex while pregnant. She'd read all about it in the *Great Expectations* book. She searched her memory. Chapter Ten, page 213, starting with paragraph three. Quickly, she scanned the page in her mind until she reviewed the text for various ways to have sex close to term. She blinked again.

Got it. Options.

"Let's try something," she said.

She turned over and rose up on all fours.

"Holy shit."

"No good?" She buried her face in the blanket. This had been a horrible idea. With any luck, he'd forget about this ridiculous evening. Heat climbed her neck. She tried to roll onto her side, but he palmed her hips, holding her still.

"Shit, Kiera, this is an amazing view."

"Is it?"

His growl was steamy enough to peel wallpaper.

"You have no idea. So sexy."

He ran his warm hands over her back, her thighs, and up the seam of her extra-sensitive flesh. She shuddered.

Tremors rippled through her body.

Jake stood at the edge of the bed and pressed himself tight to her backside, easing into her with short strokes, each thrust stretching her, filling her. Her nerve endings tingled with the friction and pressure until she matched his panting breaths with her own. Their moans echoed off the walls.

Leaning over her until his heat melded her skin, he brushed the sides of her belly until she shivered. Then he tugged at her nipples as she clenched around his length inside of her.

He groaned, "Damn, you feel—"

"I, you—" She managed to spit out the words. "More. Oh, God, more."

"You bet there's more."

His palms clamped on to her thighs as he drove into her with deep, heavy, demanding thrusts. Even though she was open, vulnerable, and literally in his hands, she knew he would never hurt her. Always knew. This was Jake.

The pace increased until the swirling sensation inside her vagina, coupled with the amazing friction, drove her right to the edge. He squeezed her hips and pulled her against him with each hard rotation of his pelvis.

With frantic movements, she tried to meet each stroke. She would never get enough of this pleasure. Never get enough of Jake.

The rasp of his rough hands over her thighs sent rough and delicious waves of pleasure through her. She panted. When he slid his fingers over her swollen folds while still rocking against her, Kiera's vision grayed out on the edges.

He sped up the deep, looping thrusts of his hips and rolled her clit at the same time. She moaned and struggled to stay upright. Light and sound exploded all around. She flew over the precipice with a hoarse cry.

Jake followed a few seconds later, and their moans blended together in the bedroom. With each relentless brush of his finger, she skimmed along, muscles clenching again and again. Unable to support herself on her arms, she lowered her chest and head into the bedding. Her abdomen tightened for about twenty seconds. Not very painful, but definitely enough to get her attention. She mentally reviewed the educational materials lodged in her memory.

Sex at term could indeed trigger some mild contractions. This cramping was normal. Not dangerous.

"Oh, my God, Kiera," he panted, half laying over her, one arm locked straight, the other arm cupping one swollen breast. The portion of his body resting on her back? Hot and slick with sweat. Perfect.

Still connected, he rolled them both to their sides and scooted up on the bed. Then he pulled the blankets over their spooned bodies.

After one more cycle of tightening and release in her uterus, her body settled down. Her heart returned to a normal rate, and sweat cooled on her forehead. Once he'd eased out of her to clean up, he returned, trailing his fingers up and down her arm, sparking more amazing tingles. With a sigh, his entire frame relaxed, and he dropped his palm over her midsection.

Over the baby.

Their baby.

Something deep down inside her soul seized up.

She refused to analyze what it meant for his big

hand to warm the rounded bump.

Her eyes burned, and she blinked hard.

His slow, deep breaths feathered the hair on her neck as his lips pressed against her skin. The heat from his muscled frame permeated her entire body.

Perfect.

Chapter Thirty

For the first time in nearly ten years, Jake slept soundly. Every muscle in his body relaxed. The relentless push-pull of virus versus sanity had abated. Every spinning thought seeped away, replaced by a comforting connection, knee to chest, with Kiera. She lay flush with her butt and back pressed against him. For a precious piece of time, he was a normal man, not a monster.

For a precious piece of time, he caught a glimpse of forever.

His existence boiled down to breathing in the soothing scent of flowery shampoo and exhaling every regret into the quiet, dark room. He couldn't move for fear of disturbing the crystalline, delicate peace. His hand, heavy and brutish, rested motionless on the curve of Kiera's hip. The other hand had gone numb as her head pillowed his arm under her. But any movement could break this spell. So, he remained motionless.

When he dared to crack an eye open at dawn, he drank in the way her dark hair tangled on the pillow in an adorable mess. He brushed a kiss across the back of her neck, loving how the smooth skin under his lips stippled with goose bumps. Unable to resist touching her, he traced her shoulder and arm with his fingertips.

"Mm." She shifted and stretched, grinding her butt into his groin and waking up the rest of his body in the best possible way.

When she rolled over, the sheet stopped just above her nipples, but the visible portion of her full breasts had him licking his lips, eager to drop more kisses on the silky skin. Even the delicate line of her nose tempted him to kiss her there as well.

The corners of her rosy mouth curled up. "Morning."

"A very good morning." He brushed his thumb over her lower lip, and she sucked the tip in, sending pure happiness straight to his groin. Then she scooted closer and nestled her head on his upper arm. Then she sighed.

A raw and beautiful emotion nailed him in his solar plexus.

Fuck it all, he'd stay right here for days if she wished. He'd do anything for this woman. Anything.

He leaned up on his side, caressing her cheek.

All his life, this was what he'd wanted.

What did Kiera truly want? He stilled the movement of his fingers on her skin.

No way did she want half of a man, Jake, with his fucked-up life.

He had no business leading her on.

He had his chance with her before and blew it. Had he learned from the experience? Contentment congealed into nasty slime in his gut.

Screwing up again with Kiera would damn near kill him. They had too many cards stacked against them. His lack of staying power in a relationship when tough times happened was the problem. That, and the presence of an experimental virus that could turn him into a hair-triggered, feral monster who had a crappy future.

Add in the U.S. government, which would never stop until it had 'repatriated' Jake back to the cage where he could resume his career as a glorified lab rat. Oh, yeah, that job had *upward mobility* written all over it.

What kind of a future picture could he paint for Kiera? Their child?

Black ink on a black easel.

Nothing. He had nothing to offer her. Except for

pain.

He was already in way too deep. Panic clawed through his lungs, taking up all the air inside of him. Things had gone too far. He needed to end this relationship now. Distance. He would start by getting some distance from Kiera.

He groaned and rolled to his back.

Damned if she didn't follow, continuing to cuddle like she cared less about all the ways he didn't measure up. If only she didn't trail those magical fingertips down his torso and dangerously close to—

"Shit, you have to stop." He encircled her delicate wrist and drew her hand away from the area of his body jumping to attention.

"Why?"

He couldn't see it, but he felt her smile with her cheek pressed against his chest. A shudder ripped through him when she feathered a kiss next to his nipple. It would be way too easy to go for round two of passion. Far too easy to lead her on until he inevitably hurt her. Again.

Time to man up. Do what was right. Rip off the goddamned Band-Aid before the damage became permanent.

Like sleep with her?

He eased away from her. "Kiera. Stop."

"What?" Her dyed brows drew together, a visual reminder of how she had to change to survive. And why.

Her rounded abdomen was a reminder of why Jake had to step away. He needed to give this baby a future, which meant he needed to give Kiera a future. That future couldn't include Jake.

"All of this. We have to stop all of it," he ground out.

She pulled back and propped her head up on a

bent arm, revealing another tempting portion of a full breast. "I don't understand."

What he'd give to replace the sad downturn of her lips with another sexy release of pleasure like last night.

Cut it out, he commanded his hardening cock. No, it didn't matter what his body wanted. This was about what Kiera needed, even if she didn't realize it right now.

He rested the side of his head on his palm, mirroring her semi-reclined position. "Last night ... shouldn't have happened."

Chapter Thirty-One

One corner of Kiera's delectable mouth rose, both temping and tormenting Jake. "Don't worry. It's not like you can get me more pregnant." She motioned toward her midsection.

"Couldn't anyway."

"What?"

"Get anyone pregnant. Anymore. They encouraged us to get vasectomies. Even if they find a cure for the virus, I don't get a choice to be a father."

"Then how did we…"

"I waited too long for the procedure. Right after that night last July, I freaked out. Next day, I got hold of Doc. The rest, as they say, is history."

"July was that bad of an experience?"

"It was that good," he murmured.

"I'm not asking you for another baby, Jake. Never asked you for any."

"That's part of the problem, too, isn't it? The baby being at risk reminds me of our past and my ex-wife…"

A furrow formed between her brows. "I don't understand. What does your ex have to do with"—she flung out a hand, encompassing the shambles of an amazing night—"this?"

"My wife had a miscarriage," he bit out.

The color leached out of her face. "Because of the virus?"

"No. I took the Morpheus Virus after she became pregnant."

"Then how does that relate to us?"

He gripped his hair, like doing so would keep his head from exploding. "Because I can't go through another loss."

Rearing back like he'd slapped her, Kiera said, "We can't change this"—she motioned toward her midsection—"and I'm worried, too. But there is nothing further to prevent. Only work through. Doc's got a good plan for us."

"Don't you get it? There are no do-overs for me. This is it. I've seen one pregnancy loss." His eyes burned. "I can't survive another one. Not with you. That would break me, Kiera. I keep thinking about what might happen. Then I think of a future with you, and frankly, I don't see it … because of all this shit."

Her choked gasp gutted him. Yeah, he'd gone there.

Gritting his teeth, he plowed ahead, "Seriously, this relationship or whatever we have. It can't go anywhere. We made a mistake."

Those beautiful hazel eyes went round. They speared him. Accused him.

There were a million ways he could said it better.

Her face went blank. "I never had any expectations that last night would lead to anything long term. Never pressured you. Never felt I was in any danger from you. I have never asked for anything, Jake. Ever." She slammed her lips together.

He winced. "Yeah, I know. It's— all of this, can't go anywhere." Like a guppy trying to breathe air, he opened and closed his mouth another few times.

"What are you doing, Jake?" The quaver in her voice speared pain through his chest.

"I'm not sure what you mean." He tried to swallow down the miserable sensation of a rock lodged in his throat.

"You're pushing me away."

He picked at invisible lint.

For far too long, she studied him. A prickle of sweat tormented the skin of his neck.

Suddenly, she got out of the bed, sheet clutched to her chest. "So. What's this *really* got to do with your ex-wife?" Anger pinged off of every word. "Because this"—she waved her hand at the room, the bed, them—"is a pattern, isn't it?"

If he'd been standing, he would have taken a step back. Instead, he sat where he was, naked and gape-jawed, staring at her. "What?"

"Come on, now. I know how this story goes." She raised a hand. "We were young and scared. I got pregnant. Things didn't go well. You walked away. You didn't want to be trapped, I get it. With your ex, she got pregnant, too. Things didn't go well. You walked away. And now?"

Scrubbing his eyes with the heels of his hands, he flopped back on the pillow. "I don't want to talk about it."

Shoving hair behind an ear while she held the sheet to her chest, she jutted out her chin. "Fine. I don't particularly care what you want to talk about."

Oh, no. He was in deep shit.

"Kiera—"

"Go ahead, come up with an excuse. Because you're walking away from the truth."

Snapping back at her, he shouted, "You want the truth? Look, I dated her, wasn't careful, and she got pregnant. Then I married her. End of story."

"Did you *want* to marry her?"

"I can't believe we're discussing this." He laid his arm over his face. "It didn't fucking matter then and it doesn't matter now."

"Did you love her?"

"What the hell? Drop it."

"Simple question. Did you love her?"

Hormonal and pissed-off was not a good look for the woman who nearly levitated in front of him. She was terrifying.

For a split second, his life teetered on the edge of a cliff. There he stood, one shaking foot suspended out over the abyss.

Unable to meet her eyes at first, he said, "My feelings weren't part of the decision-making matrix. I needed to do the right thing." He glared at her, his vision tinting red. Stupid virus churned up his insides like damned lava in a deep, dark pit.

Shit. His shoulders itched as the muscles expanded and flexed. His virus loved this fight. It wanted more conflict. Jake clenched and released his fists, over and over. *Work the technique. Talk it down.* No way would he inflict the full force of Mr. Hyde on her.

When she swallowed, he studied the line of her smooth neck so he could commit the image to memory.

She tucked the covers around and tightly over her breasts, then crossed her arms. "So, that's why you wanted to marry me, back in the day. To do the right thing."

"No comment."

"Must have been a relief when I miscarried."

A slap couldn't hurt more than her comment. "Unfair question."

"Did you ever feel anything for me, Jake? For our baby?"

He opened and closed his mouth. The words of how much he cherished her and how terrified he was stuck to his tongue like thick paste.

Sucking in a whistle of air, she said, "You can't even admit it."

He shook his head. "No, that's not it."

"What do you want from yourself and from your life?"

He shoved his hands into his hair and pulled, hard. "I. It doesn't matter." Air rasped through his burning throat. "I have had no choices."

"Bull. You volunteered for military service. You volunteered for Special Forces. You volunteered for the virus." She had a point but damned if he would admit it.

"That's the truth of my past." He clenched a pillow in his fist. "But my future? I have no choice because of the virus. No future. No legacy. Don't you get it?" He scooted toward the edge of the bed, hand held up. But he wouldn't touch her. It was exactly what the clawing virus wanted. Close contact. A target. Jake would rather die first than lay a finger on her in anger. "Oh, God, Kiera. We need to stop this conversation." Before he made it worse? How was that even possible?

"We're not done." Shoving hair behind her ears again, she pointed at him. "You just told me that what we have together isn't going anywhere. Fine. To pander to your conscience, don't worry—I never planned on a future. Kind of have a lot on my plate right now, in case you hadn't noticed. Thanks for the lack of support, by the way. Yes, I'm terrified, thanks for asking." She licked her lips, driving him to insanity from one part lust and one part anger. "But I deserve to know the real reason why you're shoving me away. Don't give me some bullshit about the virus and safety. That's not the story."

Snap, pop. The virus exploded from the mental constraints he'd placed. Everything in the room turned the color of blood. No more sugarcoating. Words tumbled out before he could consider them. "You always liked to push things, didn't you, Kiera? Back in high school with our relationship. The mission with Mateo. How far did you goad him to take risks? What percentage of his death was your fault due to your hard-headedness? What about the risk to your family now?"

Her horrified expression? The truth hurt. Hell, he owned that t-shirt in several different colors.

He cut her off when she opened her mouth. "Hell, you probably encouraged Brady to join Fallen Comrades and do those damned ads. Look where it got him. And what about Lequire? Did you lead him on, and now the entire team is in danger?"

The color blanched from her face and neck. Her chin quivered as she swayed on her feet.

The virus didn't care how badly he hurt her, but Jake sure did. Damn his stupid mouth. His character assassination of her was uncalled for. He opened his mouth to beg for forgiveness—

"Oh, my God," she sputtered. Then a hard glare fell into place as she stepped forward and poked him in the chest. "How can you say those things?" Every time her finger indented his muscle, the virus ramped up, madder and madder.

Kiera was filtered in a blood-red hue. "Stop it." His ears rang. He scrambled to his feet, the blanket still on the bed. His fisted hands shook.

Poke, poke. "While we're on the subject of failure, do you recall what I asked before you and Brady went into Special Forces?"

"Don't you dare say it," he warned her. It took all his remaining control not to grab her wrist.

It terrified him that he had an impulse to try. He planted his hands on his hips to anchor them in place.

"Should be easy to remember," she said. "As a matter of fact, it's the one and only thing I ever asked you to do: keep Brady safe."

The muscles in his gut clenched. Damn it all, she was right. He had failed. "I don't want to hear it."

"Of course, you don't. Know what? You're done avoiding the truth and hiding and running." Her voice cracked. "Sure, you have baggage and history. You got dealt a raw deal throughout your life. Welcome to the club. But maybe you should try owning your crap instead of making excuses for it." Even through his virally altered vision, he spied vivid stains tinting her cheeks. A pulse beat wildly at the base of her neck.

When he regained the ability to talk, thanks to another round of knuckle-popping fist clenches, his voice came out tight and harsh, like lashes of a whip. "See, there you go, pushing again. That's what you do, isn't it? You push until someone gets hurt."

"No," she whispered, unshed tears glistening in her eyes.

"Listen, I let people down, and I'm done with it. If I don't put myself out there, then I can't let people down. So, there's nothing I can offer you. There's no picket fence and two-car garage for us. There are no two point three children in a cozy home. There's no possibility of a long-term, secure relationship because I am a fucked-up ticking time bomb who has a bounty on his head."

He'd left logic and good sense behind sixty seconds ago. Whatever. This situation had gone to shit at the point last night where he had ripped off her clothes.

She sucked in a breath. "I have never forced you to do anything. Never."

"Didn't you? You made an advance at me at Brady's funeral."

Her chest rose and fell as haunted eyes widened. "What is wrong with you, Jake?"

"Oh, and now you're going to use tears? Here's a hint: doesn't work." Wrong. It did. The cracks in the dam no longer held back the contents. He broke, spilling his soul out. "You want more truth? Being the good guy has bitten me in the ass too many times to count. I tried to be a stand-up kind of man for you before, and then fucked up that simple task. Because I wasn't man enough. Then I tried to do the right thing again and my wife miscarried. I wasn't man enough to help her. By then, I couldn't even safely provide her with another baby."

"None of it was your fault," she whispered.

Oh, fuck, the words kept coming, like a relentless landslide of bullshit. He shoved fists against his face, half punching himself. "After my ex lost the baby, she went to a dark place where I couldn't help her. Then she left me. I sure as hell wasn't the man she needed. Sound familiar? Yeah, because *that's* the pattern. Hurting others, not being man enough, and leaving. My dad did the same thing to my mom when I was a kid. I did it to you. History repeats itself. The future is set."

When she opened her mouth, he cut her off with a slash of his hand. Then he yanked his hand back, terrified he might accidentally touch her.

Jake needed to escape. With his messed-up brain, he shouldn't be around other humans, much less be trusted to say the right things to a woman he cared for more than anyone in this world.

In jerking motions, he pulled on his boxers and shoved his legs into denim. "How's that for a fabulous fucking résumé, Kiera?" A yank and a clank of the belt punctuated his words. "Now do you get it? There is *no* future for us. There *never* was any future. You need something—someone—better than me. Don't worry, I have funds saved up from not spending while on duty and from my mother's life insurance policy. I can provide financial support for this baby for as long as I live."

He stood there, exhausted and out of breath like

he'd run a marathon, and stared down at the woman he'd left, far too many years ago. The woman he was leaving once again. Funny, he figured it would be easier this time around, what with all the practice.

Not so.

A little muscle jumped in her jaw as she clamped her mouth shut. Her pretty face twisted as she visibly struggled to maintain control. She didn't spill a tear, but they threatened to fall, and damned if the shimmering didn't make her look even more beautiful. Her shoulders went rigid. The effort to hold her shit together made him want to yank her into his arms.

Which would be yet another horrible mistake.

Damn it. At what point would he stop hurting people he…?

Fuck that. No. He was not going to put a label on any emotion right now.

After grabbing his shirt, socks, and shoes, he stormed to the door, then spun around. Damn it, the way her expression changed as agony morphed into blank resignation. The shift hurt more than being punched in the balls.

Whatever. Time to throw himself back into work for Morpheus Squad until this mission ended or his life ended. He would make Beau Lequire pay for what he had done to Mateo and Brady and Kiera. The asshole would answer for what he had done to other veterans. Now if that didn't count as fulfilling a life's purpose, Jake didn't know what would.

"I'm due for perimeter patrol. You need to meet with Hunt at 0800." The frigid tone of the words coming out of his mouth scared even Jake. "He has more questions. You can discuss your future plans then."

After slamming the door shut, he shoved his arms into his t-shirt, almost ripping the garment to shreds when he missed a hole. Balancing on one foot then the other, he had his shoes on in no time. Rage turned to nausea, but he shoved both bile and emotion down deep and clung to what little control he still possessed.

Then in a smooth movement, he headed to the front door.

A soft sound behind him stopped him in his tracks.

He listened carefully.

Nothing.

Good. Because he had work to do.

Chapter Thirty-Two

"What did you do to her? Probably said something stupid." Rodeo got in Jake's face in the garage, near the front entrance of the compound. Jake had finished his morning patrol and was starting on his next assignment per the roster. The more activities filling his schedule, the better.

Before he checked equipment, though, Jake was about *thisclose* to remodeling that guy's head. Then he'd work on Gonzo, who had joined in on the pile-on.

"It's no one's business," he gritted out. Damn, he could feel the viral monster lapping up the heightened emotions and urging Jake to swing fists. He'd never ridden the line between sanity and complete loss of self-control for so long before. Jake could go supernova in two seconds flat. A shot of antidote would help some of his problems today, but not all of them.

The antidote didn't fix stupid, unfortunately.

"Ok, *princesa*, then why did Kiera look all red-eyed and unhappy this morning when I came in from my shift? Like someone gave her the worst news of her life. Why did Stumpy say you were a jerk?" Gonzo's dark eyebrows rose as he hovered inches from Jake's nose. His teammate's hard chin provided a tempting target.

"Again, not your business," he muttered, trying to walk by the men.

Rodeo extended a dark, muscled arm across his buddy's chest. "I've got this one, Gonzo. Watch me work." Mr. Male Model grabbed the front of Jake's shirt and shoved him into the metal wall.

Dumb move.

The virus flared. Hungry. Ready. It flooded Jake's arms and torso with power. Muscles pushed against fabric. A brick-hard fist rose, ready to fly. Red tinged his vision.

No. Jake could not attack his friends. He had to control the virus. Clamping his hand at his side, he suppressed the overriding desire to remove Rodeo's teeth. At the rate he was throwing emotional chum into the waters for the virus's feeding frenzy, he'd need another antidote shot soon.

Rodeo thumbed the brim of his hat. "Not our business? Look, shit-for-brains. First of all, Kiera is a nice person who tried to avenge Brady. Brady was our brother-in-arms, therefore Kiera is our sister. Second, stress is bad for the baby. Which is yours, by the way, you dumb fuck. Finally, if you hurt that sweet woman, I will open up the biggest can of whoop ass on you and will not stop until you cease breathing. Got it?" He glanced at Gonzo. "Good?"

"Oh, yeah, couldn't have said it better myself. Very descriptive, yet still based in fact."

That smug cowboy bastard preened. "Why, thank you."

"You're welcome." Gonzo smirked.

"Guys!" Jake interrupted their mutual fawning. "Get your hands off me. I have work to do." *And wounds to lick.*

Rodeo leaned into him. "You have work to do? You haven't helped us in well over a year and *now* you want to pitch in? I call bullshit. This is a test of your character to see if you still fit on our team. Try again. Start by explaining how you fucked up a good thing. And don't tell me it's not what happened. Failure is written all over your ugly face."

Jake sagged under his teammate's crushing arm, his body limp as a noodle. "I screwed up with Kiera. Again. Worse than when we dated ten years ago. Worse than last summer. This morning, I said things I shouldn't have." A prickle of irritation made him stand up straighter. "But in my defense, she said mean things to me." He glared at them. "Don't you two have work to do?"

"We're union, fucker. This is our coffee break," Rodeo growled.

"My turn." After a tacit handoff, Gonzo crossed his arms over his barrel chest. "Let me get this straight. This woman escaped being murdered recently—twice. She attempted to avenge Brady—something we could not do. In trying to avenge him, she put her life in danger. She has taken a huge personal risk to deliver information to us."

Shit.

Gonzo sucked in another lungful of air. "And, oh, by the way, the company she might take down has its hooks deep in the U.S. government and Mother Russia, and wouldn't everyone like to keep her quiet— permanently? Despite all of it, she's still helping us. That about cover it?"

Jake glared at him. A lead weight settled in his gut.

"Oh, wait there's more." His teammate glared right back and pointed a finger. "Also, because you were a numb nut and didn't man up with the Snip-snip For Safety program, now she's carrying your child which may or may not be okay when it makes its entry into the cold, cruel world. A world which, by the way, wants to take her child and run goddamned tests on it. The one and only thing certain about her future is that it's scary as fuck." He poked Jake in the ribs. "But you? You're a superhuman powerhouse. Nothing can hurt you. Yet you have the balls to stand here and whine that she said 'mean things' to you?"

Jake's lungs deflated in a massive whoosh. His teammates were right about everything. If he could melt into the ground, he'd do it, but Rodeo's death grip on the front of Jake's shirt kept him firmly propped up in the line of fire.

Oh, shit. Gonzo wasn't done. "Because a stressed-out pregnant lady said 'mean things' to you, you ruined the one single thing in your miserable existence that is good and pure? You're *el pinche idiota*."

Rodeo let go of the shirt and flashed a tight, unhappy smile. "You are the stupidest fuck I've ever seen, bro."

"Dude, that's what I said." Gonzo tilted his head.

Rodeo scrunched up his face and studied the metal ceiling as he pulled out his yo-yo from a pocket. A few thoughtful trips up and down the string later, he said, "I like how you said it better, George. It's a really good insult. I'll have to jot that one down."

"Okay, but you have to give me credit."

"Guys." Jake slid down the garage wall until he knelt on the ground. He put his head in his hands, thoughts swarming like angry bees. "Oh, shit." The virus remained silent. Unhelpful fucker. "What do I do now?" What had he done? He wanted to throw up or beg for forgiveness. Chances of her ever speaking to him again, to say nothing of forgiving him … the probability was less than zero.

His inability to address his own hang-ups and work through his past had destroyed his relationship with the sweetest woman he'd ever known. He had done this to her. To them. To any future he might have had. Jake: destroyer of entire lives.

Rodeo nudged him with the silver tip of his cowboy boot, like Jake was a pile of manure. "You want that crow cooked medium-well or rare?"

"You can still fix this, man," Gonzo said. "I know it."

"Yeah." Jake staggered to his feet. Maybe there was a tiny chance. He'd beg if necessary. "I have to go talk with her. Apologize." Explain how he felt and what she meant to him. Truly meant. He needed to own up to his baggage. Promise to work through his shit. Counseling. Homework. Penance. Anything it took.

Gonzo sniffed. "It would work better if you had flowers and a box of chocolate."

"Dude." He spread his arms out to encompass the drab garage and entire compound. "Seriously?"

"It's a suggestion," his teammate said. "You need all the help you can get. As a matter of fact, I'm going to say a few *Ave Marias* for you."

"That means 'Hail Marys,'" Rodeo added.

Gonzo whipped around. "I know."

He thumbed his hat with a sniff. "I'm clarifying for dumbass here."

"Guys!" Jake faced down two sets of raised eyebrows.

"What are you waiting for? A permission slip?" Rodeo said. "Get out of here, shit-for-brains. Go fix your mistake."

Chapter Thirty-Three

How Kiera held herself together through the question-and-answer session with Hunt and then working with Stumpy a few hours after that terrible wake-up call, she had no idea.

Her emotions still raw from last night's passion followed by the harsh rejection, she considered her options for a plan B for safe delivery and a new life with her daughter. Kiera took a deep breath and concentrated, tugging at the blue knit top beneath her black cardigan. It was a monumental task to bring up the ledger images in her mind long enough for Stumpy to write them down on paper. If he thought something was wrong, the computer guru said nothing.

After a tasteless lunch of some kind of sandwich, she and Stumpy finished their work in the early afternoon. Kiera sighed and stretched her lower back. The soreness had as much to do with being pregnant and sitting for hours as it did with recent fabulous, earth-shattering sex.

Well, there was a last time for everything.

"Mind if I go for a walk?" she asked, shaking herself out of her inactivity.

He looked up from what he was typing. "Sure. Want company?"

"Um, I don't want to interrupt." The attempt to hit the sweet spot with a casual, carefree tone went to hell when her voice cracked.

Rubbing his goatee, Stumpy studied her a beat too long. "If you want privacy, you got it. No issues with you walking around. Perimeter is secure." He patted the computer. "Final permanent system check was completed this morning. Only the best high-tech proprietary security system the military has ever developed is good enough for our team." He pointed to a bank of monitors next to his big desk in the corner. "Cameras are online, too. Not that it matters. I'll get an alarm if anything comes within a half-mile of the compound. Also, Curly and Hunt are patrolling this afternoon. I'll let them know you're strolling."

"Good." She snagged her cardigan from where it rested on the back of a chair. "Then I'll get some fresh air and be back in an hour." She needed to exit soon before she started crying.

With a nod, he swiveled in the chair, focusing on the computer screen.

A walk. That would be helpful, right? If only she wasn't simply pacing in a glorified cage.

Hunt hadn't ordered her to stay. While she might be technically free to leave the compound, the feeling of being trapped tightened around her like a tight, wet harness. Trapped here. Trapped with Jake and by their past. She peered down the mountain as she exited the building. What waited for her at the end of the dirt road?

Freedom. A new life for this child. A new life for Kiera.

What else?

Beau Lequire.

Danger.

She rested a hand on her belly. Damn it. Willing her sore hips to cooperate, she followed the fine mesh with black boxes spaced every hundred feet or so.

The overcast skies mimicked her uncertain, heavy mood. Muffled crunches accompanied each step, and the brisk mountain air provided distraction but not clarity to her racing thoughts. She toyed with the extra factory button sewn onto the tag in the black cardigan's seam.

She sighed after another few steps. Seemed like

she couldn't stop sighing.

What the hell had happened this morning? She'd never, ever pushed Jake into assuming additional responsibility.

Hadn't she?

Maybe showing up at his house unannounced and handing him Mateo's letter constituted some pressure. Okay, a lot of pressure. In her defense, though, she didn't have options.

Sure, she encouraged him last night, but their desire and the amazing sex seemed mutual from where she stood. No pressure.

More likely answer? Jake had gotten gun-shy when he figured out all the complications that came with her.

Hey, not a problem. Once this mess calmed down, she would pick up the pieces and create her own life. A normal life did not require anyone else to be in it other than her baby girl.

Before she went, Kiera needed to sit down with Jake and hash everything out. Deal with his reaction. Make sure he knew she cared for him, but that he had his own path to travel and she was on board with that fact. Give both of them closure.

Her eyelids burned. Oh, sure, she could have that conversation. Easy peasy.

She scuffed her feet over the leaf litter as she stared at the ground. The damp soil cushioned every chilly step.

Good God, this morning. Her steps faltered, and she stared out into the dense forest. How had the mouth that had dropped passionate kisses on her lips hurled such anger?

Did the virus make him say those things?

Didn't matter.

She rubbed her shoulder and neck. At a crackle in the woods, her pulse jumped. She peered again into the misty forest.

Nothing out there. As she walked a few feet away from the perimeter mesh, her worries and concerns slotted like jigsaw puzzle pieces until she had a full picture of her failings.

Tears prickled behind her eyelids.

So much for avenging Brady. So much for righting a wrong. She rubbed the bridge of her nose. Mateo. The baby. Jake. What a mess.

A small puff of vapor punctuated her breath every few steps. Cold front coming through the region, per Stumpy's update earlier today. Fingers of mist wound through the trees, thickening the air. Anemic light from the overcast skies straggled through the fine mesh in the trees above her. Frost clung in heavy droplets to spider webs suspended between branches and undergrowth. In the thick mist, the outlines of trees and plants became indistinct. Blurred. Like her thoughts. Swirling, churning.

Another sigh, and she gave up trying to figure everything out. Better to walk.

She continued along the perimeter. The light track she and Stumpy had walked yesterday made for a reasonable stroll today. When she reached the first back corner of the compound, she turned right, toward the other far corner of the forty-acre deep rectangle which encompassed the large property. Curly appeared, ghostlike, out of the fog, gave her a curt nod, and kept walking.

Mesh-muted shadows in the forest outside the boundary played tricks with her imagination.

Then the skin on the back of her neck crawled.

She peered in the direction of the compound entrance.

In the haze, she could no longer see the buildings or hear any sound coming from that direction, and Curly had melted into mist.

She picked up the pace.

Dull, low crunches of rotting leaves and thick snaps of branches compelled her to look into the forest again. She stopped.

A second later, the crackling noise stopped.

She began walking again, trying to move faster. The only structure she could see well? The perimeter fence and the occasional security box.

She stopped walking again.

The crunches in time with her pace stopped, but with one additional step than her own.

Air rasped through her mouth.

Her muscles twitched. *Quit it.* Stumpy had said the security here was solid. They had patrols and cameras. He could see her progress and the woods nearby, even now. No way he would have let her go out if it was unsafe.

There, to her left in the forest, outside the barrier, more sounds.

Probably a deer or squirrel. She eyed the thin mesh. Or maybe a bear.

Little Bit kicked and rolled.

At a movement out of the corner of her eye, Kiera turned around.

A muffled *pop* was followed by a sting in her neck.

She frowned. Mosquitoes this soon in the mountains? She stopped in her tracks and felt her neck. Something was sticking out of it.

Pulling out the object, she stared at a small dart in her palm. She squinted to focus, but her vision blurred. What...? Blinking again, she dropped the dart and rubbed her eyes. No improvement.

She took a few staggering steps, then her legs gave out on her. Dropping down hard onto her knees and palms, she braced herself on the damp decomposing leaves, crushing them in her fists. She shook her head, trying to clear it.

When she tried to push to her feet again, she couldn't get upright without crumpling back to the dew-covered ground.

She opened her mouth to call for help. No sound came out.

She couldn't hear or feel anything. It was like bubble wrap insulated all her senses.

"Well, that was much easier than we'd planned, wasn't it? Getting my feet dirty coming with you chumps all the way out to this godforsaken hell was worth it after all." The too-polite voice sounded familiar.

One more heave to her feet? Unsuccessful. She slumped to the ground and made a feeble attempt to crawl away. She tried to look up, but gray mist blended with a gray figure.

The last thing she registered was a pair of mint-condition brown leather boots right in front of her.

Chapter Thirty-Four

3:30 PM.

"Anything?" Jake yelled as he sprinted into the main building, slamming the doors nearly off their hinges.

When he hadn't found Kiera anywhere on the compound, cold sweat broke out on his forehead and his oh-shit meter went off like a Geiger counter near a nuclear bomb.

Stumpy said she had gone for a walk a half hour ago, and she'd probably headed back to take a nap. Looked really tired, he'd said, giving Jake a nasty glare.

Jake had searched all the buildings. Every one of them. Including the room they had shared last night. No sign of Kiera. Had she left the compound? Surely someone would have seen her. The security cameras would have picked it up.

An unexpected hollowness gnawed at him. It was her prerogative to leave, right? Ill-advised, but in the end, her decision. But one of the guys would have tried to get her to stay.

His gut tightened. She had no reason to stick around, given Jake's behavior this morning.

Still, nothing felt right about this situation.

He skidded to a stop at Stumpy's bank of monitors. "Anything?"

Jake struggled. Every muscle jumped, ready for action. Something was very wrong here, he could feel it. Imaginary spiders crawled over him.

Hunt dashed in, followed by Gonzo, Rodeo, and Doc. Bald-headed Curly entered a few minutes later.

"Well?" he asked Curly.

He remained vigilant, even in the building.

"Passed her just after fifteen hundred hours on the back of the property."

"And? Jake was coming out of his skin.

"Perimeter secure. She seemed fine. On a walk. Nothing was out of the ordinary." A sheen of sweat glistened on his teammate's head.

"Let's check the back forty." Jake spun toward the door.

"Wait," Stumpy said. "Save some time and energy." He swiveled in his seat and pulled up surveillance images on multiple screens: woods outside the compound, several views inside the compound, and shots down the entry road. Bland and blander images. Stumpy leaned forward and magnified the timestamps on the screen. "Wait. What the hell? These images have been playing on a ten-second loop." His neck turned red as he tapped more keys until new video appeared on the screens. "No, no, no." There, sure enough, on the top right monitor, was Kiera, head bent, hair swinging forward to cover part of her face, walking around the perimeter of the property.

Time stamp on the film: 3:10 PM.

Jake held his breath.

She stopped and stared out into the forest.

Then she stiffened, turned, and clutched at her neck.

She dropped to her knees, hands clawing at the ground.

Jake's heart stopped.

Three men in hunting clothes passed through an opening in the mesh.

"The fuck?" Hunt exploded.

Jake's blood iced. "Some fucking airtight security system you've got here!"

Stumpy started talking to himself like an idiot

savant. "No, no, no. How is this possible? What the hell? I would have known. It should have tracked her progress on the monitors, camera to camera. What happened to the alarms?" He flipped on additional computers while the horrible security recording played out on the main screen. "We had patrols up, too." He glared at Curly, who raised his hands.

On the screen, one man wearing a fresh off-the-rack flannel button-down shirt and dark brown pants with a perfect fit stepped next to her. He knelt and pushed Kiera's limp body onto her back, one arm flopping across her body, above her rounded abdomen.

Vinyl shredded beneath Jake's grip on the computer chair.

The man grabbed her hair at the back of her scalp and raised her head off the ground. When he brushed the leaves off her face with exaggerated tenderness and gave Kiera's lifeless cheek a kiss, Jake shoved down bile forcing its way up his throat.

Then the man looked directly at the camera and produced a dazzling smile that any cosmetic dentist would be proud to claim was their own client.

"Beau fucking Lequire," Hunt growled. "I'd recognize that designer face anywhere."

Blood drained out of Jake's head.

Rodeo shoved a shoulder under Jake's arm to keep him upright.

The image of Kiera, crumpled on the forest floor, with those men surrounding her, burned into Jake's retinas. Then, before he could focus his rage, he watched two of the men grab her under the armpits and under her knees to carry her limp body back through the mesh.

The rest of the feed showed nothing but some scuffed leaves and branches. Like she'd never been there. Even the mesh appeared undisturbed.

The chair back snapped under his fingers. All objects in his field of vision bled red.

Stumpy jumped up, still typing and clicking.

Jake wanted to chop the hands off those assholes who dared touch her. His virus pleaded to be let out.

Kiera. His baby. Out there with those men. With Lequire. Jake's need to protect and then kill was the only thing tethering him to this Earth.

Hunt's voice split the silence like hot fire cracking a stone boulder. "This will not stand. What about other camera views? What's happening outside the compound?"

"On it." Stumpy flipped switches and entered computer commands—a maestro conducting a hellish orchestra—and pulled up additional camera angles. He pointed at the screen. "Look here. Motion detector cam, tree-mount, outside the compound. Why didn't the system alarm?" He rubbed his eyes. "Goddammit. I have no idea what happened. I checked the status this morning and all systems were working perfectly. Locked in tight." He paused, and the color leached out of his face. "Hold on. Hold on." He spun around and typed more commands into the system. "Holy fuck."

"What?" barked Hunt.

"Goddamn. The access code got entered right at noon." He pointed at the screen. "From outside the compound."

Jake bellowed, "Who the fuck can get into the security system?"

If looks could kill, Hunt would have incinerated everyone in the room. "Someone who knows about Morpheus Squad. Shit." He turned toward Jake. "Might be my source. Or if my source leaked the info. Or another in. I don't know, but the codes were compromised." He took two heavy strides away, then spun back around. "Son of a bitch."

"What, boss?" Stumpy turned in his chair.

The men's wide-eyed stares locked onto their leader.

He blinked. "We're fucked, boys. We need to blow out of here. Permanently and ASAP. I don't know how much time we have before Uncle Sam sends in a regiment of well-armed lemmings to pay us a visit. Or if they're feeling frisky, they'll drop munitions right on Morpheus Squad central and wipe us off the planet."

Silence filled the room.

Jake didn't care about getting outed by some loser prick and his prick senator father. Didn't care if the entire Army arrived at their doorstep. Kiera and his baby were all that mattered.

"Goddammit!" The word exploded out of Jake's mouth.

He headed for the door.

Hunt and Rodeo grabbed him. Jake fought them until Hunt's booming voice woke him the fuck up.

"Stand down, soldier!" the CO hollered. Even the windows rattled.

Jake stopped moving. "The hell! Look at the screen. Lequire kidnapped her, right under our noses. We need to find her and get her away from that bastard. They don't have much of a jump on us. Let's go."

A muscle worked in Hunt's jaw. He clamped a meaty hand on Jake's shoulder. "I get it, but hold on. We've got way more than one problem. Let's plan this op out. Gather intel."

"What the fuck more info do you need?" His muscles twitched, so badly did he need to run into the woods after her. "They have her. It's not like they're gonna throw her a cute baby shower."

"Shit on shit." Rodeo whistled.

Jake stared at his boss. "And now Lequire has access to Morpheus Squad. He broke in despite our patrols and so-called ironclad security system." Yeah, he let the sarcasm fly. Didn't care if feelings got hurt. "That man is fucking going to end her! Why are we standing here, drooling?" Not since his ex lost the baby had Jake known incapacitating terror like right now. An imaginary vise cranked down around his ribs until he couldn't breathe.

The virus swarmed, wanting to be let out. Wanting to maim. To kill. Needing release. Needing a target. Jake couldn't form a coherent thought with the damned virus churning inside of him. He could take an antidote shot, but then he'd lose any physical performance edge.

No. He'd wait on the shot for now. He would need all his unnatural strength to help Kiera. He'd deal with sanity later.

"Guys." Hunt pointed to Gonzo and Curly. "Recon, evidence, and possible retrieval. Now."

The men dashed out of the building at pace, Gonzo pulling on latex gloves as he exited.

Shit. *Focus*. Jake needed to be out there, but somehow recognized why he'd be useless.

For now, he would hold himself together if it killed him. For Kiera. *Make a plan*. He still had a chance to save both her and the baby, if he could get to her in time.

Images of his two teammates filled one of the screens as they knelt and studied the ground. Curly passed through the hold in the mesh and took off into the woods.

On the screen, Gonzo held up a small object.

"Dart," Doc murmured.

"Come on," Jake muttered. "We should be doing

more. Do you know what might happen?"

Hunt remained infuriatingly calm, but his eyes glinted with lethal intent. "I'm aware. But don't worry if Curly doesn't get to her. We can track her down."

"How?" Jake snapped and pointed at the shitty security setup. "She's out of the camera's range now. They could be taking her anywhere. We're running out of time."

"Not exactly." Stumpy tugged at his goatee and glanced over a shoulder. "Did you like her new pregnancy outfits?"

"What the actual hell?" he screamed, barely able to think.

Hunt pointed at the screen. "Stumpy here is a goddamned genius. Each piece of clothing contains an itty-bitty tracking device."

"What?"

Stumpy typed as a ghostly image of a person with bright spots on different areas of their body filled the screen. "Those dots come from her shoes, pants, and sweater."

"Holy shit. That means—" Maybe there was a chance.

Curly reappeared on the perimeter camera, his voice coming in over the radio. "Lost them at the dirt road. Vehicle peeled out right as I got there. Sorry, boss."

"Bring it in, guys," Hunt said. "On the double."

Jake reached out to the monitor display to touch the last picture of Kiera. "Tracker in the clothes?" he said, in disbelief.

"Yes." Stumpy shooed him away. "Don't touch the equipment, man."

"What if she is not with her clothes?" Jake gritted out.

Stumpy's goatee was stark black against his

blanched white skin. "Damn it." He turned and typed faster. "We'll have a general direction for now. They're still moving."

Curly and Gonzo re-entered the room, barely out of breath.

Hunt pointed to the door. "All right. Here's the plan. You all have ten minutes to pack gear for the rescue mission. We'll use two SUVs. I want equipment to cover various infiltration options and surveillance as well as ways to neutralize … anyone. The rest of the base's equipment goes in the truck. Curly, you're going to stay behind and demo the compound and vehicles with the Armageddon protocol. Then move the remaining supplies to the other site. Stumpy, get your tracking system mobile and keep an eye on her."

Gonzo raised an object. "Doc, what do you think about this?" He waved a wicked-looking orange and clear plastic dart. The beveled, razor-sharp end had a drop of blood on it.

The plunger was fully depressed.

After studying the drop of clear liquid remaining in the tube, Doc then waved the dart under his nose and frowned. "I'd have to run tests to know for certain, but I bet this is ketamine." He closed one eye and sniffed. Right, because Doc's Morpheus Virus enhanced his sense of smell. Weird extra skill, but came in handy. "Yep. Ketamine combined with xylazine."

"What the hell is that?" Jake asked. It didn't sound good.

The unflappable Doc's face twisted into a terrifying rictus of anger. "Horse tranquilizer."

Goddamned Lequire. Jake was going to kill the bastard. "What will that combination of drugs do to her?" His hand had curled into a hard fist and shook.

Doc growled—actually growled—in response.

"Depends on the dose. I've seen it used to drop big animals at fifty yards. In a human, it would hit hard and fast. Might screw with blood pressure."

The words hissed out between Jake's clenched teeth. "What would it do to the average pregnant woman?"

"You don't give it to a pregnant woman. Ever. But theoretically? It could drop her blood pressure. Could stop her breathing. Could reduce blood flow to the baby. Could bring on labor due to the drug causing uterine muscle irritability." His knuckles turned white as he gripped the syringe.

"Any other good news?" Jake's jaw ached from clamping down hard on it.

Doc didn't answer.

Hunt grabbed Jake's upper arm and turned him. "We'll get her back, I swear it. Doc, stock the vehicles with medical equipment you think we'll need."

Guilt squeezed Jake's throat until he choked. The last time he had seen her. What he'd said…

Damn it. No time to dwell on mistakes. Job one was to get Kiera away from Lequire. No telling what a vindictive, greedy asshole like that would do to a pregnant woman who had the goods to destroy his entire world.

Actually, no. Jake had a fucking fabulous idea of what the guy could do to her.

The guys hauled butt through the compound, packing two SUVs and a truck in the garage with as much critical equipment and sensitive materials as they could shove in there.

The clock was ticking.

As they stowed the last cache of weapons and medical supplies into the back of the SUVs, Stumpy exited the compound, a large laptop under one arm.

"Can you still see her?" Jake asked.

"Yep. Trackers are working like a charm." He didn't meet Jake's eyes. "They're moving south, through the mountains. I'll bet they're headed back down to Atlanta." He looked up at Doc. "Her pulse is eighty-two, oxygen level is ninety-eight percent."

"How do you get that info?" Jake asked.

Stumpy answered, "These readings are from the tracker embedded in her bra and underwear."

Over his shoulder, the CO hollered, "Curly!"

He jogged up, pointing a thumb over his shoulder. "Truck will be loaded and ready to go in five, boss."

"Roger that. Take care of the rest of the compound." Hunt said. "Okay. We're compromised. Lequire and his guys now know where we are. That means the Army may know we're here. Morpheus Squad 1.0 needs to disappear. You know the drill."

"You got it. This place will be ashes. Meet you at the designated site." Curly spun on his heel as Jake and the rest of the team piled into the SUVs.

Chapter Thirty-Five

Kiera curled up on her side on the lumpy gurney, her arms drawn over her blue knit top-covered belly. Little Bit gave a weak kick, like baby girl struggled to wake up. Or maybe she wanted to reassure Kiera. Nothing about this situation was remotely reassuring.

Where was she, anyway?

If she didn't have a clue, then probably no one else knew her location, either.

This time there would be no escape tunnel. No well-rehearsed plan. No ex-Special Forces operator keeping her safe.

Air sawed in and out of her lungs. *Oh, God.* She struggled to calm down.

Then a wave of tightness grew from her lower back, spread around her belly, and went down to her crotch, stopping her breath on a horrified cry. It felt like hours before the pain eased up. She panted. *What the hell was that?*

Once she recovered, a sense of deep dread motivated her to action. She blinked and accessed her memory. Page 271 of *Great Expectations*: Labor Symptoms. Contractions.

She rubbed her sweaty face, trying anything to clear the cloying fog from her brain. Whatever they'd shot her with packed a hell of a punch. When she tried to get off the bed, she fell, banging her knees and slapping her palms on the puke-green and black-flecked vinyl floor. She could handle discomfort personally, but what the drugs were doing to her baby terrified her the most.

She hadn't been handcuffed or tied to the bed. No one was guarding her. Blinking, she forced her thoughts into logical order and tried to think like Mateo had taught her. All right. If no one bothered to secure her, then they didn't care if she moved around. Or they didn't think she'd be able to move. Or there was no way to escape.

Bull. There was always a way out.

She grabbed the metal rails of the bed, hauled herself to her feet, and heaved back to a sitting position on the mattress, with her legs swinging over the edge. Her knees ached, and it took a minute for the room to stop spinning. Once the motion stopped, she scanned her surroundings.

Fluorescent lights and a sharp, bleachy-sweet scent of some kind of cleaning solution gave the white-walled room an astringent quality, devoid of life and warmth. On a wheeled table nearby rested numerous metal instruments on top of a large blue drape: metal clamps, white gauze, blue towels, scissors with blunt and sharp tips, and rounded metal wedges with thick handles. In the corner stood a tall machine with an overhead light and a tiny platform the size … of a newborn baby. On the platform rested clear tubing hooked to an oxygen tank, a blanket, and a plastic yellow clamp.

Oh, shit.

Her throat closed up and she struggled to draw in air.

Her heart hammered double time as sweat broke out on her forehead.

Standing once more, she fought the head-spinning dizziness and staggered to the solid metal door, careening into the wall with a knife-like pain in her shoulder. She grabbed the doorknob and twisted. Locked.

Struggling to stay upright as a wave of pain speared her belly, she clung to the doorknob and doubled over, panting. She shoved a hand against her mouth to prevent screaming while the relentless pressure passed.

After a circuit around the room, where she

touched every inch of wall, she could find no other escape route. No vents to crawl through, no trapdoors she could find. No back doors. No windows.

Footsteps sounded from outside the door. She spun around and almost fell over, searching for something—anything—to use to defend herself.

Scanning the instrument table, she selected thin, long scissors with one blunt tip and one sharp tip, palmed them, and staggered back over to the gurney. With an awkward and desperate sideways poke, she pressed and twisted until the plastic mattress cover facing the wall parted beneath the metal tip. With an aching twist of her wrist, she crammed the ends of the instrument inside and prayed the handle wouldn't be visible to whomever came through that door.

Just in time.

A beep sounded and a red light blinked green on the door. The handle turned. Her scream lodged in her throat.

Beau's elegant, too-calm visage greeted her.

She scooted as far back on the bed as possible.

"Well, hello there, Amy." His handsome features darkened into a sneer of pure disdain. One corner of his mouth twisted. "Or should I say … Kiera McNeill?"

She clamped her mouth closed.

He knew her real name. That meant he likely knew everything else: why she had been working at Fallen Comrades, who Mateo was, how she was connected to Brady, and who the rest of her family was. He knew about Morpheus Squad, of course, or he wouldn't have found her at the compound. The frantic pounding in her chest sped up.

The soles of Beau's gleaming leather dress shoes snapped on the vinyl flooring as he stalked across the room. As usual, his gelled hair was maintained in a fashionable tousle. Not a crease appeared in his fine slacks material. Immaculately presented. Classic Beau Lequire.

In her torn pregnancy leggings, dirty blue shirt, and dirt-covered black cardigan, she felt like a street urchin next to him. When he raked her from head to toe with his cold, calm stare, she tugged the cardigan around her body.

As he closed the distance, she reared back, placing a protective hand on her belly. All her best intentions were about to end here, in this bed.

Then her spine locked. No. She'd be damned if Beau laid so much as a finger on this child.

"Such a shame about your brother's death." His expression bore no resemblance to remorse. "Vets who have combat injuries are so vulnerable. He must have gotten confused and wandered into a bad area of Atlanta. Sad." His imperious sniff made her want to punch his long, straight nose. "For a disabled vet to die stateside, too. I should know how hard his life was, as I am a disabled vet, too." He smoothed his designer shirt.

Kiera would be happy to personally disable him and make it official. "Bull. You're no more combat-injured than I am."

"I can change that, sugar," he snapped, the façade cracking. Then he composed his expression back to one of infuriating calm.

Before she could rebut him, a surge of agony rushed over her like a tidal wave and crashed down, pummeling her bones, her belly, and her entire body. She collapsed on her side and writhed and whimpered.

After about a minute, she focused again.

Beau was watching her with the merest twitch of one eyebrow. "Do you like those little twinges, sweetheart?"

"No," she panted.

"I can make the pain stop." When he pointed to the table of instruments, her vision dimmed at the edges.

He stood close, so she had to crane her neck and squint against the bright lights to keep track of him. No way would she look away from his snake-like movements for even a second.

Lacing his smooth fingers together, he said, "Well, then. I believe you have some information to share with me."

"No idea what you're talking about."

"You see, I want to know everything about the Morpheus Squad."

"What's Morpheus Squad?"

"Come on now, Kiera." He pointed at her abdomen. "We don't have time for games. I want to know what they can do and how. You will share everything Brady told you about Fallen Comrades. I need to know what you mistakenly told those Morpheus Squad guys." His brief leer smeared over her like a trail of slime following a slug.

"Seriously, what are you talking about?

Back to his creepy professional demeanor, he said, "You didn't understand what I said. Must be the drugs. Let's try again. You *will* give me the information..."

Or?

Perfect white teeth flashed as he glanced toward the table of medical tools. She prayed he didn't notice the missing scissors. "Or we'll give your little bundle of joy here a birthday party to remember."

It took her a full five seconds to register his threat. "What? You can't do that."

"You're right, I can't—Oh, no, wait a minute." His cold, dead eyes glinted. "I absolutely can."

When he stepped forward, she scooted away, gripping the edge of the mattress. One fingertip brushed metal.

"See, what you fail to understand is that I can do whatever I want, Kiera. I have money. I have power. And I have you, here, in a locked room." He remained in perfect posture, not a hair out of place. "You, on the other hand, have nothing. Except a baby in there."

Hard to argue that line of logic.

His chuckle came out hollow. "Want me to tell you a secret?"

She didn't answer.

Dropping his voice to a level she had to strain to hear, he murmured, "What I really want is to see you beyond vulnerable. Beyond helpless. I want you aching for me. Begging me. I want for you to be scared enough to do anything I tell you. Anything." He inspected his buffed nails. "I know exactly what leverage will make you do anything."

Her heart tried to drill its way out of her ribs.

Beau got one of his wishes right away. The scared part was a total lock.

She couldn't hide her disgust. True, she knew about Beau's appetites and preferences. But somehow, this cold, stark room with the whole risk-of-death piece, brought the reality home in a brand-new way.

There was no way would she let him touch her. Or her child.

Between the drugs and his sadistic tendencies, she might not have many choices. Acid burned the back of her tongue.

Kiera wouldn't go down without a fight.

He licked his thin lips.

She swallowed and walked her fingers over the metal implement on the far side of the mattress.

He adjusted his shirt sleeves so the cufflinks glinted at exactly the same place on each wrist. "You choose. We can do this the easy way or the hard way. How about we start with you telling me everything you've learned about Fallen Comrades? Then we'll chitchat all about Morpheus Squad." He leaned over her, inches away from her face. "If I like what you tell me, I might let you or the baby live."

"What?" Her mind spun. What should she do? Sell out the squad and her brother's memory or put her baby at risk? A sob bubbled up. No matter what she did, her baby's life was in jeopardy. Beau's promises were hollow.

"Oh, I'd prefer to do this the nice way." His too-minty breath next to her cheek made her want to vomit. "You know, have a little fun first."

"God help me, I don't know anything." Sweat rolled between her breasts. Her baby kicked, more insistently, as if encouraging Kiera to get them both out of this place.

When she recoiled as he picked up a lock of her hair, he frowned. "You know, I always fancied brunettes. They're more mysterious, like they're hiding a delicious secret. It's good of you to change to suit my tastes. Every woman realizes that they need to conform to my preferences."

She pulled away but froze as fury warped his reddened face.

"Don't you dare move without my permission," he whispered, stroking her cheek with an icy fingertip as he rested his other hand on the mattress next to her.

Gripping the instrument, she said, "Who wants to move?" Another contraction wrapped around her midsection.

With a desperate stab of the scissors into his

planted hand, she encouraged him to step away.

Chapter Thirty-Six

"How much longer?" If Jake leaned forward any more, he'd be in the front seat and on Stumpy's lap.

What was Lequire doing to her? What was the status of the baby?

He tried to focus on the situation outside of the vehicle, but panic had removed his ability to perform even a simple cognitive task.

He gritted his teeth as Stumpy typed on the laptop and Hunt drove. They needed to move faster, but even on a Sunday the congested Atlanta traffic was slowing things down. He pressed his fisted hand to his forehead, like he could physically hold back the virus. Even now, his muscles quivered as waves of directionless power flooded all the cells.

Actually, no. He had a perfect target for his virus to unleash every last ounce of fury. Soon.

Stumpy waved a hand. "If Hunt here could drive a straight line, I would be able to focus on the screen better." A corner of his mouth lifted at the CO's scowl. He typed again and hit enter. "Right. Her signal stopped there."

"Where?" Jake snapped.

Hunt maneuvered through another slowdown. Five fucking lanes per direction and the metro still couldn't handle normal amounts of traffic.

"Hold on, I'm working as fast as I can." Stumpy typed in coordinates and pulled up an address. "Well, that's interesting. Her signal is coming from this very inconspicuous building in an office park. Property is owned by 'FC Industries.'"

"Fallen Comrades," Hunt said as he merged onto another highway.

Jake stared at the screen. "Office park?"

"One out of thousands around here." Stumpy kept typing. "Probably has a name like 'Horizon Center' or 'TechSide Business Park.' They're all basically the same idea: dead-end road with a turnaround, office buildings on either side and at the end. Sidewalks and green medians to make it seem more homey and less … business-y."

"Don't need a real estate tour," Jake said. "Tell me how to get her out of there."

Hunt spoke up. "Can you get schematics?"

"On it."

Jake turned around. A second black SUV followed close behind. Gonzo, Rodeo, and Doc.

Doc. Jake's heart pounded harder.

Stumpy scrolled through screens. "We're five minutes away. By the time we pull behind the building, I'll have plans, with options for ingress and egress, both conventional and unconventional."

"Send the address to Gonzo," Hunt said.

"Done."

"Then pinpoint her location within the building and formulate a plan to knock out any security systems they might have." Hunt navigated I-285 on the west side of Atlanta until he pulled off at the exit indicated by Stumpy. He met Jake's eyes in the mirror. "We'll get her out of there."

"Not fast enough," Jake spat.

"Understood."

Three minutes later, both vehicles stopped behind an office building 150 yards away from their target structure. The weather had turned foul as cold drizzle plinked off the hood of the SUV. Faint noises of traffic going around the I-285 loop rumbled in the background and echoed off the numerous tall glass and metal nearby.

Leaping out of the vehicle, Jake was ready to sprint out of their surveillance hide, break through the steel and glass with his bare hands, and rip Kiera out of there. His hands shook as he gripped the edge of the hood, denting the metal.

Remaining in the front seat, Stumpy worked the computers and downloaded data. Electrical schematics, floor plans, and HVAC duct and shaft diagrams flashed across the screen.

Hunt stared at the building and paced, securing and re-securing his weapons in various holsters and pockets, stopping every few minutes to mutter a question to Stumpy. Each word was punctuated with a cloud of vapor.

Damned cold snap in March in Atlanta. The temperature had dropped below freezing, and tiny ice pellets tinkled on the vehicles and leaves. Worst-case weather scenario for a technical rescue.

Doc had the back of the other SUV open, double-checking neatly labeled packets of medications and instruments. His efficient movements were at odds with the tense set of his shoulders. Last time Jake had seen him working with that much tension was when Stumpy had lost his leg.

Any other time, Doc stayed loose and fluid whenever he worked. He was the calmest person Jake knew—at least in doctor mode. Soldier mode, the guy was terrifyingly efficient.

Doc kept glancing at the building as he rolled his neck and shoulders. Shit.

Gonzo and Rodeo crouched behind a low wall, motionless and monitoring the security of their current position. Wearing a helmet with night-vision gear in place of his cowboy hat, Rodeo stared at the building like he could bring it down with a single glare.

"Well?" Jake asked.

"Got her." Stumpy clicked another few buttons. "Doc. Heart rate one hundred, oxygen level ninety-seven percent." He studied the screen. "Seventh floor."

"Out of?" Hunt asked.

"Ten."

"How do we get there?" Hunt asked.

Rodeo sighted through his gun. "Front door? Or back door?"

"Neither." Stumpy pointed at the screen. "I'm in their security feeds. There's a large group of people on the first floor, concentrated near the exits."

Jake whipped his head up and over. Too easy. Something didn't feel right.

Hunt growled. "They waiting for us?"

"Logical," Stumpy answered.

"It's nice to be wanted." Hunt's smile twisted into a nasty scowl. "Weaknesses?"

Typing, Stumpy pulled at his goatee. "Nowhere to go but up."

"Won't they see us?" Jake asked. "With thermal imaging. Plain old security cameras. Human eyeballs?"

"Our tech is low viz, high stealth to obscure what the human eye sees," Stumpy answered. "I can give their system something else to look at. Up it is."

"Yeah!" Rodeo fished in the back of an SUV for a grappling hook gun.

Jake's jaw dropped as he studied the ten-story metal and glass building. And the sleet. "No."

"It's got the least security coverage. Last place they'd expect an infiltration."

"But they have security cameras and detectors up there," Jake spat.

Stumpy nodded. "I can disable them. Actually, I could take out all of the cameras through the whole building, but it'll be too obvious. They'll know right away something's coming. I have to be choosy about what live feed I deactivate and then play bland reruns."

Jake stared at Stumpy. Bland reruns. Playing Lequire like Morpheus Squad had been played? Coincidence?

Hunt patted his vest. "Anything else?"

"Infiltrate via roof entrance, head down three flights of stairs, and take the fourth door on the right. I'll update you when I know more about what's there." Stumpy leaned forward and scowled at the screen. "Hey, Doc. Her heart rate went up to 140 for almost a minute. It's happened a few times now. Every two or three minutes, like clockwork."

Doc's quiet voice chilled Jake's blood. "She's in labor."

Chapter Thirty-Seven

Wave after wave of pain rolled through Kiera, starting from her back and clenching around her belly like a cruel vise. Over and over, the crushing gravity of agony pressed her into the bed. She couldn't change positions since Beau had zip-tied her arms to the gurney rails. She tried to count time by the contractions but lost track in the endless swirl of misery.

Whatever drug fog her brain had been swimming in had long left her system, leaving her with nothing but stark reality.

Reality sucked biscuits.

After she'd stabbed metal into Beau's hand, making blood spurt and messing up his fancy shirt, he had slapped her and pushed her back on the bed. Then he left.

The room was silent except for her pitiful whimpers.

About ten contractions later, he returned, sporting a clean shirt and a bandage on his hand. He eased the door closed until the lock clicked. His actions were too gentle. Too deliberate, even for Beau.

When he turned, he held up two syringes full of yellow liquid. Before she could question what the substance was, another contraction hit. Up, up the pain climbed, stretching the suffering higher and higher. Even breathing hurt. Then the pain plunged down to end in too-short relief. She couldn't stop sweating. Every muscle in her body endlessly tightened.

At least Beau hadn't attempted to check her for dilation. He would have lost his entire arm.

"Done with the little twinge, sweetheart?"

She grunted as she tried to suck air back into her

lungs. Tugging on her arms, she gasped as the plastic ties cut into her wrists.

"I have a treat for you." He flashed a brief smile as he paced in front of the bed. "Well, for both of us, actually."

"I don't understand."

"These." He raised the syringes. "Are courtesy of my father, Senator Lequire. Turns out, he has some interesting connections."

She stared at the liquid. "What?"

"He'll do anything to keep his re-election campaign on track. Even cave to his son's leverage. Use his security clearance to access top-secret military research facilities."

He reached out as if he wanted to pat her shoulder but stepped back. "You sure you wouldn't like to know what's in here?"

"Nope." Not interested in playing games.

Once again, the pressure in her pelvis climbed. Oh, God. The contractions were so close together. Was that normal?

She squeezed her eyes shut hard until she saw stars. Her pubic bone felt like it was breaking in two and she couldn't keep a guttural scream from bursting from her lips.

No one was coming to help her. This was so not how she planned to go through labor. Alone, imprisoned, suffering.

After she recovered a minute later, he said, "All done? Because I want you to pay attention. Your baby's future is at stake."

"Okay," she whispered. Anything. She'd do whatever it took, as long as her baby would be all right.

"Do you know what these are?"

"Again, no," she gasped.

He stepped forward and glided one capped syringe tip over her tied hand. "Sweetheart, what I have here is everything. It's power, money, and control."

"I don't understand."

"It's how I'm going to make my father proud, once and for all. I'm going to become what he's always wanted me to be."

Her brain spun, frantic, watching the syringe. If he poked her with the needle she would … what? Scream?

Wouldn't matter.

Run? Couldn't. She tugged again.

By God, she'd make him work for any torture he wanted to dish out. She would die first before he touched this child.

Had he gone nuts? "I don't understand—aaghh—"

Rocking her hips from side to side, she tried to find a position to relieve the relentless grip of the contraction. The stupid breathing exercises she had read about? Yeah, screw cleansing breaths. When one contraction stopped, the awful squeezing started up again, cranking down into tighter, harder pressure.

Was Little Bit even moving? Kiera couldn't stop writhing long enough to check. A sob lodged in her throat.

She crossed her legs and prayed that nothing would emerge from between them.

The last contraction ended on a weeping gasp.

The ending to her pain would bring a different suffering.

"Better?" Nothing in his question indicated he cared about her answer.

"Sure. Whatever." Her voice came out cracked, static-y, like a poorly tuned radio station.

"So, these little goodies"—he waved a syringe in front of her—"will be our salvation. We will be powerful together."

Pressing her head into the bed, as far away as possible, she said, "What is it?"

"Two doses of the Morpheus Virus."

She stared at him. "No."

"Yes! I'm going to take a dose, and if you don't cooperate, then you will take a dose before the baby is born."

"That's a horrible idea," she stammered. "What about—?"

His reptilian blink triggered the taste of acid on her tongue. "We'll get to find out what mainlined Morpheus Virus does to a live fetus. For research, of course."

"No."

"Well." He pressed his bandaged hand over his heart. "You'll have to help, then. Don't you want me to have power and the ability to command respect?"

"The virus doesn't earn you respect," she panted.

"Sure it does, especially when it comes to my daddy. He'll definitely respect me after I take the virus. Won't have a choice. I have the keys to his political kingdom, and he'll do anything to keep me quiet. Besides, if the virus increases men's size and stamina, just think of how much more pleasure I can give a lucky woman." He adjusted his slacks.

The next wave of nausea had nothing to do with labor.

Then another contraction climbed up and up until it finally crashed back down, leaving her panting on the bed.

"Once the virus makes me more powerful, you'll come around." His glare sent terror skittering up her spine. "If you continue to refuse, I'll find other ways to convince you. The baby. Your family. They're all at risk. I can kill any of them"—he snapped his fingers—"like that."

"Why would you want me to have the virus? Won't it make me so strong that I could escape you?"

"You'll do whatever I want if I have your baby. And for the chance at a cure, I'm betting you'll do anything I say."

"You have a cure?"

"My father does."

"Really?"

"No. Not really. But he has access to resources who can create a cure for his son. If he can get hold of a cure for me, then we'd have one for you. For junior, too."

For a split second, she considered it: giving herself to Beau as a path to save her child.

He rolled up his sleeve, Velcro'd a tourniquet above the elbow, and then lifted the syringe in a macabre toast. "Here's to Fallen Comrades' success, making my father proud, and our future together. Forever."

He jammed the needle into a vein in his arm, depressed the plunger, and released the tourniquet. "Oh, yes." His face flushed as his eyes rolled back in his head. "What a rush."

Then he froze.

Dropping to the floor, he thrashed, panting, as his ecstasy metamorphosed to pain.

She pulled on the zip ties, desperate to get out of this room.

Another contraction pummeled her, and they both curled into twin balls of misery.

Once pain no longer blurred her vision, she watched as Beau, off-balance and sweating, slowly crawled back toward her bed, inch by terrible inch. He clawed at his head like he wanted to rip it off. His animal snarls made hairs rise on the back of her neck. The man who had to always be in control had lost all restraint.

In one hand, he carried the second uncapped syringe.

Beau's bloodshot eyes appeared over the side of the bed a few inches away from her. She pushed back.

No place to go.

Then a hard contraction seized her body hard enough for sound to fade away.

Her legs jackknifed around her tight abdomen.

Tears slipped out as she tried to clamp down on a scream and failed.

Beau grabbed her arm.

Chapter Thirty-Eight

Grappling hooks sailed over the lip of the building's roof and seated with *clanks* and tooth-grinding metal *scritches*.

Silently, Jake and the team clipped on jumar ascenders and shimmied up ten stories. Each man moved like a ghost floating up a sheer wall. He had forgotten how well-trained his teammates were. Gonzo, Rodeo, Hunt, and Doc slithered over the edge, unhooked from the cables, and pulled out their weapons. Rodeo slid around the edge of the roof and took out the two patrolling security personnel with his silenced Sig, the breezy *pops* barely audible.

Jake clambered over the roof edge, his foot slipping on the icy rim. He pitched toward the sheer drop-off, heart thundering in his chest. Grabbing the frigid, slick metal, he managed to take a few breaths.

Shit.

It had been a while since he last practiced this maneuver. *Pay attention. Get to Kiera.*

In silence, Jake unclipped the ascender and pulled the wire up, coiling it neatly next to the other piles. He could barely make out what the other team members were doing. Their movements appeared as mere blurs in the shadows.

After a com check with Stumpy, who monitored the building's security systems from the ground, they all got in position. As one, they moved across the tar and gravel roof, their booted footsteps making no sound. Every instinct urged Jake to sprint ahead and rip the building apart to find Kiera. His virus rose and flared. He wanted in there. Wanted her in his arms and away from Lequire. Now. Even in the night, his vision turned red.

He fought to concentrate on Hunt's hand signals.

In silent unison, the men slunk to either side of the access door. Gonzo flipped up his night-vision goggles and fished around in a pocket. He took out an electronic gadget, stuck a probe to the lock, and with a few pushed buttons, the keypad light turned green. The door opened inward to darkness.

They froze.

No alarm. First hurdle cleared.

Stumpy remained one electronic step ahead.

Hunt led the way. Their muffled steps scraped on the concrete and echoed off the hollow walls of the stairwell. Every tiny sound activated Jake's nerves. Each door they passed could hold someone barging through to try and stop them.

Let them try. Pulverizing anyone who got in his way would be a pleasure.

He gnashed his teeth at the slow and deliberate progress as the group wound slowly down the flights of stairs. After what—minutes? hours?—they reached the seventh-floor landing.

No one moved.

Hunt held a hand up until the electronic lock on the door flashed green, then he slowly opened the metal door into an empty, lit corridor.

The men all flipped up their night-vision goggles.

At a dubious glance at the security camera, Hunt motioned the team to follow him down the hall.

Hopefully, Stumpy could keep feeding the system fake footage.

This mission was too easy. Too easy.

Jake's head whipped back and forth.

Past three more doors, they approached their target destination.

In silence, Rodeo and Gonzo readied their guns

for entry into the room.

Hunt raised his fist again.

Jake's heart thudded double time as every muscle in his body tensed.

"Guys, stop!" Stumpy's voice crackled through their earpieces. "Don't move. Goddamn it. *Stop!*"

No one so much as breathed.

The voice in their earpieces continued. "Whatever you do, don't fire your weapons on this floor. Repeat. Do *not* fire weapons." Clicking of computer keys blended with static for a few seconds. "Shit, shit, shit."

Jake didn't move. He didn't breathe.

Kiera?

"Holy fuck, I knew it was too simple. The reason you had no problems getting here and there's no welcome wagon? This floor is fucking rigged." Tapping punctuated his harsh breaths through the com. "Here's the deal: any gunfire will set off a shit-ton of explosives. The bombs are wired into special pressure detectors in the ceiling. If you shoot, every last one of you—including Kiera—will die. The entire building may go."

Jake's head heated up. His heart pounded. He carefully replaced the safety on his gun and eased the Sig back into his thigh holster. The other men followed suit.

Explosives. Kiera. The baby. A trickle of sweat down his temple tormented him, but he didn't move.

A security guard came around a corner at the end of the hall, about forty feet away. No one moved.

Right as the man opened his mouth to yell, Rodeo whipped out a short, sharp knife and hurled it with cold precision into the man's left eye with a muffled *thunk*. The guard dropped. Rodeo peered back at the team and grinned. "Who needs a gun?"

Shit.

No one else was in sight in the corridor. Made

sense. Fewer victims if explosions happened. Besides, what kind of security did a very pregnant woman require?

Not much, if she was incapacitated.

Muffled voices came from the other side of the door before them.

Then a gut-wrenching scream emanated from within the room and virtually shredded Jake's spinal cord.

Chapter Thirty-Nine

Fuck going slow and steady.

Jake exploded into the room, shucking off control of his virus as he burst through the metal door and ripped it from the hinges. His shoulder and chest muscles popped and grew, braiding joy and horror together and sucking up even more viral strength as it coursed through every cell of his body.

His ability to think fled. His vision bled red.

His teammates flowed into the room behind him, Rodeo securing their exit.

Through the haze, he saw her. On the bed, a small figure in a blue top writhed and screamed.

Looming over Kiera was a man in slacks and a button-down shirt. Lequire. He wielded a syringe filled with liquid. He pressed the point into her arm. Zip ties bit into her skin as she strained away from him.

A wave of déjà vu stopped Jake. Flashes of a similar syringe, used on a base in Afghanistan, in an empty clinic room, flooded his mind.

All sounds blended into a dull buzz. His entire world narrowed down to Kiera.

Through a rictus of pain, she popped open her eyes wide.

The needle tip pierced her skin. A dot of blood bloomed red on red within Jake's altered vision.

Her scream arrowed into his soul.

In two steps, he bounded across the room, horse-collaring Lequire and flinging him away from her. Shit, the guy was solid. Off-balance, Lequire windmilled and crashed into the opposite wall, the syringe falling out of his hand and rolling across the floor. A drop of liquid clung to the needle tip.

Kill.

Jake stalked over to Lequire and unleashed his viral strength, pummeling the ever-loving hell out of the man. Every connection of his fist into the bastard's flesh? Relief. Bliss. Release. Bizarre communion with the virus, and God help him, it felt fucking amazing. Between the roar in his ears and the film clouding his vision, he had one goal: grind Lequire into a pulp. The crunches of bone and sprays of blood satisfied Jake's ravenous virus. Every time the man fell, Jake propped him up again for another blow.

Through the rush of destruction, a high cry penetrated his altered hearing. He glanced back and paused. Kiera struggled on the bed. Doc approached her. It took Jake several seconds to process the situation.

Kiera. In pain.

The baby's life at risk.

Beau's fault. He stared at Beau's mangled face then whipped his head back up and stared at Kiera's desperate shriek.

Wasn't even a decision.

He dropped Lequire's body to the floor with a thud, but the man staggered to his feet and wiped blood from the corner of his snarling mouth. And laughed.

Impossible.

The force of the impacts from Jake's enhanced upper-body strength should have killed a normal person. Even his teammates couldn't withstand the full power of his fists.

Kiera cried out again.

"Hunt?" The word ripped out of Jake's mouth, a shredded, incomplete sound.

"On it," his CO growled, right behind Jake. "Gonzo? Incapacitate Lequire."

"With pleasure, boss." Gonzo strode over and

pulled a knife.

"Ah, ah. Don't do that," Lequire snickered. "Booby trap. If I die, this place blows. Kill switch is keyed to the presence of my heart rate."

"Boss?" Gonzo said.

"The fuck," Hunt snarled. "Jake, get Kiera out of here now."

"You won't be able to kill me," Beau snickered.

Jake turned back to Kiera and tore through the zip ties like they were paper.

She immediately curled into a ball and trembled.

"Kiera," he whispered.

She flinched and moaned. He had to get her out of here.

The only thing grounding him through his mental fog was Kiera's sweet face, creased with pain. When she looked at him, those hazel eyes controlled the rage inside of him. Brought the monster to heel. Color seeped back into his vision.

Hunt hollered into the com, "Stumpy! Kill switch status on Lequire."

Beau rotated and stretched his neck like he was popping back into place. A bloody grin cut across his bruised face. "Gentlemen. You can stay and try to take me out, but I promise you, it won't be easy. Then you'll all die."

While Hunt and Gonzo cornered a seething Lequire, who grew larger with each passing minute, Jake turned his attention back to Kiera. He rested a hand on her shoulder, and she recoiled, her wounded cry gutting him.

"Kiera, I'm here," he murmured.

She lifted her head, then let it drop back on the bed. "Jake?" she whispered, squinting up at him through puffy eyes.

Tendrils of damp hair stuck to her forehead, and she clutched at her stomach and moaned. With shaking hands, he wiped her brow.

Doc ran his hands over her in a rapid assessment, making quick work of a stethoscope and another handheld device briefly placed on her abdomen.

"Doc?" Her voice cracked like breaking glass.

Or Jake's shattering heart.

Doc frowned. "We're getting you out of here, Kiera. Right now. Your job is to breathe through the contractions. We'll take care of the rest."

"Okay." She reached up. "Jake? You're here. How—" Her trembling fingers on his jaw felt like heaven and hell.

"I'm not leaving you." When Jake grabbed her icy hand, she clutched at him like he was a lifeline.

"Move!" Hunt called from his position next to Gonzo and Lequire.

It took everything in Jake not to crush her delicate fingers. Damned virus had gone all haywire, wanting to destroy and protect at the same time. He blinked, and the red filter went back into place. Jolts of viral energy continued to pour through his muscles.

"The baby?" Tears leaked from the corners of her eyes as they helped her sit up.

Doc pressed on her abdomen, too calm. "We'll take care of the situation."

He hadn't answered her question.

It took all of Jake's willpower not to walk over and end Lequire.

Hunt shoved his knee into Lequire's spine and sat on him while Gonzo trussed the man with thick metal zip ties, using at least ten of the ligatures for arms and legs.

When Lequire opened his mouth to yell, Gonzo temporarily shut him up with a rage-filled hammer fist which left Lequire sprawled halfway on his back. His buddy's eyes had gone feral. Good. About time someone else besides Jake lost control.

Stumpy's voice crackled through the earpiece. "Incoming. First-floor security team headed your way."

Hunt turned to Gonzo. "Stop. We can't transport him out of here and can't end him right away." He pulled his serrated Gerber Mark II from his lower leg sheath and plunged it into Lequire's chest. "With luck, he'll take a few minutes to bleed out," he gritted out the words.

Fuck.

Hunt spoke into the earpiece. "Prepare for extraction. And incoming fire."

Doc and the CO exchanged a look that chilled Jake's blood.

In an economy of movement, Hunt slid out the door and back into the hallway, followed by Gonzo.

When Kiera stood up, another contraction hit, and she cried out. Her death grip on Jake's arm was solid.

Doc murmured to her, his voice soothing and insistent at the same time. "Kiera, I need you to move quickly. I know it's hard with the contractions, but you have to try. We'll help."

With an expression that blended pure misery and determination, she nodded. Jake wanted to hug her.

Then he wanted to disembowel Beau Lequire.

Time for payback later.

Jake swung her into his unnaturally strong arms and half walked, half ran from the room and down the hall. Rodeo took rear guard behind them.

As they entered the stairwell, she stiffened and clamped her jaw shut, muscles standing out stark on her neck. She grabbed a fistful of Jake's shirt and tucked her head into his shoulder with a muffled cry.

Something primal and powerful expanded inside

him. A moment of pure clarity. Yes, he wanted to be the one she turned to when she was hurting. He needed to be the one who took away her pain. The one who defended her from everything bad in the world.

After breathing hard for forty-five seconds, she let out a shuddering whoosh of air and a groan. Sweat rolled down her forehead, but at Doc's murmured encouragement, she clung to Jake as he kept climbing stairs.

Hunt and Gonzo opened the door to the roof while Jake, Kiera, and Doc rushed through.

The stairwell ten stories below exploded with shouts.

"Go!" Hunt yelled.

They raced into the sleet and sprinted to the edge of the roof.

Gonzo jammed his grappling hook under the slick lip of the roof. After flinging the coil out into the night, he threaded a figure-of-eight rappel device, clipped it to his harness, and flew over the edge of the roof with a high-pitched whine of metal on wire.

Rodeo knelt behind a utility vent halfway between the access door and the edge of the roof and took aim. "I assume firearms are okay now, boss?"

"Do whatever the fuck you have to," Hunt said as he quickly threaded equipment.

Jake clipped his rappel device into the front of his harness.

Hunt touched his ear. "Stumpy says they're on the sixth floor. We've got less than a minute. They're going to start exiting from the bottom of the building soon." He looked up. "Rodeo, you copy?"

The silent man gave a thumbs-up as he remained in a rigid position, Sig aimed at the access door. Rodeo was a deadly shot, even before the Morpheus Virus enhanced the speed and accuracy of his precision. No one dumb enough to come through that door had a hope of survival.

"Let's go, fellas," Hunt said. "No time to get a harness on her. Go, Jake."

Jake stared at his CO. Then he looked down.

Ten stories. With an unharnessed pregnant woman. In icy conditions. Fuck.

Shouts transmitted through the access door.

Jake pressed his palms to either side of her head. "Kiera, you have to hang on to me for all your worth, got it? It's the only way." He prayed his strength would be enough.

"You've got to be kidding." She gasped, peering over the edge.

"Gonzo will control the rope and slow us down. I will keep you from falling."

Hunt motioned to him. "Stop talking. Go. Now."

With a weak nod, she faced his side and wrapped trembling arms around Jake's neck. When she twined her legs around his waist, awkward with her belly, he used his free hand to steady himself as he sat on the edge of the roof, Hunt securing the hook.

Jake's hand slipped on the icy rime, and he dug his fingertips in to hold on. The metal bent and creaked under his grip. He allowed his rage to rocket every last bit of the virus's power into his upper body.

He looked down at the ground.

Fuck.

He locked his other arm under her butt.

Doc threw the wire down the side of the building as Hunt maintained the hook's placement.

Jake never had problems with heights, but that was before he had to carry Kiera down ten stories without any safety device on her.

Footsteps and shouts grew louder behind the access door.

"There's going to be a little drop, okay?" he whispered and let go of the roof edge.

They fell.

Chapter Forty

They fell…

For six feet until the rope went taut.

The free-fall and sudden stop stole Kiera's breath.

Curling her body around her belly and Jake, she hung on with everything she had, arms shaking.

Pressing her chest into his, she manacled her arms around his chest and back. Over his shoulder, she stared out into the night. Gonzo was a mere speck on the ground below them.

A gurgle escaped her lips, and he tightened his arms around her. Her belly was squished between them, stealing her breath.

Without Jake holding on to her, she would be dangling from a rope.

No. Without him, she would be dead.

"Hang on, honey." The rumbling growl of his voice bolstered her nonexistent confidence.

The sway and shift of his thick legs as he walked them down the side of the building? Terrifying, but safer than that hellhole.

On the ground, Gonzo adjusted the rope tension and lowered them quickly.

They might do this.

Another contraction hit.

Her entire body tensed again, and she clenched her arms. Anything to hold on. All she wanted to do was curl up in a ball. "Help," she cried, every muscle in her belly on fire.

"I've got you." Over a hundred feet off the ground, icy pellets pinging into her, with armed killers about to attack, his voice gave her hope.

As they passed by a window, Jake's foot slipped

out from his braced position on the wall.

She yelped as they rotated and careened to the side. Their collective weight landed square on his shoulder as they crashed into the metal window frame.

His grip loosened.

She bit back a scream.

He grunted, but kept his arms locked firmly around her.

Hold on. Hold on, she pleaded to her trembling arms as the contraction continued. *Do this for Little Bit. Almost there.*

After a few more seconds, the pressure in her belly eased off.

A few seconds more? Solid ground. Her knees buckled under her, but Jake held her upright as he unclipped his rope.

Hunt and Doc whizzed down right behind them.

Kiera's legs wobbled. She rested her forehead on his chest, wanting to kiss him. Wanting to stay in his arms. Wanting him to never let go of her. Ever.

"Go!" Hunt bellowed into the com and looked up at the structure. "Rodeo! Damn it, move your ass."

Out of a cloud of sparking light and a hail of gunfire, a shadowy figure launched himself over the side of the building and slid down the rope.

The second his feet hit the ground, Rodeo ran toward them, flinging a smoking leather glove to the ground with a rakish grin.

A burst of bullets thudded into the wet ground as they sprinted toward the building that hid the two black SUVs. Jake swung Kiera back into his arms and hunched around her. Doc kept a hand on her shoulder and protected their flank.

Once at the vehicle, Jake set her down, flung open the back door, and shoved her in. Awkward and off-balance, she scrambled over to the far side.

Doc dove into the front seat, and Rodeo had his foot pressed on the gas before the doors closed. No one took off their harnesses. They simply buckled into the seats. Nearby, Stumpy's vehicle was already rolling as Hunt and Gonzo vaulted into front and back seats.

Jake tugged at her to lean toward him.

Another contraction folded her in half. Good God, was that awful, beaten animal sound coming from her? He cradled her head in his lap as the car lurched around a tight corner.

She peeked up at him once the contraction ended. "Are they coming after us?" she whispered.

He shifted with a rattle of gear. "Yeah. Stumpy says there are guys pouring out of the front entrance. Another group on the roof." He leaned forward. "Rodeo, man, they're pulling out in vehicles. Let's get lost in a hurry."

Doc talked into the radio, "Roger." He motioned to Rodeo. "We're splitting up. Stumpy's going to try and draw the pursuers away from us."

Kiera's heart hammered against her ribs. *God, please let this baby be okay.*

With the next contraction, the voices around her became muffled as she saw double.

In the backseat of the SUV, her reality split into two agonizing pieces: during and not-during contractions. On and on it went.

Her anchor in the waves of pain tossing her body in all directions?

Jake.

Solid. Steady.

Right there.

She opened her mouth to speak, but the words got lost in another burst of pressure threatening to rip her apart.

****

As Kiera groaned every two minutes like clockwork, Rodeo maneuvered the vehicle through several suburbs, weaving in and out of traffic, and making sudden turns onto different highways that flipped Jake's stomach upside-down. With the icy drizzle pinging off the windshield, Jake expected to skid off the road at every jolt and lurch. One wrong swerve on the slick roads and they could all die. He kept his arms wrapped around Kiera, like his own life depended on it.

Because, hell, his life did depend on her survival.

Rodeo found a balance between speed and safety. Once they were certain no one followed them, Rodeo hauled ass on a deserted secondary road.

Free.

They were safe. She was going to be okay.

He exhaled as Atlanta flew by them. Color returned to the world around him.

His head lolled against the seat back. Tension seeped out of his muscles.

They'd done it. She was safe. Mission accomplished. He closed his eyes and took a big, deep breath, enjoying the relaxing exhale.

Then the most god-awful scream he'd ever heard burst from Kiera's lips, shattering his calm into shards of razor-sharp terror.

"Oh, no!" she called out. "My, my—"

Doc swiveled around.

Jake stared down at her shaking frame.

She lifted her hand from her lap. Damp.

Chapter Forty-One

Jake knew very little about pregnancy, but he sure the fuck knew that wetness *down there* wasn't good. At least not while they were doing fifty-five on a county road in icy conditions.

Shit.

Rodeo glanced in the rearview mirror, the whites of his eyes stark in the reflection of his dark face. "Guys, is there a problem?"

Doc shrugged. "Amniotic fluid."

Rodeo sputtered, "Fuck that shit in the same zip code as me. I am burning this car after we get home."

At her next brutal contraction, Doc said to Jake, "I need your help here. Now."

Here? Now? No.

Doc called out rapid-fire orders.

Jake unbuckled and scrambled to obey, movements awkward with the harness still attached and their gear taking up too much space. He banged his elbows and knees against the roof and sides of the vehicle.

Somehow, he managed to fold down one of the back seats down, scoot Kiera over on top of it, and shove supplies far back and to the side. Taking care not to hurt her, he crawled across and folded down the other side until he had both seats down, creating a larger flat area.

After pulling the front passenger seat forward as far as it would go, Doc then clambered into the back of the SUV, yanked over a large canvas bag, laid out supplies on a folded seat back, and flipped on a compact machine. He pressed a probe to her belly. Whooshing beeps filled the vehicle. Eerie sounding. A digital representation of life. Faster than Jake's heart rate.

Sweat broke out on his upper lip.

As the vehicle careened around a curve, Kiera bit down on another scream. The terror on her pale face… Jake would never forget it.

"Oh, my God. Baby coming!" she gasped.

The beeping sound slowed down. Jake knew nothing about baby monitoring, but his heart sank along with the lower tones.

"You're going to be fine," he crooned, trying to project a calm confidence.

He was about to throw up.

Also, the unanswered question remained: no one knew how an exposed baby would do.

Exposed? Hell, that kid was conceived by sperm permeated with Morpheus Virus.

That kid? No. *His* child. His.

Doc called over his shoulder as he shrugged out of his vest, "Rodeo, fold the front seat toward the dash. I need more room."

"Roger." Keeping one hand on the wheel, Rodeo reached over and pulled the lever, cramming the seat back up against the dashboard. Not missing a beat, he then signaled a lane change and smoothly steered the vehicle onto a two-lane state highway.

"Where are we going?" Kiera asked in between contractions.

"The compound," Jake said.

She grabbed a strap on his protective vest. "No! Beau… He knows where the compound is."

Doc shook his head. "Second compound. Morpheus Squad had a plan B."

By now, the original empty compound would be ash, if Curly had completed his work on schedule.

The beeps from the monitor seemed very fast. Too fast? Doc met Jake's stare.

"Do you want a hospital?" Doc asked Kiera, snapping on vinyl gloves with crisp efficiency.

"Yes, but won't Beau find me in a hospital?" Her voice, ragged and desperate, ripped through Jake.

Doc's nod, a mere shifting of shadows in the lights of passing headlights, iced Jake's veins. "Possibly. But if you want a hospital, we'll go to one. We'll make it work."

Their cover would be blown wide open, too. Jake didn't care. He'd trade his freedom for this baby's life.

"Can you take care of everything, Doc?" she panted. "Will the baby be all right?"

"It's safer in a hospital. But I don't know if we'll get there in time." He blinked. "I have delivered babies before and am trained to take care of newborns. If you're okay with the fact that I'm neither an Ob-Gyn nor a pediatrician, then yes, I can do this. It's your call."

"No, will the baby. Be. All. Right?" she cried. "With the virus."

"Seems to be doing okay right now," Doc answered.

Another non-answer.

"Good enough for me—" Another contraction had her puffing hard and groaning.

"At the end of this contraction, let's scoot your pants off," Doc said.

Damn, he was calm. The guy said it like he was commenting on paint color or the weather.

"We're really having the baby? Here. Now." she gasped.

"Here? Now?" Rodeo hollered, voice in soprano range.

"Shut up, Rodeo," Doc snapped.

His teammate clamped his mouth shut and stared at the road in front of him.

Doc turned back to Kiera. "Not so much *we*. More like *you*. I will help. You're having this baby. Soon."

With his assistance, she shoved the jeans leggings and underwear down and away. Doc positioned a thick cloth and plastic pad underneath her and placed a papery drape over her bare hips and bent legs.

Jake's head spun. By God, he would not pass out, but fuck him sideways, they were really going to do this right here in the car.

What about his damned viral monster who gave Jake his super strength? That lily-livered bastard wanted no part in this clusterfuck, cowardly little shit.

As the SUV rumbled and lurched onto the shoulder of the road with a stomach-turning swerve, Doc barked at Rodeo. "Eyes on the road, soldier! You have one job: don't get in an accident."

"Roger that!" The vehicle made a violent swoop back onto pavement, sending Jake's heart into a nosedive.

Shit. Doc, yelling? Never happened, unless things were going south in a hurry.

"Crank up the heat, Rodeo!" Doc turned on a headlamp he had positioned on his forehead. "Make it a sauna in here."

With a gloved hand, he examined Kiera. Lines formed next to his mouth. "You're completely dilated, baby is almost here."

She panted. "I could have told you th—" Another squealing scream burst from her lips.

Holy shit. The death squeeze she gave his arm? Impressive. This woman could choke out a grown man with that much strength.

"All right. Bear down, Kiera. Good job. Excellent." Doc's voice became low and comforting, almost singsong, relaxing everyone in the vehicle.

Well, maybe not Rodeo, if the whites-of-the-eyes horror reflected in the mirror was any indication.

Memories swamped Jake.

Images of Kiera's pregnancy loss back in high school, his ex-wife's cries of despair and tear-streaked face, Kiera's current terror and pain—all barreled into him with a one-two punch of past and present which left him reeling.

Air burned his lungs. He grabbed the handle of the back door. He wanted to run.

Instead, he turned and cradled Kiera on his lap, brushing the matted hair back from her sweaty forehead. Screw his personal demons.

Could he do right now what he couldn't before: stick with her, no matter what happened?

No matter the outcome.

The baby's heart rate slowed down. *Beepbeepbeep. Beepbeep. Beep.*

Beep…

Fear choked him.

Beep…

The shit that was important to him crystallized in a split second. And what was most important in his life screamed bloody murder from the back of a speeding SUV.

What about their future?

Right about now, he couldn't give two fucks about any future beyond the next minute because there was a human being coming out of Kiera.

Her next scream filled the car and then some. His ears were probably bleeding.

"There you go," Doc encouraged her. "You're doing great, Kiera."

How in the hell could he remain so calm? Was he

on pills? Could he share?

"Keep going, Kiera. Push, honey," Jake babbled. He had no idea what all he said, only that he didn't want things to get worse.

Worse?

She was cranking out a baby who may or may not be affected by a top-secret military virus, while lying in the back of a moving vehicle as it traveled on icy roads at a high rate of speed. There weren't many ways it could be worse.

Actually…

In a burst of paranoia, he glanced out the back window. Okay. Good. No one followed them.

"One more time, Kiera," Doc crooned.

Her grunt and primal scream rattled the glass in the windows and made acid churn in his gut. Kiera clamped down on Jake's arm and made an admirable effort to do a full sit-up with him attached.

He felt a silent shifting sensation as her body tensed and then relaxed on a big whoosh of exhaled breath.

Doc's shoulders and arms moved vigorously as he grabbed towels and a round, plastic squeegee thing.

Silence. Except for the rasp of cloth on wet skin as he worked. A few presses of the squeegee bulb *blurped* in the quiet vehicle.

Jake couldn't breathe.

Oh, shit.

"Doc?" Kiera panted.

Doc didn't look up. Kept moving his hands back and forth. His shoulders had gone tense. His jaw went hard.

Her head lolled back on Jake's lap. "Is she okay? Jake? Please, tell me."

Doc reached for another towel.

He continued working, big hands chafing a tiny body.

Please let the baby be okay. Please.

The bulb thingy made more noises as Doc suctioned again.

Silence filled the hot SUV.

"Please, is she all right?" Kiera's voice cracked.

Jake caught sight of a tiny pasty-white arm.

He stared at that arm as sweat rolled down his neck.

Then a feeble, thin cry emitted from the wiggling baby.

His baby.

Kiera gasped and squeezed Jake's hand.

Then their fighting baby grabbed a solid lungful of air and screamed for all she was worth. Jake winced. Like mother like daughter. The best fucking sound he had ever heard in his entire life.

Two tiny feet kicked in the air. Doc did a clamp and cut routine with the umbilical cord.

Doc's shoulders relaxed. Sweat dripped off his chin. "Can I put her on your skin, Kiera? It will help keep her warm."

"Yes, anything she needs," she said, her voice hoarse.

With Jake's help, she lifted her shirt and reached for the kicking, mewling baby. Doc opened a reflective heat blanket and tucked it over the baby and around Kiera.

While Doc finished his work down below, Jake stared in amazement at Kiera and her living, breathing baby girl.

His baby girl.

Something was wrong with his eyes. He had to keep blinking away blurriness.

"You did it," he said, leaning over to drop a kiss on Kiera's damp forehead.

Her head lolled back on his lap. "All because of you and the guys." Her chin quivered. "If I were still there…"

"Shh, we're not going to think about that."

"How did you find me?" she whispered.

He smiled. "I'd love to take credit, but Stumpy gave you wearable GPS tech."

"Wow." As she nuzzled the baby, Kiera's amber gaze went liquid. She cupped the baby's head. "Oh, my gosh, look at her hair. She's got so much. I wish Mateo was here to see her. He would have been the best uncle."

Mateo. A lead weight dropped into the pit of Jake's stomach, and he swallowed. "Yeah, and she's beautiful, like her mother."

Still terrified that the virus would make him do something stupid, he stroked his daughter's soft, round cheek. But carefully. He had to be so gentle. Why did his fingers shake?

"Thank you, Jake. So much." She lifted her head from his lap. "You too, guys."

"Happy to help," Doc said, a relieved smile the only betrayal of emotion. "Rodeo, you good up there?"

With a weak wave of his hand and an incoherent whimper, his teammate remained strictly facing forward, gripping the steering wheel.

Doc rolled up the waste into a plastic bag and placed a special stretchy undergarment on Kiera. "All done. Um, you'll have to use the sheet for now." He tucked the drape around her hips and knees and leaned back on the folded front seat.

"Works for me." She beamed at her cooing baby.

Her face glowed in a way Jake had craved since the day he'd first met Kiera.

He'd lost his chance before. He had almost lost his chance again tonight. There was no guarantee of a future together. Not after what he'd said to her.

Something twisted in his chest. He made a silent promise to at minimum be there for this baby and Kiera for as long as he possibly could.

Lequire was still out there, enhanced with the virus. The guy was even more dangerous and unhinged. Morpheus Squad's mission to destroy Fallen Comrades wasn't even close to over yet. Kiera's family was still in danger. The team had work to do.

For now, though, Jake would enjoy the brief peace, for as long as it lasted.

But before he started his work of keeping Kiera and her baby safe, and before he helped the team destroy Lequire…

Jake had one more mission to complete.

Chapter Forty-Two

"Hey, buddy. I know we haven't talked in a long time, and for that, I'm sorry." Jake stared at the decorative urn he'd carried into the woods behind the burnt-down Atlanta house.

Less than a week since the explosion, the air near the house still carried the scent of fire. Kiera had escaped a horrible death.

Mateo had not.

Thanks to Stumpy's computer work, Jake had become Mateo's next of kin, which allowed him to claim the remains.

But Morpheus Squad still had to remain secret, so Mateo couldn't have an actual funeral. As much as Jake wanted to, he couldn't let any of Mateo's real family members know what happened. For now, his friend had to literally stay a ghost.

There was no way Jake would walk away without laying his friend to rest. The woods behind the house Mateo and Kiera had lived in during their mission was as good a place as any for last respects. Even the mid-March sunlight filtered through the trees this morning, picking up bright sprigs of early green grass, iris shoots, and spring leaves on the trees. A perfect day to be outside.

Mateo would have loved it.

Jake sat on a fallen tree near a creek and carefully set the urn on a flat rock. Dropping his head in his hands, he calmed his churning thoughts. At least he'd taken a dose of antidote as soon as they reached the new compound.

He stared at the receptacle with its muted but elegant design. Amazing how a life could be boiled down to such a small object. "I need to discuss some things with you. About me. And Kiera." He glanced at the sky. "I'm hoping you can run this past Brady, while you're up there, my friend."

Lifting his head, he continued. "So you know how Kiera was pregnant with my child? Yeah. Well, that woman is amazing. She gave birth to a beautiful baby girl. Thank God that child didn't get my ugly mug." He pushed hair back off his forehead. "We have the cutest kid on Earth. All the worry about the virus? Baby is perfect. Strong and brave. For your part in caring for Kiera during your mission together, thank you."

His voice cracked as he picked a few pieces of grass and slowly tore the blades into pieces. "You would have been an amazing uncle, Mateo. Tell Brady he would have been, too." Under his ribs, a sucking emptiness carved out more space inside of him. "Mateo, I wish I'd been there when you and Hunt set up the team stateside. It's amazing what you created. We're going to help other vets and help our country, but without being government lab rats or pawns ever again."

He tossed the pieces of grass to the leaf-strewn ground and propped his elbows on bent knees. "Brady's digging might have cost him his life, but you used his intelligence to infiltrate Fallen Comrades. What you both uncovered… Not only do we have a chance to destroy Fallen Comrades and take down Lequire, but we may get to have some fun screwing with the U.S. Government. Maybe unearth some shady Bratva connections. Once it's all done—and done properly—we'll shut down the department that did this to us. All of this happened because of you."

Jake picked at the bark next to where he sat. Clearing his throat, he said, "So, about Kiera. I would gladly lay my life down for her and the baby. The mistakes I've made, shit, you would be impressed by what a colossal fuckup I've been." The words rolled out of him. "I got stuck not-handling my past baggage to see the amazing woman in front of me. My mistakes almost cost Kiera her life."

He swallowed. "I came here to lay you to rest and to make peace with Brady. But I also want to say this to you both: I will spend the rest of my life making up for past mistakes. Keeping Kiera and her baby safe should be job one.

"I'd love to know if you approve, but I'm not going to get an answer and the reason why sucks. It's also up to Kiera to decide if she wants me in her life." He stood up and scuffed his boot on a tree root. "What I'd give to talk with you one more time, buddy. Both of you."

Jake rotated in a circle, taking in a deep breath. Fresh air and rustling leaves swirled around him. When he turned back around, a blue jay perched on the top of the urn. With a cock of its head to the side, the bird blinked a dark eye and flew away.

A single blue feather remained.

Well, blue jays were some of the fiercest protectors, like Mateo.

Jake picked up the feather and the urn. With a smile, he looked up to the sky. Jake wouldn't take the message lightly.

Chapter Forty-Three

With a sigh, Kiera leaned back in the wooden rocking chair while little Mattie made smacking noises as she fed. Her baby's warm skin against hers was the most perfect feeling in the whole world. Thank God they had a safe place to go after the first compound had been shut down. How was it only a week ago?

The living room she sat in, like the rest of the new compound, was built into a limestone cave system.

The entire structure was an engineering feat. Turned out, Mateo had a hand in the creation of this second Morpheus Squad base as well.

She'd always wondered what he had been working on in Atlanta, staying up late those many nights. His computer screen had been full of blueprints and schematics, and when she'd asked, he always told her, "A little side project."

According to Hunt, Mateo had hit *send* several months ago, and the rest was history, as the skillfully honed walls of the structure attested.

Some side project. She looked out a window set perfectly into solid rock and took in the vivid green foliage, still glinting with morning dew.

Kiera pulled the quilt around Mattie. A nearby unit emitted cozy heat that warmed the stone enough to make the dwelling comfortable on chilly days.

The property was located deep in forested mountains around Jefferson, North Carolina, several hours north of the first compound.

No need to use radar-blocking material. The solid rock above them provided perfect cover. The new compound contained several bedrooms and private living areas, as well as the ubiquitous strategy room, complete with a kitchen, dining area, and group work area.

Stumpy had all of his computer equipment set up, exactly the way he wanted it. He would have the security cameras and motion detectors operational within the next few days. Still upset about the security breach at the first compound, he labored for hours to ensure the system would be impervious to a breach this time around.

The small clinic area had been restocked to Doc's specifications. He was in his element, organizing all the labeled supplies into neat bins on shelves. With a few modifications, the large exam room could convert into an operating room suite or a hospital bay for several patients.

God willing, they'd never see any casualties. Her heart skidded a few beats. The team hadn't heard from Pele in over twenty-four hours, and Beau's men had been spotted near Reagan's workplace. *Trust Pele*, the guys said. *He's a professional.* Easier said than done. Kiera couldn't wait for the nightmare with Beau to end.

She looked down at her daughter's sweet face. How long had it been since Mattie's birth? Kiera ticked off her fingers. Six days.

Doc had examined Mattie every day, measuring her weight and length and checking her heart and lungs. He monitored for jaundice or other complications of being born a few weeks early. For her part, Mattie ignored the fact that she was slightly preterm and thrived with the attention and love.

Speaking of attention, Kiera cringed as she adjusted a piece of pink frill erupting out of Mattie's pink onesie. Gonzo made a show of reluctantly volunteering again when it came time to shop for baby clothes. From the looks of it, the guy had cleared out every pink piece of zero- to six-month clothing from the local big box store.

The guys were wrapping up work developing the interior of the structure. Even though they had to focus on getting the compound functional, it was obvious by their conversations that they wanted to return to their original mission: take down Fallen Comrades, destroy Beau Lequire, and unearth the government and foreign dealings.

The comment Lequire had made about his father having access to the development of a cure for the Morpheus Virus? Maybe there was a chance of normal lives for the guys.

She stroked her daughter's soft cheek and silky strawberry-blonde hair. Doc had run numerous tests. No evidence at all of any problems due to the Morpheus Virus.

Mateo and Brady would have loved to see Mattie. A catch hit Kiera right in the chest, and she rolled her head to the side. She hadn't had time to mourn the loss of her brother or her mission partner.

She shifted Mattie to suckle at the other breast and tucked the quilt back around her.

There was unfinished business between Kiera and Jake. But if the future comprised of only Mattie and her against the world, then so be it.

She could find a job in accounting. Once things settled down with Fallen Comrades and exposing Beau Lequire, she could move back to Chattanooga where her father lived, or disappear into a small town and create a life there.

She sighed, a dull pain in her chest.

Mattie fell asleep, and Kiera dabbed a bit of milk from her daughter's mouth and then pulled her own shirt closed. Rolling her eyes at Mattie's pink disaster of an outfit, Kiera wrapped her in the pink satin-trimmed receiving blanket. With flowers on it, no less. Tucking the swaddled form into her arms, she pushed the chair into a slow rocking motion while gazing out the window.

The sound of a small waterfall cascading next to the cave dwelling provided a peaceful background noise. The stream gave them fresh drinking water. Better yet, the guys said they'd have hydroelectric power in a week.

It wasn't home, but it felt good.

Each of the Morpheus Squad guys kept checking in on Kiera and Mattie. Incessantly. It was as though Mattie had inherited a bunch of overprotective, brawny uncles. Even Rodeo, who clearly had misgivings about small babies and laboring women, stopped by regularly, mumbled a few words, and left.

Not all of the guys came by.

A bubble of pressure grew in her chest, and she tamped it down, hard.

After the delivery, Jake stayed at her side until she and Mattie were completely safe within the new compound.

He had run. Again.

No. She had no right to criticize. He'd put his life on the line to save her and Mattie.

Her head rested on the back of the chair.

A door opened behind her. A whiff of aftershave and hickory wafted past.

No way. Her heart skipped a beat.

"Hi." Jake stopped a few feet away from her. He had circles under his serious gray eyes.

"You're back." She tried to keep her voice neutral. God knew, he'd far exceeded any obligations when he had risked his life and freedom for her.

"I—yeah." He shoved his hands in his jeans pockets. Despite the cooler temperatures here in the cave house, he still wore a t-shirt, his massive arm muscles bulging from beneath the fabric. And his chest holster. Of course.

He stood next to her and stared. A muscle jumped along his clean-shaven jaw, though his gaze softened when he looked at Mattie. He ran a single finger over her fuzzy reddish-blonde hair. There was a peacefulness to his expression that Kiera had never seen before.

Swallowing, she studied his hard features. "How are you doing?"

"I should ask you the same thing." A flash of sadness drew his brows down again. "Yeah. Every day is better."

Damn his closed expression. "Are you sure?" she said.

"Kier—"

"What's on your mind, Jake?" She no longer had the patience to dance around hard topics.

"Nothing." He shifted from one foot to another.

Sleep-deprived and grumpy wasn't the best way for her to have this conversation, but she needed to cut him a little slack until she understood his explanation. "Try again."

His shoulders slumped. "Well. My house is gone."

"Gone?" Her jaw dropped.

"Burned to the ground."

"Oh, God, I'm sorry." Nasty shame flooded her. Of course, he needed time to take care of his property.

"It'll be okay. I have other funds available to rebuild. But I was thinking that I might stay here for now."

Something fluttered in her chest, like a piece of her was trying to take flight. "Here?"

The muscles in his arms tightened. "Yeah. Seems I've officially rejoined Morpheus Squad."

They both stared out at the early spring day as she rocked Mattie.

He blew out a deep breath. "I, um. Put Mateo—his remains—to rest."

"Really?"

"Least I could do. He sacrificed his life so you could escape and Mattie would live."

"Wow." She swallowed. "Thank you. I know he's looking down and appreciates what you did."

"Maybe. He supported and helped you after Brady died. Putting him to rest gave me a chance to say some things to him." He shuffled his feet.

Another period of silence filled the room.

Time for her to buck up and make things … not necessarily better, but at least not bad. "Jake. About the other day, before… When I accused you of letting your past control you. I never had a chance to apologize."

"You were completely right."

She pitched her voice low so as not to disturb Mattie. "No. You're a good person. You're not defined by your parents, your past, or by things out of your control."

Shaking his head, he said, "But how I've responded to those things. That's what I could control. I'm ashamed of the mistakes I've made. I'm not proud of what I said before … Lequire took you." He blew out a big breath. "What I said was wrong. You've never put pressure on me. Never. The problem was with my insecurities."

Her eyes burned. "You've never owed me anything, Jake. Ever."

Leaning forward, he pulled his hands out of the pockets and clenched them. "But I wanted to owe you something." His rumbling voice made something twist deep inside her.

When she opened her mouth to reply, he held up his hand.

"Let me finish. I made mistakes with you years ago, and there's not a day gone by when I haven't regretted them." He stared out the window. "You know why I went into the military so long ago? It was to get away from you."

When her jaw dropped, he winced.

"That came out all wrong. What I mean was, I ran away from you."

Tucking hair behind an ear, she said, "Sounds much better."

"Shit." He cringed. "Let me try again. Years ago, you were everything good in my world. When I thought you were pregnant back then, I was shaken to the core. I knew I had to take care of you but had zero confidence that I could pull off the job, given the crappy role models I had growing up. When it turned out you weren't pregnant, I was relieved not to have to fail you."

"So you joined the Army, ran to the opposite side of the Earth, and volunteered for a dangerous mission? Hell of a crisis of confidence." She rubbed her neck.

He shot her a wry grimace. "You're right. But by then, keeping myself free of entanglements had become second nature. Then later, I got a woman pregnant and married her because I wanted to do the right thing." He tapped his toe on the floor.

"You didn't cause the miscarriage. Her sadness wasn't your fault."

"In a way, her issues were partly my doing. I could have been there more for her. More supportive. Open up about my feelings and intentions from the start. But like before, I ran. I checked out of the relationship." Shifting from foot to foot he said, "Don't you get it? When the chips are down, I run."

"You didn't run this time. Not in the back of the vehicle when Mattie arrived."

"Mostly because of your death grip on me."

"Poor super soldier."

Thank goodness for the tiny lift of his mouth.

"I ran afterward."

True. Although he technically did it to gain closure. "You came back."

He knelt in front of her. "Listen, I'm sorry I doubted you. I'm sorry I doubted myself. My misjudging of your character put you in danger."

"We've both made mistakes."

His hand drifted over Mattie's head again. "Yeah, but your mistake is a hell of a lot cuter."

"It's *our* mistake." She sniffed. "And she's not a mistake."

"You're right."

For a minute, he simply watched Mattie until Kiera's breath caught.

Finally, he said, "Look, I don't have any right to ask this." His Adam's apple bobbed. "Do you think two people can start over again?"

Her pulse jumped. "I think it's possible."

A hint of a smile lit up his handsome features.

"Because I'd love to get a crack at being a dad to Mattie and a long-term partner for you. If you're willing to take a chance on a defective guy without any solid future who has some serious hang-ups. If so, then I'd love to be that guy." He groaned and dropped his forehead onto his palm. "Not good."

His effort melted her heart.

His voice was muffled. "This shit never does come out right."

"Jake?"

"Yeah?" He lifted his head, but there was no

smile.

"Let's try."

"Let's try what?"

"The together thing." She reached for his hand. "We'll take baby steps. All three of us."

"Yeah?"

"I love you, Jake. I always have."

He stared at her like she'd grown a second head. Then he laughed and tugged her hand to his cheek, kissing the palm. Blissful sparks shot through her fingertips.

"Kiera, I have loved you since the day we met, all those years ago. You're an amazing woman."

"You're just saying that because I cranked out a six-pounder in the back of a moving vehicle."

"Well, it's one reason. I'll tell you the other thousand or so reasons over the next however many years."

When he leaned over the chair and kissed her, the tenderness in his touch made her heart catch once more. He stroked her cheek and neck, and then leaned his forehead against hers.

Between them, Mattie's quiet breathing filled the space.

He eased back, still holding Kiera's free hand between his two large palms. "As long as I have you and Mattie, that's all I need."

"Are you sure?" she asked.

"I love you, Kiera McNeill. Not because of the baby, but because of you. I will protect and love you and Mattie with everything I've got."

Her eyes burned with happy tears. "I love you."

As they leaned in for a long kiss, Kiera sighed.

Jake.

After all these years, she had found her safe

haven and home.

The End

Author's Note
Pregnancy, Sex, and Body Positivity

As many of my readers know, my day job is that of a rural FP/Ob (family doctor who provides obstetrics services). I've been honored to be a part of well over a thousand pregnancies and deliveries over my career! Many of the conversations had in the office and in the labor room (precipitous deliveries, especially) form the inspiration for Kiera's story, not only depicting her as a fabulous mom-to-be, but also as a heroine who is desirable and capable at all phases of her life.

I can't tell you how many times I've been asked by patients about whether it's safe to have sex during pregnancy. And yes, part of our discussions often end up being about "the laws of physics" where 'Slot A' and 'Tab B' don't line up like they used to when someone is super duper pregnant. At that point, I recommend that the couple try alternative positions for enjoyable sex. When we get to the point where I offer to draw up a diagram, most couples can't stop laughing and generally beg me not to draw a picture. Hopefully they feel more comfortable and confident in their bodies and partnerships and healthy expression of sexuality while pregnant.

I believe that the concept of healthy bodies doesn't have to be a serious topic. Healthy bodies aren't perfect. Sometimes what we do in various expressions of human sexuality can be silly. But talking about sexual health at every stage of life is still important.

If anyone wishes to read more of my thoughts, I'll post them on my blog at jilliandavid.net. If you go to the categories list on the right side of the landing page of my website, you can click on either "Funny Medicine" or

"Medicine" to see all of my thoughts on this and other medical topics. Some of the more serious blogs about death, happiness, illness, and new life—those encounters also inform my writing. Experiencing loss and hope and fear and joy with my patients has allowed me to make my stories that much more real for readers. In my heart, I thank each and every one of my patients for allowing me access to their most sensitive moments. I hope readers can feel that connection on the fictional page.

As always, nothing I write in my books or on my blog or on social media should ever be construed as medical advice! Please check with your doctor for any medical questions or concerns!

Thank you all for taking a chance on this wild and crazy romantic suspense series that starts with a damaged but determined couple and a motley team of imperfect soldiers who will do anything to stop injustice and keep their comrades safe.

Acknowledgements

This particular book and series have been floating around in the ether since early 2016, which is either a testament to my dogged determination or an inability to let something go… To be fair, I knew in my gut that this book was special and the concept—I had to see it to completion. To find a home for this series has been wonderful, and I appreciate Evernight taking a chance on my books!

Early on in writing and querying this manuscript, I was fortunate to have three amazing beta readers Mickey, Carmen P., and Lisa C. who provided valuable feedback. I was also blessed to have various levels of critiques by Bev Katz Rosenbaum, Patricia Elrond, Diana Gardin, Kelly Garrett, Gwen Hayes, and Tara Cuskaden. Gwen especially kept saying, "More alpha. Over-the-top alpha." So here we are with literally the most alpha alphas to ever exist, so much so that I gave them a virus that made them "Alphazillas."

One of the best things I ever did was swap a beta read a few years ago with fabulous author Crista McHugh, and she brought such wonderful suggestions for improvement and steadfast encouragement to keep going. Big thank you to Diane Wiggs who turned a "last minute" read around in a week or so. And lastly a warm thank you to Anna Richland, a writer who herself has served in the military and who brought layers upon layers of military insight to this manuscript. That said, any details that are incorrect are solely my mistakes.

Lastly, I cannot thank enough my amazing agent, Jana Hansen, at Metamorphosis Literary. Jana also took a chance on this wild story, and she has been such a cheerleader for my work. I am lucky to have her as a partner in the publishing journey.

And to Hubs: You know the drill. So sorry but there is no bald guy on the book's cover this time. When we need a short, bald, ~~aging~~ wise cover model, I know who to call!

JILLIAN DAVID

EVERNIGHT PUBLISHING ®

www.evernightpublishing.com